The Gryphon's Glade
Impossible Love: Book I

LINDA L. ZERN

LinWood House Publishing

Once upon a time . . .

Out in the fogs of the humid springs and wet summers along the Tannin River, near the 'Taintsville Bridge, locals joke and laugh about seeing bouncing balls of supernatural light: ghost lights, spook-lights, maybe will-o'-the-wisps.

Now I'm not saying the 'Taintsville lights are up there with those Marfa, Texas ghost lights, but the Friday night gang down at the Gator Bait Bar and Grill, out on Highway 46, can hold their own in the unexplainable sightings department. Admittedly they're mostly drunk when they're talking ghost lights, but still, it can be exciting for a kid to think about living in a place where the earth's skin is thin, and the woods are thick and dank and full of cloudy mysteries.

Most small towns can claim an urban legend or two. My hometown is no different. My name is Reed Baye Hunter, and I'm from 'Tainstville, Florida.

Welcome to 'Tainstville

A place that 'taint Oviedo and 'taint Lake Pickett.

Population

Fluctuating

CONTENTS

Shooting Boxcar

Overhead, a slow swirl of feathered bodies glided in a familiar holding pattern. The vultures kept to their patient circle—nature's version of a neon arrow in the sky, pointing to death.

"Boxcar, buddy, what happened to you?"

At the sound of his name, the old water buffalo managed a wheezing moan. The sound shocked me. I thought the big bull beyond hearing, let alone capable of producing a noise.

Half-submerged in mud, he lay where the creek faded into a slough of muck and sawgrass, a favorite spot for our ranch's herd of Asian water buffalo. Boxcar had been happily wallowing in that mud and fathering buffalo babies for as long as I had been around.

Judging from the furrows cut in the mud by his horns as he'd thrashed, he'd been down a while. His tongue lolled from the side of his mouth.

The buffalo's side barely moved. Hours. He'd been suffering for hours, and it might take hours more for him to finish dying. Walking back to my mare, Cantara, I pulled my uncle's Smith and Wesson 500 out of the saddlebag. Mr. Stillbee, our ranch hand, liked to call it a hand cannon—okay, whatever, as long as it did the job.

"Goodbye, old man."

Pushing the pistol against Boxcar's head, just behind his ear, I angled the shot into his brain and fired. I'm not a big girl, and I knew enough to two-hand the pistol so as not to let the barrel come back and smack me in the face. Still, the recoil rocked me back a few steps.

I'm a ranch-raised girl. I knew what to expect. I also knew to expect the hollow spot that opened up in my heart when I felt for a pulse in the animal's heavy neck and didn't find one. One more bit of Gilded Oat Ranch crumbling away. Boxcar: I'd given him his name.

I checked again for a pulse—nothing. Big gun—efficient.

I had no intention of letting the vultures get at the old bull. The exotic animals we raised weren't pets, but we knew them, and we cared. Pulling out the ancient walkie-talkie in my saddlebag, I pushed the talk button and waited for the screeching whine to fade.

"Mr. Stillbee, I need you. I'm out just past the Clear Water Spring. Mr. Stillbee, it's Reed; Are you there? Over."

I released the button and waited. Tried again.

"Mr. S., it's Boxcar. I had to put him down."

The walkie-talkie in my hand started to crackle to life.

"Reedy-Girl, it's me, Mr. Stillbee. Roger. Roger. Over. Over."

Who else could it be? Mr. Stillbee had been around longer than Boxcar. He almost had me smiling.

"Yes, Mr. S., I know it's you. Listen; it's Boxcar; he's . . . well . . . I need you out here, and bring the backhoe. Can you?"

"That bad?"

"Yeah, bad enough. Most of him is stuck down in the mud. Hard to tell what brought him down. I finished it. He'd suffered long enough."

I walked over and squatted next to the body of the old bull. His eyes had that glassy, fixed look that felt sickeningly familiar. "Had to finish it."

I heard Mr. Stillbee sigh.

"It'll take me a bit of time, but I'm coming."

He didn't sign off. He never did. I looked at the now silent walkie-talkie in my hand and made a mental note to see if I couldn't get Mr.

S. to switch over to a cell phone, something from the 21st century at least. Flopping onto my butt in the mud, I checked the safety, rested the pistol across my knees, and dropped my head to wait for Mr. Stillbee with the backhoe.

By the time we got the hole dug and a chain wrapped around Boxcar's horns, the day was close to fading out into dusk. Mr. S. had to keep the tension on the chain for a good four or five minutes to break the suction of the mud. Boxcar had been in the creek a long time. With a sucking, wet pop his body slid out of the muck to the open pit.

Caked in mud, the body didn't show any visible signs of blood or trauma until the buffalo's legs slid free.

"Cut the engine. Mr. S.! Hold up," I screamed over the groaning backhoe, slashing at my throat with my hand. "Mr. S., stop. Stop! Jump down here."

He let the machine idle as he climbed down. I saw him grimace as he made his way from the machine. I knew better than to offer my help. He'd only make rude noises through his nose and tell me what I could do with my twenty-seven-year-old self.

Besides, I had a hard time taking my eyes off of what was left of Boxcar's legs. They were shattered so badly they resembled broken tree branches.

Mr. Stillbee huffed and puffed his way over to me.

"What's got you looking all heebie—"

He quit grumbling when he saw what I saw.

"Yeah, *what* is right?" I shuddered. "What could have done this? Or maybe who? I don't see any blood, and there's so much mud. Shattered. Not just one, but all four legs."

He circled the bull's body.

"Could a younger bull have done this?" I suggested. "Challenged the old boy to a duel?"

He glanced at me. The lines of his face settled into a familiar pattern.

"There are two younger bulls coming up. They might have roughed him up some, maybe a broken rib or two, but look at his body, Reed."

He poked at the body with the toe of his work boot. It wobbled like gelatin.

"Maybe got a broken leg, but not this."

I squatted in the mud.

"Then someone did this to him. Poachers? Sadists? I haven't seen anything like this since Iraq."

It was a mistake, mentioning my deployment. I knew better. It still bothered him, my enlisting in the Army. I saw him flinch. In his mind, I'd abandoned the farm, my uncle, and, in the end, Mr. Stillbee too. It was a subject better left alone-for now.

I studied the frown on his face.

"What? What are you thinking?"

He shrugged and bent down to fiddle with the chain.

I stood up and searched the ground around the creek. I knew how to look for something, anything, out of the ordinary: IED's hidden in dead dogs' corpses and trip wires under tires.

"No tracks. No trail. I can't even tell which part of the ranch Boxcar wandered in from? There's no sign. It's like—" I said, hesitating.

Mr. S. frowned, pushed his ball cap back and scratched at his forehead. He shrugged again and then pointed at the darkening sky. The sun dropped behind the tallest trees of the surrounding hardwood hammock. Dusk arrived. The light faded and the mosquitoes showed up in squadrons.

"Let's get this done and then you can tell me what I'm not seeing, Reedy. I don't care to be out here when it gets full on dark. We'll get chewed on. Why don't you start on back to the barn? There's no more for you to do here." He dragged himself back into the seat of the backhoe. It rumbled into action. Boxcar slid closer to the hole.

"Go on. I'll be along," he yelled and waved. I brushed dried mud from my hands.

He was right. I headed Cantara toward home.

The temperature dipped. The sky's colors leached away. The woods filled with the glowing eyes of the shy, wild, night creatures. They watched and waited as I rode by. As Cantara trotted through the growing shadows, I thought of what might have happened to our old water buffalo: old age, disease, rustlers, injury, infection. None of that.

It reminded me of a time I'd seen a Chinook helicopter lose the jeep it had been hauling. There hadn't been much left of the undercarriage or tires or axles or jeep when it hit the ground.

Boxcar looked like that. As if a Chinook helicopter had dropped two thousand pounds of water buffalo right out of the sky.

A To-Do List

I stared at the door latch. It had come off in my hand in a shower of sawdust. Was anything not falling apart around here?

"Dry rot."

Mr. S. pulled a screwdriver out of a random pocket of his overalls and started prying the tack room door open.

"It's late, Miss Reed, for a body to be riding out on the Refuge Trails; that's all I'm saying. It's just not the time to be starting out. There's park hours and rules and stay-on-the-trail-we-tell-you-to signs. Since your parents gave them governmental folks all that land along the river, it's been restricted to death."

He banged and complained inside the tack room. Then he popped his head out of the door, handing me a saddle pad. I carried it to the hitching rail and flipped it over the cross post, relieved when the posts didn't wobble. I started the ritual of brushing Cantara's dark sorrel coat.

He didn't mention Boxcar or any new theories he might have about how the big bull had died. I didn't mention my Chinook helicopter theory. It was absurd. The best I could do was settle on sadistic rustlers. When Mr. S. didn't offer up any ideas, I let it drop. We'd fallen back into the see no evil, speak no evil pattern of my childhood. He treated me like a twelve-year-old, and I tried not to worry him.

Hopefully, Boxcar was the end of it. I couldn't afford to hire help to patrol the perimeter fence. Dry rot wasn't the only problem eating away at Gilded Oats Ranch. The place was swimming in red ink.

I threw the saddle pad across Cantara's back and smiled at the familiar disapproving mutters booming inside the two-story barn. Mr. Stillbee had worked for my family all my life, always been there in the ranch's big, cantilevered barn kicking up dust and hay and disapproval. He limped down from the tack room to the hard-packed clay of the center aisle; my dressage saddle slung over his shoulder.

"You've probably forgotten all about them spook lights out there along that river."

I laughed. It had been a long time since anybody had threatened me with supernatural, floating lights. I hadn't forgotten about the ghost lights of my high school years. It had been the best way in town to get your date all shocked and clingy: bring your date out to the bridge over Highway 13 and talk up the rumor of creepy, floating balls of glowing fire.

"And here I thought you'd be pulling the poacher card on me. Spook lights? Come on, Mr. S. I thought Uncle Rulan pronounced once and for all that there's no such thing as the 'Tainstville lights. Just methane gas from swamp rot; isn't that what those professors from the University proved? Or did they decide on ball lightning?"

Cantara sidestepped as I tightened the girth.

When he reached for a pitchfork, I noticed how deeply the lines around his eyes now cut into the dark leather of his face. His once black hair was completely gray. My friend had gotten old while I'd been gone.

"Bah! Swamp farts! There's proof, and then there's truth, Reedy-Girl, and now that you've brought up them poachers that went after Boxcar. That's no joke."

Not fighting fair, using his pet name for me.

"Oh no, you don't. I'm not going far, and I'm not looking for any trouble."

"Reedy-Girl," he said it again.

And there it was, the unexpected prick of tears. Cripes, I was twenty-seven years old; I'd been a staff sergeant in the US Army; I'd been to war. I was too old and too disciplined for sentimental silliness. I was tired, that's all. Just needed to catch my breath. What I needed was to ride away from the latest chapter of my life for a while.

Leading my horse to the mounting block, a hunk of solid cypress carved into a step up, I paused. The block still had the sheen of a half-dozen layers of shellac Uncle Rulan had painted on it. He'd made it for my tenth birthday, one of his beloved "art" projects.

"I promise to be careful of spook lights or ghost lights or swamp farts or whatever it is that's out there in the woods," I said, trying to sound serious and mature. "And any self-respecting poacher is going to have a full day's head start on me. They'll be way out of town by now."

He tapped at his watch as I swung my leg over the saddle.

"Before dark. Be back here before dark; I'm too old to be waiting up for you to come in from gallivanting around like I did once."

Trying not to laugh, I didn't bother reminding him that I was a veteran of foreign wars.

"You'll check in on Uncle Rulan for me; won't you? I sat with him, but there was no change."

He nodded.

"Thanks. He shouldn't need anything, and Mrs. Jonas won't leave until six." I gathered the braided leather reins of the bridle.

He nodded again and propped the pitchfork against a stall. He crossed his arms over his chest, "Home before dark. Don't forget. Trouble comes in the dark—"

"And nothing good happens after midnight." I finished for him. "I haven't forgotten." And then I did laugh.

Cantara shifted restlessly beneath me, full of pent up energy, needing the stretch and burn of muscles moving in ground-eating exercise, maybe sensing my pent up frustrations.

Before I headed out, I turned in the saddle.

"Mr. S., thank you. For all of it. I mean it."

He dropped his eyes, maybe wrestling with his tired emotions.

"And don't worry. I'm all grown up. I don't gallivant anymore."

He snorted.

I pushed Cantara into a canter and headed away from the weight of having to run the three thousand acres of Golden Oats Ranch with nothing more than the help of one old man and a failing uncle.

Twenty minutes later, I was at the Tannin River gate, confident I had worked out most of Cantara's bucks and kinks. By the time I reached the boundary fence, her dark red coat looked black and gleamed with sweat, but she'd finally quit snorting and twitching her lush black tail.

Riding a horse, riding a bike, you never forgot how to do either. I felt my knots and kinks relaxing as I concentrated on keeping my heels down and my chin up.

Stroking her wet neck, I jumped down to open the gate.

The gate needed a coat of Rustoleum, but the fencing looked solid. Designed for the exotic animals we raised, the fence was eight feet high for the antelopes and gazelles, and made of galvanized net wire.

The river gate was a smaller version of the black wrought iron main gate, complete with the family motto in Latin: Cum Gryphae Equis Iungunt.

Pushing the gate open, I could hear Uncle Rulan's voice, the way it had sounded before his stroke.

"When pigs fly, that's what it means, Reed: Cum Gryphae Equis Iungunt. Big impossible things, that's what our family motto means. I like to think that it means believing in miracles like flying pigs." He'd laugh his booming, happy laugh.

"No, that's not right; it's not about pigs, Uncle Rulan," I would correct him, in my best bossy-kid voice.

"It's about gryphons and horses having babies together, but they hate each other, so it's not about anything real anyway because gryphons aren't real. It's all pretend and kind of silly. Besides, it's embarrassing to have a family motto."

That's when he'd mess up my already wild mop of curls with his calloused, work-reddened hand and smile.

"Be careful, Reed, because it's only the people who believe in impossible things that get to see miracles up close."

As a teenager, I'd been self-conscious about the idea of family crests and symbols and massive iron gates. Everything had embarrassed me then: my crazy mismatched eyes—one blue, one green; being an orphan, alone and lonely; and living behind gates with Latin mottos. I'd been a brat, no argument there. Now I just hoped Uncle Rulan was right about the miracle part.

I took a minute to be grateful for the miracle of good fences and gates that only needed painting, not replacing.

As I pushed through the river gate, flaking rust covered the palms of my riding gloves. The hinges screamed. I slammed shut the notebook I carried around in my head. I would think about paint for rusty gates tomorrow. Right now I was going for a ride and to enjoy being home. Finding poacher tracks would be an added bonus.

I turned Cantara away from the setting sun, heading east, down the Refuge Trail toward the haunted 'Tainstville bridge of my bratty teenage years.

Chapter 3

Lights

The Tannin River ran like a brown satin ribbon along the boundary of Gilded Oats Ranch. Acid from the cypress trees leached into the water, dyeing it a solid rust color. It turned the water opaque, close to black in some places. To a kid with too much imagination, the water might have looked like old blood.

Live oaks and magnolias and thickets of palmettos lined the riding trail, and the woods rustled with tiny anoles, lizards, and scrub jay. The massive trunks of oak trees supported dense arching limbs curving low to the ground while their tops grew as high as fifty feet: ancient trees as enchanted and magical as in any fairy tale forest, dripping with Spanish moss, presiding over a cushioned carpet of leaves.

My father and mother had donated the land along the river to the state to become the Toad's Head Refuge and Recreation Area when they were first married. Their generosity had made me feel better about our big iron gates and stuffy family motto, even if I'd had nothing to do with it. Laughing, I forgave myself for being such a juvenile prig.

The air along the river was so clean that breathing it made me dizzy. I wasn't used to this; I'd forgotten what it was like to breathe air that wasn't full of burning garbage and blowing sand.

Home. It was good to be home. I felt lighter already.

Next to the river, the air took on a heavy expectation as if the sky held its breath. The thick air grew heavier, and I caught the faint hint of ozone, promising rain.

"Well, it won't be the first time we've gotten rained on out here, will it?"

I leaned forward in the saddle and stroked Cantara's neck, then wiped my damp face with my sleeve.

Her ears ticked forward; her attention fixed on the trail ahead. When her head came up she snorted, and I began to pay more attention to the path ahead. Something was bothering her—wild hogs, maybe another horse and rider.

"What do you hear, girl?"

Behind us, from the west, the faint rumble of thunder came like a leper's bell, warning of the approaching thunderstorm. The big oaks on my left and across the river to my right trembled when quick gusts of wind slapped at them. The temperature dropped five degrees. I shivered in my sweaty T-shirt.

Cantara stayed riveted on the trail ahead. I was more worried about lightning and wind coming up behind us or getting conked on the head by a falling tree limb. Her ears never flipped backward, not once, letting me know that she had not noticed the random echoes of thunder. We were too far out to try to make it back before the storm broke.

I pushed her forward into a trot.

"Come on, let's make the bridge and stay out of the lightning or ghost lights." I laughed at my own joke.

She rolled into a gentle canter.

The storm came up behind us fast, filling the woods with chilled gusts of wet wind. Thunder cracked louder as the sky darkened. Cantara arched her muscular neck and snorted. We rounded a blind curve in the trail, cantering past a massive old oak, its branches dripping with Spanish moss that fluttered like lace in the rising wind. The bridge was just ahead.

We moved passed Indian mounds that lined the banks of the Tannin River. Maybe all those dead Timucaun Indians had the best reasons of all to be haunting the cypress stands and hardwood swamps with mysterious fire and lights. Good for them.

Rain pocked the surface of the river. Cantara snorted again, and underneath me, I felt her body suddenly tighten, coiling like a closed fist. Her ears flattened against her head. I could feel the buck coming. Rain slashed down.

"Oh no you don't," I said, yanking her to a stop and thinking that I would lead her the last bit to the bridge in front of us.

I swung my leg out and over the saddle, throwing myself to the ground just as the woods exploded with fire followed by an earsplitting clap of thunder.

Storms didn't so much begin along the river as they erupted. Cantara shied backward, thrashing against my hold on the reigns. I managed to pull her head back around as she panicked, skidding sideways in the instantly slick mud of the trail.

Blinding light and the sound of thunder made my mouth go dry. It was too much like artillery. I had forgotten how violent the thunderstorms could be here. The dry season was obviously over. My horses' panic radiated through the reins to my hands as she jerked wildly. Forcing myself not to slip back into memories that had the power to crush me, I felt sick to my stomach. I smelled blood when there wasn't any. I smelled gunpowder in the middle of a flooded trail and heard soldiers screaming. The flashback held all the elements of real panic.

My horse could feel it, I was sure; but she brought me back, trying to yank away and head home. Her fear was greater than mine. I focused on the problem at hand and managed to pull her head back toward me. Calling her name, I talked to her, silly soothing stuff.

Down the trail, the Tannin River Bridge disappeared behind a solid sheet of water. Rain slammed into the dirt of the trail. As the water sought the lowest point, it carved gouges in the riverbank.

A razor of lightning hit a date palm across the river, setting its ruffled top on fire. Rain sizzled as it hit the burning palm fronds.

My horse reared, her front hooves pawing air.

"Cantara! No! Stop fighting me," I screamed, trying to out-pull a thousand pound horse. "Stop!"

I'd gone stupid with my reaction to the storm. Get my horse to the bridge, and there'd be help; we'd be safe. It was all I could think.

She wasn't buying it and acted as if the lightning and thunder lived under the bridge. She skidded backward thrashing hard enough to pull me ten feet back the way we had come. Mud kicked back by her hooves splashed up into my mouth and eyes. I could taste dank leaf mold and rot. Lightning continued to rip the sky apart.

"Move, damn you!"

I saw her eyes roll in her head; her nostrils flared blood-red and huge. I tried to drag her forward.

She lunged in complete and mindless terror, and I knew. She wasn't frightened because of the storm at all, not something behind us. It was something in front of us, under the bridge, beyond it maybe. I turned to face the bridge as Cantara squealed, dragging my arm backward. Pain shot down from my shoulder to my fingertips, and I dropped the reins. She bolted and disappeared into the murk.

A hot blaze of light blinded me. More lightning? But where was the thunder?

When I tried to open my eyes all I saw was light and more light and glitter and sparks arching everywhere through the rain. I covered my eyes with my hands. What was happening didn't feel like ghostly or spooky or anything. Could I have been struck by lightning? Was it possible? I kept my eyes closed.

A screeching roar from the bridge tore through the air, and I squinted into the slowing rain. Against the ink of the sky and rain, I could see the faint gray outline of the bridge and there, on the railing, stretching up and out like a vision were wings. Wings formed of fire and shadow—a winged monster, or maybe just the blinding after-effects of too much adrenalin.

I was halfway to believing the second theory when the air from the 'Taintsville bridge exploded with another furious roar. It ripped at my ears. I turned away, thinking that Cantara had been the smart one.

Before I could take a step, something raked at my hip and thigh, and a downdraft of furious wind pushed me facedown into the mud of the trail. My mouth and nose filled with muck.

There was an unrelenting pressure on top of my back, forcing me down, hard into the mud. My last conscious thought lying face down that way was how bizarre it was going to be to drown in the mud of the Toad's Head Nature Trail donated to the state by Jon and Starlyn Hunter, my parents, who were dead—like me. Like I was going to be.

Chapter 4

Lost

"I wasn't gallivanting. I promise, Mr. S.," I said, sounding twelve. I swallowed, tasting pennies—copper pennies.

"Hush now; don't worry. Shhhh." It was a man's voice. He sounded mildly impatient. "There was an accident, but you're fine. You fell from your horse."

He pressed a cup of water to my mouth. A hand lifted my head so I wouldn't spill. I swallowed and grimaced, tasting more blood.

"Don't worry," he repeated. "You've bitten your lips, that's why you have blood in your mouth, but you should not worry."

Despite his reassurance, I wrestled to make sense of the darkness and the dreams. Why couldn't I see? My mouth wasn't working anymore either. I tried to ask a question but only managed to gag. I could smell camphor somewhere close.

The man's arms came around me, pulling me to a sitting position. He held the cup to my lips again. The water stung as I sipped a little but the blood was still too thick in my mouth; I turned my head. It was the only protest I could make.

"Can you tell me your name?"

"Why can't . . . I see?" My voice was so hoarse I barely recognized it. "What's wrong with," I began again and then had to swallow a wave of nausea, "with me? My eyes? I don't remember falling . . . Not off of my horse. Pushed. I was pushed."

The water I'd sipped finally hit my stomach, and I tasted bile. Moaning, I tried to warn the man holding me.

Without a fuss, he bent me gently forward while I threw up what little I'd managed to swallow.

I leaned into the man's strength.

I managed a whisper.

"Sorry."

"For what? Surviving?"

I didn't understand his sarcasm, and I wanted to; I wanted to badly. "Cut off." I could feel the shaking start when I tried to remember their faces that day in Tikrit. "Ambushed. I should have done more."

His arms tightened, and he gave me a little shake.

"Do you know where you are?" he said. For the first time I heard the worry in the man's voice, and then, "Tell me your name." It was an order.

I knew an order when I heard one, and a terrible possibility occurred to me. That I was still back there, in Iraq, and they had me, and no one was coming for me.

"I only have to give you my name, rank, and serial number," I mumbled.

In the quiet that followed, I could hear rain against the rattling leaves of palmettos—not the desert, not the stinging sound of sand blowing. The sound of rain brought me back to the thunderstorms, swamp, and mud of home. Back again.

"Reed, you were caught in a storm. Can you remember what happened?"

"Hey, you know my name already. Why did you ask me?"

"Spell it."

"R-e-a-d like to read a book."

"Now you have me truly worried if you can't spell your own name. And you know that's not right," he sighed.

"You do know me," I whispered. "How? Do you?"

I could feel a faint tremor radiate from the man's body into mine—a small tight laugh, the kind that didn't come easily. "I'm Reed Baye like weeds along the water." Another small laugh and then I drifted away.

Sometime in the night, when the sound of frogs pounded into my eardrums and I was still blind, I screamed. Claws tore at my hip and thigh. Acid poured into my leg. My muscles cramped with the tension the pain brought. My jaw ached from grinding my teeth.

When the man took my hand, I gasped—cool flame seared through my skin.

"Make it stop." I knew I was breathing too fast. "Please. "

"I can't. Not yet. Soon."

"Home."

"Tomorrow, I'll take you home tomorrow."

"But my family. They'll worry." Even if the only family I had left was Uncle Rulan, who couldn't hear me, and Mr. Stillbee, who'd tried to warn me.

"They know where you are. It will pass Reed. It will."

He didn't touch me again, which was worse; it made me feel desperate and alone. I needed to tell him what I remembered so that he could tell my family.

"No. I didn't fall. Something on the trail. Attacked us—Cantara and me. My horse."

"I know. A worry for another day. Quiet now. Listen. Try to listen."

He began to speak, too low to understand individual words—not English, not any language I understood. At first, his words were a weak counterpoint to my clenched misery. But as the words continued I began to hear a cadence and a rhythm that drew me, called to me. It was the music of the words that got through the pain that had settled around me like a fog. He continued to speak until I couldn't feel anything but the music in his words. I slept and dreamed of trees. Pistachio trees. Like the ones in Iraq . . .

Chapter 5

Awake

Window blinds snapped and rattled. It was a sound that I knew down to my bones. It was time to get up, and I was in my own bed. A wild, thick relief welled up inside me.

Sunlight rushed across the bedspread. I balled my fists in the warmth of sunshine and silk across my lap and forced my eyes open. In my crazy dream, I'd been blind.

"Don't try to do too much, Miss Hunter, and don't sit up too quickly. Let me assist you."

"Mrs. Jonas?"

"Here now, let me help you."

She had her arm wedged behind my pillow before I could protest. It was time to sit up; that was evident. Mrs. Jonas, sturdy and squat, had an efficient take-no-prisoners style of nursing.

"Thank you, but really . . . I think I can . . . , " I sputtered, confused by the attention, "remember how to sit up."

Stuffing another pillow behind my shoulders, she watched me carefully. She leaned forward, bracing her hands on the bed. She was close enough for me to see that powder had settled into the wrinkles under her eyes.

"Any dizziness, head or neck pain?"

I pushed myself back into the pillows away from her.

"Mrs. Jonas, shouldn't you be checking on my uncle at this hour in the morning?"

Ignoring me, she pressed two fingers against the inside of my wrist. I jerked my hand away.

"Mrs. Jonas, really! What is this about?"

She looked at me, frowned, but then walked to stand at the foot of my bed, my narrow twin bed. I was wearing a nightgown with cows on it; a favorite, sure, when I was sixteen. There'd been no time for shopping for grown-up clothes since I'd come straight home when Uncle Rulan got sick.

One of these days I was going to need to make a run to Fort Campbell to get my stuff out of storage. I started to swing my legs over the side of the bed.

"Miss Hunter, you are not even aware that it's almost one o'clock in the afternoon. It is possible that you are not ready to leap out of bed yet."

"Yet? It's one o'clock, why didn't anybody get me up? I need to start checking on the fence line and . . ." I pushed to my feet. A bolt of pain in my hip took my breath away.

Mrs. Jonas moved to take my arm when I leaned away from the unexpected throb in my leg.

"What in the world? My hip. Damn."

No answer. But like a game of association, thinking about my hip made me remember being knocked to the ground after wrestling with Cantara. The storm. Because of the storm and the lightning and riding out too late to Mr. Stillbee's way of thinking. It came in a mushy rush, some of it, along with the haunting taste of copper pennies. There'd been a man's voice.

"I fell. No, that's not right. Something . . ." It was all a muddle. "Because of the storm."

"And that's about all for today. We need to get back to bed now," Mrs. Jonas said, her voice impersonal and bossy. "And I'll be back to bring you something to eat."

I rolled to my side. My hip burned.

"*WE* are not going back to bed. We have to pee."

She shrugged, glancing at her watch.

"Apparently, you won't be passing out and hitting your head against the edge of your dresser either, so I'll be packing my stuff up to go home." She stomped out of the room. "I'll leave something for you in the kitchen."

Her voice echoed from the hallway. Mrs. Jonas was worried about me fainting?

I needed action to hold the panic at bay; I stood up and stumbled to my white provincial dresser with its decals of pink roses and twisting green vines. There was laundry stacked on top of the dresser. I tried to imagine Mrs. Jonas doing my laundry and couldn't. It wasn't part of her job description.

Ignoring the ache in my leg, I pulled a pair of jeans and a black T-shirt on. They didn't fit. Somehow I'd lost weight—overnight.

In the mirror, I looked more like the child who'd grown up in this room than ever. My eyes, my strange bi-colored eyes, were still too big. Strawberry blond hair kinked up against my head because of the relentless humidity, making it look shorter than it was. If I wasn't careful, I was going to wind up with Shirley Temple curls. Brushing my hair as flat as I could manage, I pulled it into a ponytail.

I smiled thinking that one of the reasons I'd joined the military was to earn a little gravitas. In the Army, they'd handed me a rifle, a job, and nobody had patted me on the head or called me cute. Since I'd been home, I'd managed to slip back to the beginning—a child in a little girl's bedroom.

Looking down, I saw that I'd tied my shoelaces in double knots. Great. My head pounded from bending over, but the ache in my leg eased a bit as I stretched it. My heart thudded in my chest.

Walking down the hallway, I trailed one hand along the dark wainscoting and counted to ten, a little trick that Uncle Rulan had taught me.

"Slow down, count to ten, Reed, and you'll have to eat your words a lot less."

That's what he'd told me, and sometimes it even worked. I carefully navigated the stairs.

"Ten," I said, under my breath, standing at the edge of the parlor rug. I looked at the front room of our big farmhouse with new eyes. The carpet needed cleaning. Mr. Stillbee stood in the corner of the front room, looking uncomfortable, his hands jammed in his overalls' pockets. He lifted his eyes to mine and was obviously relieved when he saw me.

"It's good to see you up and moving and everything."

I started to deliver the apology I'd practiced when I saw the door to Uncle Rulan's sick room closed up tight. It had been a study before.

"You know that I don't want my uncle to think he's shut up away from us."

"Miss Reedy, hold up."

Telling myself that my limp wasn't all that noticeable, I pushed the sick room door open and jumped when it smacked against the wall. The boom multiplied and bounced off the walls.

"Oh my God."

My words echoed in the empty room.

Dust motes drifted through the glare of light at the bare windows. The curtains were gone, everything stripped, removed: the hospital bed, the chair where Mrs. Jonas sat to read Lost Horizon to my silent uncle; it was all gone.

"Mrs. Jonas," I called, my voice too high and squeaky. "Mrs. Jonas."

"Home." He swiped the back of his hand across his forehead. "She's done gone on home."

"Mr. S., what's happened here?"

He ducked his head, managing to look like someone waiting to be slapped. I rubbed my hip and tried not to flinch. Mr. S. glanced at my leg and flinched for both of us.

"He's gone, Reed."

I hobbled to the window.

"While you was sick and not around, he took a turn. He took a bad turn, Reedy-Girl."

Chapter 6

Gone

"No, that's not right. He was fine yesterday. It was yesterday, and he was fine."

I gripped the windowsill.

"I rode toward the bridge, the storm came up like they do, and then there was something, something about the Tannin River Bridge that frightened Cantara." I shook my head. Trying to remember what had happened was like rooting through a bag of lint.

A glitter of dust motes swirled in a shaft of sunlight; all stirred up by my trip across the room.

"Okay. Fine. Where is he? Which hospital?"

The question surprised him. "Oh no, Reedy-Girl . . ." He started, stopped, hesitated, and then scratched at his bald head. I watched him search for words as he shoved his hands back in his pockets. "No, no there's no hospital."

"What? What are you talking about?" He stared at me.

I knew what was coming, had known what was coming, from the moment I'd walked into that space, and it made my stomach cramp. I walked to the window and pressed my forehead against the windowpane, felt the cool of the glass against my hot face.

I could see his face reflected in the dusty glass, turmoil washing over it. He decided to give it to me straight, the way he had when I was a kid.

I didn't have long to wait for Mr. S. to make it official.

"It was that night. The one you're talking about. He went to laboring to breathe something fierce, and by morning he was gone. Mrs. Jonas stayed with him, and we, me and her, were there at the end."

"No one thought to call an ambulance and get him to a hospital?"

"No, he didn't want that. He left us his wishes from before he took sick. Your Uncle was not a young man, older than your father by a dozen years or more."

So many people I cared about, dead. I dragged my finger through the dust on the windowsill, wrote my name slowly as I took it all in.

"Was he . . . ? Did he go easy?"

"Now don't you worry about that, he never woke up. I would have come looking for you but it was that night, you see."

The apology I'd planned wasn't going to be enough; too little, too late. But at least I could do right by remembering him.

"I guess we should talk about what's next then. Did he say anything about what he wanted," I paused, "us to do? I mean, did he talk about what he wanted us to do for his funeral?"

He made an exasperated clucking noise behind me. It was the sound he made when I was, to his way of thinking, either not paying attention or not trying hard enough to pay attention.

"What he wanted's been done. You're not understanding me."

I turned to him, trying to focus. My head still felt like the inside of a quilt. Maybe he was right? Maybe I wasn't paying enough attention?

"What?"

He pulled his hands from his pockets and held them out to me, palms up.

"We buried your Uncle Rulan a week ago today, over there at the 'Taintsville cemetery. Pastor Danes said the words."

I felt the blood leave my face. Suddenly, it was too much to stay on my feet. I collapsed back against the wall and slid to the floor.

My voice sounded thin, even with the echo in the room.

"Last week, but it . . . was yesterday."

I couldn't look at him; I didn't trust myself to believe what I'd see on his face. The way I couldn't trust my internal clock. It was like standing on the beach when the waves washed the sand out from under my feet. Solid and steady until the sand collapsed and I lost my balance and had to stagger to keep from falling.

How much sand had I been standing on and for how long?

I heard my uncle's voice in my head, telling the girl that I used to be how it was going to be: sure of me, sure of the future. I remembered his gentle, handsome face.

"You're a little girl, Reed, and Gilded Oats is a big place, but you'll keep the gates painted, the pastures full. I know you will."

We'd ride, me on my fat pony and him on his big rawboned Tennessee Walking horse and look for the new sambar deer fawns every spring. And he'd teach me: ranching, animals, the meaning of silly family mottos.

He'd been counting on me, and I'd gone and broken his heart and joined the Army, signing the papers the day after I'd graduated from high school. I'd made attempts to explain why I'd wanted, no needed, to enlist, but he'd only smiled sadly and patted me on the head like an owner of a slightly stupid puppy. And now he was gone.

Too late for me, too late for him and too late to tell him I was home for good. I'd come home from war and found the frail shadow of the man who'd raised me. I'd come home too late, too late.

Folding my legs into my body, I hugged my knees. The pain in my hip had faded, was much less painful than when I'd first come into the room. It was happening again, healing so fast that my doctors couldn't explain it, even when I'd been wounded in combat.

"How long?" I stared at him, daring him to evade or dance around the truth. He knew what I wanted to know. He'd been waiting for the question and didn't hesitate.

"Weeks. You've been on the mend for two weeks."

"On the mend? What happened to me? For two weeks! I've been 'out of it' for two weeks? Maybe I should have been nicer to Mrs. Jonas since she seems to have 'mended me.'"

He snorted, scuffed his worn work boots on the wood floor, and shook his head.

"Wasn't Mrs. Jonas who fixed you up. She wouldn't have known how. You weren't even here most of that time." He stopped, maybe realizing he'd said too much.

"Not here. Was it that bad? The hospital, doctors, the police?"

He shook his head as his wrinkles collapsed into a frustrated frown. "No, no hospitals, no police. Not here. Not there."

"I was missing. Two weeks missing and you didn't think that you should have reported my disappearance to the police?"

He shot me his look again.

"Reedy, I said you weren't here at Glided Oats."

"What am I not hearing?"

"I said not here. I didn't say missing."

The fist in my stomach contracted to a knot; misery rolled over me in a gush. Confusion made me lightheaded.

"I don't know why I would be calling the authorities." He shrugged again. "I always knew where you were and who had you."

Chapter 7

Missing

I watched dust dance through the air.

"Gone," I continued, "while my only living relative died," I said it, but it still didn't feel real, not yet. It was a reality about as substantial as dirt dancing through space. "And not just died, but buried too. What? What happened to me, for two weeks? Because none of this can be right."

A memory ghosted through my head: a man's voice, a man's strong hands, soothing away the pain and fever. I rubbed at my hip again. The pain was almost gone.

Mr. Stillbee shuffled his feet against the bare wood of the floor.

"I saw how you were for myself after your Uncle passed." He paused, picking his words like he was picking at sandspurs without gloves. "You never wandered back from your ride. You had fallen. Then you were found. You were taken care of the best that you could be. I did warn you that you might be going out too late."

I couldn't believe my ears, any of it. I had a huge chunk of time to account for, and he was telling me, "I told you so."

"Are you just going to sit there?" He frowned down at me.

My jaw started to ache from grinding my teeth. I knew what Mr. S. was trying to do, picking at me until I got up off that floor and walked out of that empty bedroom. Old doesn't mean dumb, I realized. I stood up.

Pain shot from my hip to my knee. I almost buckled. And then it was gone. When Mr. S. made a move to help me, I stopped him with an upraised palm.

"Mr. S., I can't. I can't hear this right now. I've got work to do." I walked to the door without a limp. "But don't think that I won't want to know and that you shouldn't be ready to tell me all of it."

I put weight on my foot, testing, perfect. The truth of it was that I wasn't sure I was ready to hear.

"I'm going to the barn. Please, just stay here. I bet Mrs. Jonas left something to eat in the kitchen. Eat. Stay. I want to check on Cantara and try to sort this out in my head if I can."

I opened the door; sitting on the floor should have made my hip and leg stiff, but it felt good as new. He shuffled out of my way, but then he caught my elbow.

"No, there's more, and you have to hear it," he said.

Tears burned. Really? More? I wanted to be outside and away from this empty bedroom.

"You won't find Cantara in the barn, Reedy."

My heart dropped from where it had landed near my belly button; this time it fell all the way down to my shoes. I made it as far as the living room couch. "Because?"

"Because she didn't come back. I'm sorry to say that the bad news isn't over yet and that your horse is the one that's been well and truly missing. She hasn't come back since you rode out to the trail."

Enough. Explanations would have to wait. Cantara was one thing I could save.

The sheriff's office smelled of shoe polish and after-shave. It was full of masculine colors and textures: worn leather, out-dated paneling, a bookshelf of random books, a couple of fishing magazines.

"Cantara, my Arabian, is gone, or missing, or maybe lost. I can't figure out which word does the job best, but I thought I'd come in and at least go on record or fill out a report or alert the media or something, in case someone finds her or hears something. If she's wandering around the Refuge saddled and bridled, she's going to get snagged on something, somewhere, where she can't get to water or grazing. I've been kind of under the weather and—"

"Take a breath, Reed."

Jackson Rogers gently smiled as he sat behind the sheriff's antique desk, probably aware of just how good he looked back there. He was Oviedo's answer to Denzel Washington, but then he always had been. Star quarterback at Dr. Denton High School and my AP biology lab partner our senior year. He'd been the one voted most likely to become a superhero, married to another superhero, living on a private island. I'd been in the running for-most-likely- to be someone's governess.

He'd been off to West Point when a poor choice of keg party and a ride home with a drunk buddy and the resulting car accident had ended more than his appointment to West Point. Jackson had come close to dying too. A couple of the other kids in the car had died.

Back then, he'd been tall and lean, all shoulders and narrow hips. Now he'd added a solid, mature bulk that I suspected was muscle. There was a harder set to his jaw and a leaner look through his cheekbones. He'd grown up from being a beautiful boy with an easy flashing smile to being a good-looking man with unusual light brown eyes that watched me intently.

I bit my lip, embarrassed. I usually didn't have to struggle with control. I was the one who calmed everyone else down, helped get order back, been trained to react under the worst conditions, kept the team going forward . . .

"Earth to Reed." He folded his hands on a desk blotter and pushed his laptop out of the way.

"Wow, sorry! And you're right. I know I'm a little bit all over the map these days."

I took a deep breath and wiped sweaty palms on my jeans.

"Hey, it's okay, I was sorry to hear about your uncle, really surprised not to see you at the service, but your Mr. Stillbee filled me in. He said you were staying with friends. You'd had some kind of accident. But you're okay, right?"

He watched my reaction with those eyes of his, two wells of gold-brown, lion's eyes. I felt guilty somehow.

"Fine," I started, then stopped and took a deep breath. "Almost fine. A little shaky." I gave him a little smile. It felt crooked on my face, but I didn't want him to think something was up. "You were there? At his service? Thank you. But of course you would be there, and I wasn't, and that's part of this whole 'have you seen this horse' problem. A couple of weeks back, the night my uncle died, I was out on the trail, got caught in a pretty bad thunderstorm, Cantara, my horse—" I had to stop to gulp.

He nodded, making encouraging noises in his throat.

"Well, she bolted, and I got—" I searched for words that wouldn't make me sound ridiculous. I wanted to say attacked, but then gave it up. "Well, I got dumped."

I let the sentence drop, refusing to shrug. I just didn't have anything to tell him other than hazy impressions: a huge downdraft from above, a hot solid body slipping by, pressing me into the mud, and . . . feathers. Great, I'd been attacked by a giant mockingbird.

Oh no, I'd rather show Sheriff Jackson the fading bruise on my hip in a French cut bikini than give him my feathers-in-the-face report.

"My God."

When he finally spoke, I realized I'd done it again, been holding a one-woman conversation in my head.

"What do you mean 'dumped'?" he asked, not quite frowning. "Thrown? You were always the best horsewoman around. You're rocking my world here, Reed." He leaned back in the desk chair, making it squeak.

"If you're going to get on a horse, you're going to come off—one way or another. That's what Uncle Rulan says. I mean said."

I dropped my eyes and tried not to choke on the lump in my throat.

"But you're okay, now, right?"

"Yeah, sure. It was the storm. I got dumped and then flattened by a microburst; that's all, and a little banged up. I was out of it for a while." It felt like a lie, but it was the best I could do. I was pretty close to cracking wide open, and I think he knew it.

He tried for a lighter tone.

"Did you have a close encounter with the Tannin Bridge lights, Reed Hunter?" He leaned forward in the leather chair, resting his elbows on the pitted surface of the desk. He grinned at me. We fell silent. "You still do it, you know?"

His eyes roamed over my face. I suddenly felt like there wasn't enough desk between us.

"What?" I pressed back into my chair and folded my arms across my chest.

"You still chew the corner of your lip, when you're worrying over something. You used to do that, the lip biting thing, when you were sweating a biology exam. And your eyes, I'd forgotten how pretty they are."

I reached up and tapped my bottom lip. Great, more kid stuff and now here he was mentioning my mismatched eyes.. I thought I'd outgrown the self-conscious part of me. I shrugged it off.

"Well, that's one for the yearbook archives, and probably why you're the sheriff now," I said, really needing him to stop looking at me like he was getting ready to give my description to a police sketch artist. "Because you're the details man. So I was hoping you'd be able to give me some backup. Is it okay if I post a lost horse flyer around town, maybe on the map board at the trailheads? Is there someone you could recommend to contact at the state level maybe? Someone you trust? I can't imagine you haven't done hiker searches out there."

He shifted in his seat and did a pretty decent job of plastering on a concerned frown, but the laugh lines at the corner of his eyes kept giving him away.

"A few, sure, but the Toad's Head Refuge is huge; you know that. A thousand horses could hide out in those woods, or even a couple of pretty big elephants."

I could tell he was trying to be encouraging without telling me straight out that there was nothing he could do—officially.

"Don't be discouraged. The flyers are a good place to start. I'll make a couple calls for you to the parks people. Have you done any scouting around? Horses usually do a pretty decent job of knowing where they live. She'll show up. I'll bet you."

"Probably, I, well, actually . . . "

Even I could hear the way my voice trembled as I tried to reply, and I was on my feet before he could make it any worse. I could see it there, the questions bubbling up in his eyes. Questions that I wasn't prepared to answer.

"Okay. You'll tell me if there's anything else you need, right?" This time he watched too carefully, searching. Time to change the subject.

"Right. And I need to let you know that we've had some poaching trouble out at the ranch." I launched into an abbreviated version of Boxcar's demise and the only explanation I could come up with. "But so far, there hasn't been any follow-up trouble, just the one incident."

"Jesus, Reed, why didn't you tell me this up front? I know you're all about getting your horse back, but if you've got bad guys wandering around the farm smashing up and murdering your animals, you've got more trouble than just a missing pet."

He turned to his computer and started typing. "I can find out if any other ranches are reporting problems in the state. These jerks move through counties like locusts."

I bristled at the "pet' reference.

"She's not just a pet, you know. She's been my . . ."

I'd almost said friend, but I was done sounding twelve.

He glanced up from the screen. "Hey, don't mind me. It's part of the job description to be an insensitive hard butt. I know you've been through it since you've been home and after Iraq, too." He hesitated, watching me again. "That couldn't have been easy."

"I'm fine. It's all good. Flyers, check. I'll bring one by when they're done. Phone calls to important people, check, check. Thanks for talking to me, Sheriff Jackson."

I shoved my hand at him across the desk like a warning flag. He ignored it and stood up, coming out from behind the desk. He felt taller than I remembered, or I felt smaller. He took my hand in both of his. His hands felt bigger than I remembered.

"I know you're really worried, Reed." He glanced at the corner of my mouth. "I can come out and help you look—unofficially. I've got some time coming. I mean it. Let me help. It's been a while since I did any serious riding, but I think I can still keep up. Let's go find--your pet." He was teasing me. I could feel some of the tension drain from my shoulders.

"I could use the help. It's just me and Mr. Stillbee now."

He nodded. I got the feeling I wasn't telling him anything he didn't already know.

"You know every time you bit your lip like that at school over a test, I knew that I was screwed, because if you weren't going to make it then I wasn't coming close to passing."

Laughing, I wondered out loud, "You passed just fine. Come on, wasn't it West Point for you?"

He let me go. It was his turn to look uncomfortable.

"A story for another day. How can I get a hold of you?" He handed me a notepad.

I wrote down my cell phone number, waiting for another day to tell him that the landline at the ranch had been disconnected. We exchanged goodbyes as I walked to his office door.

"It's the side with the freckle," he said.

I turned and looked at him, baffled.

"The side of your mouth that you bite. It's the side with the freckle." I walked out of his office biting my lip.

Chapter 8

Flyer

In the Handy Way parking lot, Mrs. Newton's face looked like a billboard advertising sympathy for sale. I hadn't gotten my door open all the way before she was on me and had me backed me up against the running board of my red Jeep Sport.

"We were so sorry about your uncle. He was a pillar. He was just a complete pillar. I hope you liked the potato casserole. Food, it's silly, but it's all people know to do when these things happen. You did like it?"

She looked at me through thick lenses that made her eyes look like the bottom of a goldfish bowl.

I nodded, hoping I appeared sufficiently mournful and appreciative all at once. There were so many casseroles stuffed in the refrigerator at home there was no way I could know which one was hers. That and I hadn't been able to eat more than a spoonful of anything for a while.

"Thank you; everyone's been kind, way too kind."

Which was true, but I didn't mention that it was driving me crazy. "Now Reed, you're one of our own, and we take care of our own."

She gave me a head to toe inspection. "You should be sure and eat my potato casserole. You've gotten very thin. You're too pretty a girl to be so skinny. I'm sure all that soldiering wasn't easy on you." Her eyebrows came close to taking on the shape of question marks—

almost. If she wanted a blow-by-blow description of my deployment, she was going to be disappointed. I smiled and shrugged.

If it weren't for having to get the flyers about Cantara out, I would probably still be hiding out at the ranch, licking my wounds. Not being questioned in the parking lot of the Handy Way was also high on my list. What I wanted was to be home waiting for Mr. S. to fill in all the gaps of the last few weeks. He had been remarkably absent since he'd promised me answers. After he told me that Cantara was missing, I hadn't stuck around to hear whatever explanations he had. Probably should have stayed put instead of abandoning the only family I had left.

I waved the stack of papers in my fist, hoping Mrs. Newton would understand the important errand I was on without my having to explain it. She didn't.

"Is that something you want me to see?"

And I was caught.

"Yeah. Maybe you can help me? She's missing."

I handed her a paper with a picture of my little fifteen-year-old mare, her neck curving in a classic Arabian arch, her thick black mane and tail shining. I'd included a small picture of me with my arm around her neck when she was a foal and I was a boney twelve-year-old. I watched Mrs. Newton's face go from sympathetic to tragic.

"Oh, Reed, I didn't know . . ."

Fending off more sympathy, I pointed to the flyer in her hand.

"My cell phone number is there if you should hear anything, thanks so much." I gave her a little hand wave and slammed the Jeep door shut, hustling into the store.

I didn't recognize the guy behind the counter. He was new to me. The last time I'd been home on leave, Delores Snyder had still been running our one and only convenience store. Must have finally retired to the grandeur of her bass boat and the Saint Johns River.

Giving the counter clerk the short version of my pitch, he promised to get the okay to display the picture of Cantara in the window.

Nodding my thanks, I walked outside. I'd been so busy trying to escape from Mrs. Newton on my way in that I'd rushed past a card table manned by teenagers. Two girls sat at the table, and a couple of boys lounged behind them, tilted back in their chairs, propped against the wall. A poster pinned to the tablecloth blared its message: STOP THE BUTCHERY.

"Would you like to sign our petition?" one of the girls asked.

Caught again.

The girls at the card table looked so expectant under their black lipstick and big, round eyes dripping with eyeliner and mascara I had to stop and check in. They gestured to an enthusiastic stack of papers, holding out a ballpoint pen.

"And what are we protesting today, ladies?" The breeze ruffled the girl's dull black hair and the edge of the red plastic tablecloth.

"A travesty! A crime against the earth and the earth's children." The shorter of the two girls took the lead in presenting their righteous cause.

I tried not to smile at their passionate indignation. Underneath all their Goth war paint and black nail polish, the girls' sincerity sparkled through like sunlight through a dirty window.

"Oh, wow, that is certainly worth taking a stand against, so . . . okay," I said, resigning myself to a few minutes of the spiel. "Tell me all about it."

Holding their personal stack of flyers, the taller girl smiled shyly, waiting while her friend gave the speech. Under the slashing makeup, the shorter girl's round face reminded me of a baby bird.

"Are you familiar with Gilded Oats Ranch?" the baby bird began breathlessly.

Chapter 9

Confrontation

My stomach did a slow roll. If only this was going to be about wanting to put up another trail marker on refuge land or building a couple of new bat boxes, but I knew better. I sighed.

"Yep, little bit familiar."

She pushed their flyer at me. In bright red ink, the words *End the Slaughter Now!* echoed the posters hysterical warning. A pixilated picture of our ranch's main gate appeared just under the blazing red letters.

"Are you aware that Gilded Oats Ranch is an exotic animal farm that provides rich hunters easy targets for trophies?"

I glanced down at the fluttering paper in my hand. Pictures of horned antelope, goats, and a few species I didn't recognize marched along the bottom of the page.

"Right here, under our noses, hunters butchering animals for kicks, for fun, for blood sport." The girl waited for my reaction, hopeful. Her companion nodded.

"I see, and your petition is to stop . . . what exactly?"

"The blood sport, of course, and to raise awareness."

The taller girl jumped in, eager to contribute. "To make a difference," she added.

The two girls nodded in tandem: two crow chicks. I skimmed the flyer, noticing that the pictures were generic and straight off the Internet. I glanced at the boys behind them and realized they weren't as young as I first thought. Their faces were pierced and their hair was artfully glued in various sharp shapes, definitely older and a lot less innocent looking than the girls.

"And you know for a fact that the owners of Gilded Oats are raising animals for . . . How did you put it? Blood sport. Is that illegal?"

"They tie the animals to stakes and let people walk up and shoot them. It's barbaric. Fish in a barrel."

"Wow, that does sound terrible." I took a pen from the table. "Hey, you know I was born around here, and I heard that rumor, but there was never any evidence to back that up. And I also heard that they were dumping nuclear waste out at the ranch. Not true, of course. And then there was the time that people thought there was a secret missile silo on the property. Again, not true. You pretty sure about this?"

They had the good sense to look a bit uncomfortable.

"Hey, I tell you what. I'll sign if you take some of my flyers to the school, Denton High, right?" I explained about Cantara, and their murmurs of sympathy and condolence were decidedly on the sweet side. It was hard not to smile at the contrast between their harsh, black uniforms and their warm concern.

The shorter girl read my name off of the flyer.

"Reed Baye Hunter, hey don't the Hunters own Gilded Oats . . ." Her voice trailed off.

"You might like to know that the Hunter family donated all the property that made Tannin River Conservation Area possible, including the Eagle Rock Historical sight?" How many times had I picnicked with my classmates at the little park next to the pile of stones, made to look like an eagle by the Native Americans? From the observation tower my family had paid for, the eagle always resembled more of a vulture to me, but I had to respect the effort they'd made

hauling chunks of coquina stone fifty miles inland from the coast—
even if they did get the eagle's head a bit wonky.

The girls looked stricken when they realized who I was. Another
boy, who had just come out of the bathroom, joined the protesters. He
wasn't wearing the group uniform like the others. His hair was a
reddish-brown, a bit on the long side, and he looked like he might be a
member of the basketball team rather than this wannabe Goth gang.
He held a little blond girl by the hand. I noticed that one of the black-
lipsticked girls at the table, the first one, and this boy shared the same
hazel eyes, same as the little girl. Siblings, maybe? A family?

"What's the damage?" one of the pierced boys demanded. I
ignored him. "Hey, we just want donations." He pointed to a coffee
can on the table.

"Maybe it's not what you think, the exotics? Maybe?" I suggested.
I tapped at the pictures of the animals on the paper, trying to win
friends and influence protesters.

The girls glanced at the boys behind them. One of them, the one
demanding cash, shot out of his seat and grabbed the flyers from the
girls' hands.

"If you're a Hunter, then you're responsible for this . . ." He made
sure to let me know what a badass he was with some creative
swearing.

I almost laughed in his face, thinking about my drill instructor, a
true master in the art of profanity, and what he'd do with this kid in
the black eyeliner in front of me.

"You should be careful someone doesn't do something to put a
stop to this, or you can just kick in some cash." He shook the paper in
my face and then balled it up, which sent one of the girls into a fit of
giggling.

"Brian, don't." It was the tall boy with the little girl.

"Shut up, Ryder."

The other punk, the one with enough hardware in his face to start a
jewelry kiosk at the mall, jumped out his chair and came around from

behind the card table, doing his best to loom. It wasn't a terrible strategy, the looming; I'm only five foot two in my stocking feet. Still, he was relatively quick, jumping straight into the intimidation, and it caught me by surprise. It made me look more carefully at his face. His eyes looked like windows into a felony drug conviction.

"I'd love to stand here and discuss the difference between conservation, animal husbandry, and ecological fanaticism, but I've got one of the largest herds of sambar deer in the United States to feed, inoculate, and watch over. Conservation: it's not for the lazy."

I turned to leave.

That's when hardware-face made a mistake and grabbed my wrist. It was more like breathing now than martial arts—the hapkido. Without even a thought, I stiffened my hand, slipped my wrist free, grabbed his hand and pressed his thumb halfway to his elbow. I walked the idiot, yelping and hissing in pain, straight backward into the plate glass.

"Sorry, it's just self-defense you know. It happens without my even thinking about it anymore. You know?"

He made a silly growling sound. I pressed a fraction harder. He slumped against the window. Through the glass, I could see that our banging around had gotten the cashier's attention. He looked like a coiled spring behind the counter. Frowning, I shook my head at the question in his face. He picked up a cell phone and started punching numbers.

Behind me, there was the sound of bumping and rustling. I spoke over my shoulder.

"Stay! Or I'll dislocate his thumb." I leaned in and tried not to gag on B.O. "Are you going to be a good boy?"

He was high but not insensible. He nodded—barely. I let him go.

"Good enough." I backed away, into the parking lot. The boy they called Ryder held the little girl against his chest in a bear hug. She struggled in his arms. He mumbled something to her and then to the girls at the table, and then to me he mouthed the word, "Sorry."

"Seriously, isn't this a lot of hostility for a humanitarian effort?" I kept right on backing out of there.

The girls had gone from baby bird innocent to vulture watchful. Great. "Okay, this was painful and really unnecessary."

The cashier pushed his way through the door.

"You've just lost permission to set up your table out here. You're going to have to leave." He pointed at the bunch. "Out!"

"Geez!" The short girl started scraping papers off of the card table. "I'm just trying to work off my crappy community service."

"Sorry about all this," Ryder called out to me. "Silly stuff, right?"

Ryder caught my eye again as he folded up the card table. He looked genuinely embarrassed. I swung into my Jeep, determined to forget about the latest attack on my family business. As long as they kept their protests confined to the parking lot of the Handy Way, we would co-exist just fine.

While I waited to pull out of the parking lot, a fancy black SUV made the turn into the store.

In the mirror, I watched the driver unfold from the front seat. Ignoring the scrambling teenagers in front of the store, he caught me watching him in the rearview mirror, and I was trapped.

Trapped in the startling blaze of his eyes—ice and fire—he held my gaze without a word or gesture and frowned as if he was disappointed at finding me in the middle of all this childishness. I shook off a vague sense of annoyance and made the right-hand turn toward home.

Chapter 10

Reward

"What do you mean I don't have clear title? Are you saying I don't own Gilded Oats? I don't own my family farm?"

A drip of sweat wobbled on the tip of Mr. B.T. Snyder's nose. I didn't bother to tell our family attorney that I'd turned off the air conditioner to save money. The single drop splashed onto my uncle's last will and testament.

He swiped at his damp forehead. Who was I kidding? He probably knew the financial situation better than I did. Yellow gingham curtains fluttered at the kitchen windows. At least there was a breeze.

"No, that's not it, Miss Reed. You are the single inheritor of Gilded Oats, and the heart of the property belongs to you. It's the edges. The borders of the property are in dispute since, well, from before the frontier days apparently and the original agreements were written on vellum. Honestly, it's possible that the ranch came into your family's possession via a game of chance, a poker game."

I couldn't decide if he sounded impressed or disgusted with my family's lack of legal preparation.

"Bottom line: I can't subdivide any part of the ranch."

"Or sell. Not without clear title. I'm sorry, Miss Reed, but . . ." He took a breath. "Could I bother you for a paper towel?"

Mr. Snyder was melting. I brought him a loose roll of paper towels.

Guilt! Guilt cut across my brain, a knife's blade through my gray matter, because it had crossed my mind to sell. A fact not to be shared with Mr. Snyder or anyone else. In a way, it took the pressure off to know that the ranch was not going to be for sale—now or ever. My struggle now was to find enough money to keep the day-to-day operations going.

Watching Mr. Snyder use up six paper towels to mop his face and neck made me glad that I'd gone with a tank top and Levi shorts for our meeting.

"Mr. Snyder, I'm sorry. How about some water?" I jumped up and went to the cabinet with my mother's glassware.

"Only if you hold the water and splash something with a kick into that glass."

"Sorry, no one's ever been big drinkers around here after . . ."

"Well, no, that stands to reason after your parents were . . . I mean the accident and the drunk driver, of course, my apologies."

"I don't remember them. Don't apologize."

"Miss Reed, if you wish I can begin the process of trying to iron out the border issues with the various parties."

I must have frowned.

"Well, you can think about it," he said.

"Parties" sounded expensive and complicated. He started to shuffle papers together; I knew that it was his signal that he was ready to get in his air-conditioned Cadillac and head back to his office. I got ready to walk him out.

"I appreciate you coming and making the long trek out to the ranch. It wasn't necessary. Who is it? Is it against the rules to find out who it is that disputes the boundary line?"

He handed me a copy of my parents' will and then my uncle's.

"No, of course not, and don't worry about my retainer's fee. It's all paid up. And a nice drive in the country was just the ticket. I enjoyed getting out of the office."

I noticed he didn't offer up a name.

Walking him to his car, a behemoth antique Caddie, I wondered how many times he would bottom out before he made it back to pavement. Our rutted dirt road looped past the house, trailed by the front of the barn, hooked around the bunkhouse, and then finally spit the visitor back out at the front gate.

He huffed his way into the front seat, throwing his briefcase onto the bench seat next to him. He looked so much older than I remembered, another fragile thread waiting to snap.

"And Miss Reed, if you don't mind the personal question, I was wondering where you found enough money to offer such a substantial reward for your horse?"

He pulled a familiar flyer from under the briefcase on his front seat.

Stuck in the bottom corner of my flyer, slapped across the picture of me and my horse in our wild youths, was a sticker that read: Reward: $50,000 and our phone number.

I looked at our lawyer's face; curiosity made him look like an inquisitive pumpkin.

"I didn't put that there. I'm flabbergasted," I said, peeling the edge of the sticker up. "I didn't put these on the flyers. You already know. I don't have . . . any money."

"It's on all of them." He hiked up a hip and pulled a white handkerchief from his suit pants, dabbing at the beads of sweat on his lip.

"I sent my office assistant around to check."

"Who would do this?" I said, spluttering like a brainless kid.

"I don't know, but you're going to have more attention on this than you might want. I just thought you should know. Well, Miss Reed, I'll be off. Slow and steady, that's how I have to be to get out of here."

"Sure, absolutely." I couldn't quit looking at the big, black letters on the flyer sticker. "Thank you again. Slow. Steady. Absolutely."

He must have seen my shock and worry and took pity on me.

"The Warricks dispute the title. Primarily, one Ari Ben Warrick. They've owned property on the river forever, next to your family. I could approach him about a settlement if . . ."

"No, not necessary." I waved as he started to inch his way out of the yard. I didn't drop my head to study the paper in my hands. I more sensed than saw his slow and steady departure.

Suddenly, I was very thankful that the landline had been turned off so that I wouldn't have to explain to a thousand people that a fifty-thousand-dollar reward was not in my budget. Shoot, the phone bill wasn't in my budget, and my cell phone was on its last past-due notice. Might be smart to let it ride. On the flyer, I'd written instructions to leave any information with Miss Mable at the tiny 'Taintsville post office—no phone numbers.

"Great. I've been reward hoaxed. And I think I know a bunch of kids who might consider this payback." I balled up the flyer and tried to remember where I'd plastered all those stupid papers.

Chapter 11

Neighbor

The leather under my hands started to gleam with saddle soap and oil. The tack wasn't in much better shape than the latch on the feed room door, but this was something I could fix. It felt good to see something improved by my efforts. I tried not to dwell on my afternoon of crappy legal news, focusing on the fabulous smell of well-oiled saddles and bridles.

Mr. Stillbee stuck his head into the tack room. "I thought I saw that Snyder fellow creeping his way to the front gate. Would have been faster to carry that big-A car on his back. What was he worrying you about?"

I looked at my grimy fingernails and sighed. "Well, I don't own the important bits of Glided Oats, most of it but not all, and someone slapped a ransom sticker on my flyers that I can't pay, could never pay, and if I don't figure something out, I'm going to lose the ranch."

"Who else would own the Gilded, if you don't? Makes no sense to me."

"It seems that someone named Warrick claims he owns the edges and I don't have clear title."

A strange look settled into Mr. S's crinkles and crow's-feet.

"What? What do you know? Mr. S.?"

"That's the one." He sounded out of breath and worried. He was having trouble meeting my eyes.

"What? The one what? He's the one what?"

"Well . . ." he said, lifting the freshly cleaned bridle out of my hands. "He's the one, who found you and doctored you," he stopped and scratched at his day-old beard. The scratch, scratch sound made my teeth itch.

"Ari Ben Warrick? A doctor? What kind? And he's the man who is disputing my clear title? And didn't bother to call 911 when he found me—" I stopped to catch my breath. "And . . . it looks like it's time to pay a visit, a nice neighborly visit, to Mr. Ari Ben Warrick." I handed my filthy rag to Mr. S. and headed out to meet Doctor Dunn, our vet. One more chore, and then time to go meet the neighbors.

Pretending to be disappointed that it was too dark to ride Mr. Stillbee's old quarter horse Einstein to Mr. Warrick's house, I told Dr. Dunn for the twelfth time not to worry about running late. The sky had just started to turn into ribbons of sunset when we'd finally finished the health inspections and inoculations for the Thompson's gazelle fawns. Born in the spring, they were six months old and bounded around the temporary holding pen like bouncing balls. I'd planned to start early in the morning, but the vet had had an overnight emergency and hadn't been able to start with my bunch until after lunch.

He handed me the bill for services rendered.

"I know you're still settling in, Reed. Don't feel like you have to rush payment on this."

I almost rolled my eyes. I'd gone through an eye rolling mania in my teenage years before the military and was grateful for the discipline I'd been taught, but the mention of money owed, money needed, or money rewarded was putting my military discipline to the test.

"Thanks, I appreciate that. I'm still trying to sort through quite a bit of stuff."

"I know. It's all over town."

"Great." This time I did roll my eyes.

He laughed. I remembered that Doctor Dunn had seven daughters, so he was probably immune to a little eye rolling.

"Not like that," he said, in his best calming vet voice. "People around here are concerned, not just nosy. You know it's true."

I felt gently chastised, and I thought I might know what it was like to be one of the seven Dunn girls—just for a second.

"It's going to the top of the pile, Doctor." I waved the invoice at him.

"Not worried," he called out, his arm waving from the truck window as he started to leave.

The sun hesitated just above the tree line of the big pasture. Mr. S. watched the Tommy babies skipping through the open gate of the enclosure. He'd assured me that he'd be able to handle taking down the temporary enclosure even after I'd asked him to wait until tomorrow so that I could help him. Tomorrow morning we'd see who was boss. I was pretty sure I already knew.

Heading to the house, I thought about washing off the big chunks before meeting my neighbor and apparently personal physician.

I settled on a soft, elbow-length cream sweater and jeans, in case it got chilly. Besides, it was one of the least juvenile things hanging in my bedroom closet. I didn't need help looking younger. I zipped up a pair of leather ankle boots and grabbed a greeting card I wanted to give the mysterious Mister Warrick. You know, just to be neighborly.

I should have asked Dr. Dunn about him. Dr. Dunn knew every one's story, and by the time I had maneuvered down the third dirt road that winded around to the Warrick residence, I was kicking myself for not doing a little bit of intel of my own. At the end of a double-rutted road, I came to a fence of field wire with a gate. There was no mailbox or no trespassing sign, which was good in case I'd overshot my directions, and this wasn't the Warrick place at all. It was completely dark by the time I got to the edge of what I hoped was their property. The lights of my Jeep cut a path through the dense darkness on either side of me. I headed into the last length of the lumpy dirt driveway.

Soft porch lights ringed the charming river house. I couldn't see the river, but as soon as I jumped out of the Jeep, I could hear the endless song of the bullfrogs at its edge beyond the side and back yards. It was built on pylons for one of the perennial problems of living on waterfront—too much water. The house sat like a softly glowing jewel in the middle of the heaviest kind of semi-tropical rainforest. It was beautiful.

I looked at the card in my hand. It suddenly seemed as inadequate as I felt. I heard rather than saw the screen door opening, its creaking complaint a funny counterpoint to the croaking chorus of frogs. It made me laugh. How hard could it be to say thanks to a man whose front porch door needed oiling?

I walked towards the house to meet Ari Ben Warrick.

Chapter 12

Myth

I kept my eyes on my feet as I climbed the steep front steps of the river house. Tripping and giving myself a concussion was probably not the best way to say thank you. At the top of the steps I looked up, and found myself staring into a disapproving pair of startling blue eyes. I smiled.

The man above me did not.

He loomed in the shadow cast by the porchlight, staring down at me. His face stayed hidden in shadow and darkness. The halo of light behind him hurt my eyes.

Refusing to be intimidated, I smiled harder.

"Hi, I'm Reed Hunter; I was told you're the one I should thank for finding me, and then there's a matter I would like to discuss . . ." I lost my train of thought, and any sense I might have been making faded away.

He didn't help. I had the feeling that he was just fine with my fumbling attempts at civility.

I caught a glitter of light in his eyes. I tried again. Holding out my hand, I kept going.

"Reed Baye Hunter. I sure hope this is the Warrick place, and if it isn't, I sure hope you're not armed and dangerous."

I gave him my most disarming laugh.

Come on mister, be a prince. He sighed, and the sound popped a bubble of tension in my chest. Anyone who could sigh over unwelcome guests is someone I could understand.

He stepped back.

"I'm sorry to come without warning, but I was told you didn't have a phone, which is something I get. I don't have a phone either, but probably for different reasons." I waved my hands around, flashing the card in my hand, and experimented with another small, social laugh.

Nothing. He waited, shadow and glitter and silence.

I was quickly running out of icebreakers and started thinking that maybe I could just shove the card at him and make a quick getaway and then call my lawyer for the legalities.

"Come in before the mosquitoes descend on us like . . ." He stared into the darkness over my head. "Well, just come in, since you're here."

He held the door open for me.

I hesitated. Parts of the invitation seemed—well the whole invite was—brittle. I almost used the word prickly, but he hadn't sounded even that warm.

I congratulated myself on my straight, ramrod posture as I climbed those last steps of Ari Warrick 's front porch.

As I walked into the huge, screened, wraparound porch, he quietly closed the squeaky door behind me. Finally, we were on a level playing field.

Turning, I looked into the beautiful, lean face of Ari Warrick, the same man who'd arrived at the convenience store, as I drove away. I remembered those blue eyes, following me as I retreated from the teenage do-gooders.

Standing in the light of the porch he'd been a figure crafted of shadow: dark hair, smooth tanned skin, black turtleneck. He wore his black hair cut neat and close. His skin held a hint of olive and looked Mediterranean; as if he'd sprung up from one of those hot, sun-kissed places—exotic-places. That was the second word that came to my mind after brittle: exotic. So here was the man given to finding lost souls in the woods, and then taking them home. He didn't look like any doctor I'd ever met.

He turned toward the front door, and the light fell full on his face for the first time. When he turned his head away, I gasped.

In the military, I'd seen my share of wounds and burns, and I liked to think that I was savvy about what happens to the human body when it's damaged. But this was something else. I couldn't imagine what could have left marks like these. Maybe it was the shock of it, but suddenly I'd lost my breath and found myself raising my hand to touch his wound. It was so instinctual a gesture I was shocked.

He frowned. I dropped my hand, but not before I'd registered the ragged ridge of scar tissue that sliced from under his left ear down his throat, to disappear under the black sweater he wore. The skin pulled and puckered as if he'd stitched it up while staring into a bathroom mirror. Someone had tried to cut this man's throat.

I was horrified because I knew better than to stare. I knew how badly people who'd been wounded wanted to be seen as people, despite their scars or in spite of them.

I started to apologize, but he didn't give me a chance. He pushed passed me and led the way into the house.

"Good going, Reed," I murmured.

He'd disappeared by the time I'd followed him through the front hall into the great room, and I was alone. The room I stood in had a massive fireplace and a soaring ceiling. Floor to ceiling French doors lined either side of the fireplace and opened out to the screened, wraparound porch. The walls of the room that weren't gleaming glass were lined with bookcases floor to ceiling. It was a house built around a central living area, beautiful and elegant.

I walked to the huge bank of window glass and squinting, tried to see the river. It was out there hiding behind the darkness like a tantalizing clue. He came up behind me and pushed open one of the doors. Night noises teased from the blackness.

"When the weather's good I stay out on the porch all night so I can listen to the sounds the river makes," he offered.

He walked and stood next to me, handing me a paper grocery bag.

"And sometimes when I can't sleep I ride the Refuge Trail. That's how I happened to find you." He clasped his hands behind his back—parade rest. "I thought you'd been hiking and fallen and only later did I realize that you'd been out riding. It seemed later than it was because of the storm."

"Mr. S., sorry, Mr. Stillbee explained that you took care of me." I looked at the living room, the furnishings, the hallway leading to what I guessed were bedrooms. "You kept me here because—you're a doctor?"

Instead of answering me, he pointed to the paper bag in my hands. I opened it. It held my riding gloves, pants, and shirt. It was like that little bag of stuff the nurse hands you at the hospital. I shuffled through the layers, noticing my bra and panties, looking pretty worn out and sad. Oh jeez.

I sneaked a look at him out of the corner of my eye. He was watching me paw through my stuff. I blushed.

"I don't suppose you employ a full-time nurse, do you?" I joked.

Still no smile or laugh. He just kept watching me with those piercing eyes. "I'm sorry, no. There was no nurse. I took care of you."

"Wow, I wanted to say thank you, but now I'm wondering if I should be expecting a bill or royalties from the online snapshots."

"Look around Miss Hunter. What do you see?"

I studied the living room. "No television, no computer, no phone."

"And you won't. Your stay here was very private. I promise. We like to live simply here at River House.

Chapter 13

Night Noises

The edge of his shadow melted into the blackness. His intensity was like a physical touch. I turned away for a moment. Circles of porchlight fringed the edge of the river jungle like pearls. I counted each one.

When I turned back to the open door, I could smell the rain and damp coming, and the living green of the jungle outside—something else—clean and sweet.

He looked at me, studying my face. "One green and one blue. I thought so."

I reached up and touched the side of my face, suddenly remembering the sensation of being blind and a voice in the darkness and singing. Someone singing to me, and the smell of clean and sweet—and blood.

A young girl blasted into the room, out of breath, close to frantic. "Ari, it's the Lights of the Limits again. They're not holding. The lights aren't—"

Then she saw me, and shock replaced frantic worry.

She was as exotic as Ari, but instead of dark mysteries, life bubbled around her like seltzer water. I felt the man next to me tense and become a singing wire in a high wind.

"Eden, we have a visitor."

She didn't take her eyes off of me. Her hair was a black curtain, her eyes a pale blue echo of Ari's.

"But, Ari, they're having . . ."

He cut her off. "My sister, Eden."

She gulped and then looked at him, gathering herself like a dog shaking a wet coat, and walked toward me with her hand outstretched.

"Don't mind my brother; he prides himself on being mysterious. Do. Not. Pay. Him. Any. Mind."

She pumped my hand in greeting and then bounced around the room: a happy, normal, energetic teenager.

"Yes, I'm Eden, and this is my brother, Ari the Grim." Her laughter was the brightest sound I'd heard in a long time. It was easy to laugh with her.

Ari looked at his sister, and I saw his mouth tip up at one corner for the first time. Well, how about that? He's charmed by her.

Together they were dazzling. He was the dark mystery in the room, and she was the black cherry in a cherry coke. I felt a little bit like the answer to paper or plastic; either way, I was the boring one. I needed to hand over my lame thank you and get the heck out of there. But then Eden Warrick grabbed me by the hand and had me plopped on the leather couch in front of the fireplace before I could make my escape.

"I'm so glad you found us again."

She looked pointedly at the card in my hand and then at me. Ari stood with his back to the French doors, watching us.

I handed her the card.

"And you brought us something. How nice is that? How nice is this, Ari?"

She acted like I'd brought them an envelope of cash wrapped in a year's worth of lollipops.

"It's really nothing, no really, I mean it," I said, embarrassed by her enthusiasm and trying to slow her down a bit. "After what I was told you did for me, I hardly knew what to do or say or bring. Mr.

Stillbee tried to explain . . . things." I left it open in case she wanted to jump in with details.

Instead, she popped open the envelope and pulled the card out. It looked sadly generic. Eden acted liked she'd never received anything so amazing in her whole life.

"It's wonderful. I love it, and Ari loves it, too."

She jumped to her feet and rushed to show her brother.

I used her distraction as a chance to stand up and maneuver myself closer to the hall leading to the front door and my exit plan. I was becoming increasingly sorry I'd come. I told myself it was because it was so late, that I was tired, and not the unrelenting silence of the man with blue eyes and the dreadful scar. I cut my eyes to the front door, judging the distance to freedom. He was beside me before I knew it.

The shock that ran up my arm when he touched me made me gasp—again, louder this time. My heart pounded. I looked down at my arm and realized his fingers were pressed to the pulse in my wrist. Surely, he could feel my heart thundering all the way into my chest.

"You really should learn how to control your emotional responses to surprises, Miss Hunter. I wouldn't want to be responsible for your demise should your heart explode."

"I'm fine." If he hadn't felt the frisson of electricity between us, I wasn't going to try to explain. It didn't occur to me to check his pulse. He didn't drop my arm. I wanted to jerk away but couldn't.

"It's just that I've had a lot to think about since Mr. Stillbee told me that while I was . . . here . . . Well, I lost my uncle, who left me in charge of a two-thousand-acre ranch, with a mountain of debt—" I stopped, wondering why I'd started trying to explain any of this to them.

Eden stood across the room, but didn't attempt to join us. I hoped she was better than her brother at reading the subtle signs of panic that had crawled over my skin.

"Never mind," I said. "I really did just want to say thank you."

Eden waved the card at me.

"And I'm sure you were a big help for your brother while I was here."

"Oh, but I wasn't here then. It was all Ari's doing. He cared for you. I was visiting," she paused, "friends."

Stepping back, my paper bag of underwear clutched in my sweaty hand, I felt my face get hot.

"No, she wasn't here," he said, not elaborating.

I had a feeling that it was going to take a crowbar to get any more information out of him.

He gave his sister a look full of raised eyebrows and clenched jaw.

I held the paper bag against my chest like a shield.

"You seem much better, Miss Hunter." He looked at my face again as if I was the answer to some puzzle he'd been working on for some time.

Enough of this. I pulled my wrist free of his grip.

"Your heart rate is elevated, Miss Hunter."

"Actually, this isn't just a social visit. I don't know if you've heard." I directed my words to Eden. "But I was riding the night of the storm, that night," I said. I needed to settle down. "Cantara, my horse, has been missing since the accident."

"Oh, no! That's just awful. You must be anxious." She shot her brother a fiery look.

"And my tack. I was hoping that you might have found something: Cantara's bridle, something. If she's snagged it on something she may not be able to eat or drink. It's part of the reason I'm a bit worried." Wiggling my wrist at him, I tried defending my pulse rate.

Ari Warrick nodded and said, "I can understand your worry about that possibility. It's okay, although it's been my experience that a determined animal can manage to snap the best leather in an emergency. There's no need to worry." For him, it was a long speech. He had one of those voices that sounded authoritarian without having to work at it. Strangely, I felt my pulse slow a bit.

Then I remembered the shock of his hand on my wrist and felt my pulse leap again.

"I'll be happy to watch out for both, the horse or any sign of her."

"Ari rides that trail every day. Lucky for you."

Yeah, lucky for me. Eden came to stand next to her brother.

"And Ari is good for it. He's an incredible horseman. If anyone can figure out what's happened, I'm sure he—"

He tipped his head slightly to her again, cutting her off.

"You'll have to excuse my sister's enthusiasm. She gives me way too much credit." She reached over and took his hand.

"No, I don't. Ari saved me."

Somewhere beyond the wall of glass and the porch, out beyond the invisible black river, an insane howl—half shriek, half-metallic car crash—shook the glass in its frames. The house trembled. It felt as if the night sky had decided to roar through metal teeth.

Eden's face ghosted white as she looked at her brother. She tried to say something, but he raised his hand to quiet her, cut her off. The noise faded. I felt the skin crawl on the back of my neck.

"What was that?" I said too loudly, but Ari ignored me. I had to grab the arm of the couch to keep from falling when the house shook again. In the middle of the next squeal, someone pounded on one of the French doors—a blond guy looking suspiciously familiar. Then I recognized him. It was the cashier from the Handy Way: a nice guy, I remembered, the one who took my flyer. When he saw me, he shook his head and then banged until Ari opened the door.

The sound had faded away, but I realized Eden still cowered and covered her ears.

Ari turned to me.

"Stay with her." It was an order.

It made me mad, him ordering me when I knew he was going out to it, whatever it was. He must have seen my anger. He crossed back to me, took me by the shoulders and I felt it again, the heat and fire when he put his hands on me.

"Please. Keep Eden calm. I know you can. You will." He didn't wait to see if I would obey. He knew, maybe before I did. "Loud noises." He glanced at her and then the blond boy and shrugged. "It upsets her."

He disappeared into the dark with Mr. Convenience Store. Eden fell to her knees. I went to the girl, pulled her to her feet, and held her while the quiet settled around us again.

"See, it's gone. Just a big, crazy noise." Without a clock, I had a hard time deciding how much time had passed.

Eden buried her face in my shoulder. I stared into the blank night, waiting for it to start again, glad when it didn't. She trembled then hiccupped.

"Eden?"

She pulled away and dabbed at her wet cheeks.

"What are the Limits?"

She did not answer me. Another bullfrog sang its boom-boom song outside.

She excused herself, mumbling about getting a tissue to wipe her face.

It didn't take long after the quiet for Ari to come back, to smooth things over and give me an update. A blade of the big intake fans in the horse barn had tipped out of balance, metal on metal, sounding like the whine of a straining jet engine, enough vibration to shake the house. When his sister wandered back into the room, he took her chin in his hand and told her to relax. He turned to me and smiled.

I forgot what I wanted to ask him, forgot why I'd come in the first place, and wondered how I could have ever thought him wounded in any way.

It made me stupid, that smile.

"Nobody hurt, I hope."

"No, not at all, of course not. Blair, the young man at the door, just needed help getting it all balanced up." He gave Eden a quick glance.

"Just one of those annoying mechanical difficulties that come with farming. Our barn is just next door. You understand."

And I did, until I looked at Eden, still shaking and teary eyed.

He chucked her under the chin and murmured something, low and brotherly I guessed.

Then he put his hand on the small of my back and steered me toward the door and out, away from his silently weeping sister. With his hand on my back and the paper bag squashed against my chest, he ushered me onto the front porch.

At the front door, he stopped, maybe realizing that there were still quite a few gaps in his story about me, his care of me.

"I did find you, and I kept you here, but it's probably not as dire as you might think. You don't just seem much better. You are much better."

And I was dismissed. He pushed the door open for me.

"But I can't remember any of it. Two weeks of my life are like a black hole. And when I woke up, it was to be told my uncle had died. I'm trying not to think that if you'd gotten me to a proper hospital that I might have had more of a chance to at least say goodbye. I can't figure it out."

"Reed, Miss Hunter, I promise you it would not have mattered. I have proper training, and you were always in good hands."

I shook my head.

"Yours, your hands. You're not my doctor."

"I wasn't aware that you still had a doctor here. You'd been away."

"Of course, I do. Okay, my pediatrician, but I'm pretty sure the hospital is full of E.R. doctors and—"

He caught my chin between his fingers and looked at my eyes again. "You do look good."

Before I could comment his hand was on my back, and I was being escorted out across the porch. The front screen door squealed, and then he was waiting for me to step onto the top step.

The woods surrounded the house, right up to the porch, hugging the building, there was hardly a yard. I couldn't decide if it was cozy or smothering. After the sky had stopped its bizarre roaring, nothing moved or sang or chirped. It was easy to imagine hearing the river whispering beyond the house. Light from the porch trickled down the steps, barely making a dent beyond the gloom of the front yard.

It was hard to see the Jeep. I hesitated, telling myself I was listening to life beyond the perimeter of the house, thought about bringing up the clear title stuff, but thought better of it; I didn't know where to begin without a rumpled lawyer sitting at my elbow.

He must have taken my hesitation for fear. He started to follow me down the steps. It annoyed me. He may have taken care of me. He may have seen me naked. He may have even wiped drool off of my chin, but, he wasn't going to treat me like a kid afraid of the dark.

When I turned to shake his hand, he bumped into me, and I tipped backward. He caught me in his arms, pulled me close to his chest. I thought I saw something more than starlight in his eyes. Concern?

Chapter 14

Broken

I pushed him away, and said, "I just need to find out what happened to my horse. Sheriff Jackson's getting the Volunteer Mounted Posse out this coming Saturday."

I'd done it again, rattling off the bits and pieces of what kept me up at night when I couldn't keep my brain from filling in the empty spots, the lonely spots.

He listened to me fumble to fill the silence, slipping back behind a mask of stern indifference. I'd run out of things to say, and I shivered, but not with cold.

Ari recovered his composure quickly. "I didn't want to say this in front of my sister. She's very . . .," it was his turn to hesitate, "childlike. She upsets easily. I didn't want to upset her. But, Miss Hunter, I'm sorry to inform you that your horse is dead."

It was done bluntly and cruelly and cold. First, that heart stopping smile and then this. I wasn't prepared for the rush of nausea that choked me.

"I am sorry," he continued.

He did say that he was sorry. I'd heard him say it. But nothing in his tight, clipped voice made me believe him.

"Your bedside manner," I spluttered, "is terrible." It didn't matter; defeat settled over me like a cloak. I tasted bile and then took a breath. "Are you sure? How do you know? Where's your evidence?"

His eyes narrowed. I heard his sharp intake of breath. Ahhh, so the great Ari Ben Warrick with his childlike sister wasn't often challenged.

"I found your horse's bridle and your saddle, scratched, damaged."

"Isn't that to be expected if she's been out bumping around the refuge? Of course, they would be damaged."

Several bullfrogs started up a sudden chorus of riverside singing.

"No, Miss Hunter, they were severely damaged, almost destroyed, and I found them down on the riverbank and very near a known American alligator hole; it's the one nearest to the switchback bend in the river, before the—"

"I'm familiar."

It wasn't that he sounded condescending, it was that he sounded impatient. Give the annoying intruder the facts, and hopefully, she'll be on her way—soon. Rage replaced nausea.

"I'm just wondering if you're familiar with American alligators. Are you trying to tell me that an alligator ate Cantara, a gator who took the time to grab her and unsaddle her before dragging her under, and then death-rolling a thousand-pound horse, and then stuffing her under a log to soften her up for a couple of weeks? That's some smart gator, oh, and that's how locals say it—gator, not American alligator. You're not from around here, are you?" By the time I got to the end of the question, the strain of the visions in my head was too much. I'd started into the sarcastic description with every intention to come out of it royally pissed off, but the images from a hundred scenes on the Discovery Channel of gators and crocs dragging down animals a lot bigger than my beautiful mare started scrolling through my head like a slide show. "Seriously, that's some forward-thinking, big-planning gator."

I should have stopped. I knew I should have stopped even before the next words were out of my mouth, but I couldn't. His arrogant hawk's face registered nothing—no emotion, no sympathy, nothing.

The way he watched me. The way he'd taken the card without a word of acknowledgment from Eden. Maybe he was one of those men that assumed if he showed any emotion around an emotional woman she'd implode. Too late, pull the pin, I was halfway to self-destruction.

"What, nothing else? That's all you've got? You let me sit there thinking there was hope, you arrogant—"

I lifted my hand and slapped him. It sounded like a bone snapping. Too angry to be afraid, I watched a stillness come over the man in front of me: a rigid, stony control. The frogs fell silent.

"You should call off the Mounted Posse, because I'm quite confident she is gone and—" he began.

"Stop. I'm not going to let you end that sentence," I said, turning towards my Jeep and clawing at the keys in my pocket. "And tell your sister that I think she's very sweet and that it made my night that she was so touched that I brought a thank you card. And you ought to invest in a new fan blade for your big-A fan if the noise upsets her so much."

I flung words over my shoulder at him as I retreated before he could fill in any more blanks. I'd heard enough for now. I wasn't ready to listen to any more.

The door of the Jeep groaned when I yanked it open. It sounded the way I felt. I already had my foot on the running board when I felt his hand on my elbow. This time the electricity from his hand sent flares up my arm and made the hairs on the back of my neck stand up.

I looked down at his hand on my elbow. He had long, lean fingers. Uncle Rulan would have called them piano fingers. They were elegant and incredibly strong. When I looked up at him again, I was pretty sure he would be able to see the glint of light from the porch in the tears on my cheeks. I didn't know when I'd started crying, maybe right from the beginning.

"What? Do you want to describe the teeth marks in the leather before I leave?"

He looked confused.

"Why are you crying? I thought you would want to know so that you didn't continue to wonder. It's finished. Isn't that a good thing?"

"Yes, very sensible of you. You're right, of course, but if you say, 'Just get over it' I'm going to shoot you. Maybe not right now, because I left my gun at home, but I have a big gun. I shoot buffalo with it."

He let go of my elbow and leaned over me, his hands braced on the frame of the Jeep on either side of my head.

"What? What now?"

"You have beautiful eyes, and I am sorry. Sorry that it's made you cry."

"I don't cry. I'm a Staff Sergeant in the United States Army, or was. I was. Never mind. Wow!" I took a rasping, tired breath, and squeezed the steering wheel until my knuckles went white. "Then let me make a suggestion that you figure out a better way to tell someone that the one thing on this planet from her childhood that mattered to her was eaten, Mr. Warrick. Maybe your sister seems so childlike and easy to upset because you are an upsetting jerk?"

He stepped back. I yanked the Jeep door shut. I tried not to look in the rearview mirror to see if he watched me as I left, but I did. And he watched, standing at the edge of a pool of porchlight in the middle of a jungle made of darkness and humidity.

Chapter 15

Gifts

There were a dozen more urgent chores on my to-do list than pressure washing the chicken coop, but it didn't cost anything and hadn't required a trip to the hardware store. Plus, it was going to make me feel better to be able to mark off at least one of the items on the list. I was counting on the feeling better part.

I wanted to look for Cantara, refusing to believe that she was dead, but I was running low on pie-in-the-sky faith after my chit-chat with the neighbors.

Sweat dripped off the end of my nose as I blasted away at chicken manure. At least I hoped it was sweat that dripped off the end of my nose.

I'd thrown on an old white tank top, passing on the whole bra thing, and covered up with a pair of candy-pink overalls I'd dug out of the back of the closet. Tucking the ragged legs of the overalls into purple polka dot rubber boots, I was a wet, pink, mucky mess.

It was hot work, the main reason I'd forbidden Mr. S. from doing it. He'd grumbled, but not too convincingly. It was a sweltering, filthy job.

Our small flock of chickens scratched and clucked their way around the coop. I kept an eye on Rody, our rooster, as he stayed busy trying to seduce his hens with promises of imaginary worms. He clucked and they came running, falling for the trick every time.

One of the fat, older hens tried poking her head into the coop to check on the condition of her nesting boxes. I shot a spray of water in her direction. She squawked and flapped away toward the vegetable garden that resembled a weed jungle. The jet of water hit the corner of the coop where a pile of chicken muck had piled up. Water and manure exploded back into my face and hair. Lovely. I turned the power washer off while filth dripped from my hair.

Overhead, someone had started banging away on the sheet metal roof. Swiping at my face, I tipped my head back and yelled, "Mr. S. get off that roof before you keel over. I said I'd get to that." The banging continued, a steady, rhythmic sound— stubborn. "Seriously, get down here and talk to me. I don't need you falling off of there."

I took a broom to what I'd missed with the pressure washer inside the coop, knocking down some stubborn spider webs in the corners. The hammering sound stayed steady. Impossible old man.

"Hey, I went to say thank you to Mr. Warrick last night."

No answer from the roof. I rapped the broom handle against the tin over my head.

"Hear me? His sister's awfully sweet. She seemed glad to get the card. He was less impressed," I let my voice drop to a murmur, "and less impressive." I said it, trying to shut out the memory of his glittering blue eyes.

The hammering stayed steady. "And he has the bedside manner of a wounded bat. He told me not to look for Cantara. He told me to give up."

The hammering slowed but didn't stop.

"Seriously, get off of there. You're going to die, and I cannot take that right now."

I stepped out of the coop and looked up. Whoever was on the roof appeared as a black outline against a dazzling halo of morning sun. The light hurt. It was a strangely familiar sight. I brought my hand up to cut the glare. The hammering stopped. Then came the unpleasant feeling that it wasn't Mr. S. on my chicken coop. The figure stood up.

This was not an old man. There was the impression of height and width, of dark hair and broad shoulders, long arms relaxed at his sides, the outline of a hammer silhouetted in one hand. The figure above me might be capable of filling the entire sky instead of only most of it. I recognized the surge of adrenalin that jump-started my heart.

Sheet metal buckled beneath his feet as he walked to the roof's edge. When he jumped down, landing in front of me, I gasped, swiped at my watery eyes, and took another step back, tripping over the hose connected to the power washer. I flopped backward.

A hard hand grabbed my wrist, pulling me back to my feet.

"Careful. I've got you."

"Good grief," I stuttered in surprise at the feel of his hold on me, controlling me, balancing me. Good grief. "You can stop catching me now. What are you doing on my chicken coop? And with a hammer?"

Still not smiling, Ari Ben Warrick looked at me as if he were itemizing my face, again, lingering on my eyes, nose, and finally my lips. He lifted his chin.

"Okay, enough with the face inspection. Didn't you figure it out last night?"

"What?"

"The puzzle that is my face, apparently." I shook my head. Wet hair flapped against my cheek. "Never mind."

He stepped back, putting distance between us.

"Besides, I think it's my turn; don't you think? I'll stare you down, and we'll compare notes." I pushed the drippy wad of hair behind my ear. Sighing, he handed me the hammer. I slipped it in the loop of my overalls.

I looked down. My T-shirt was drenched and see-through. I was hardly dressed for visitors. Plucking at the bib of the overalls, I pulled it higher.

"So what you were doing on my coop roof? Apologizing?"

"No," he said. He arched one dark eyebrow. "Eden let me know that I ought to work on my 'bedside manner,' as you suggested, and I noticed a loose edge of sheet metal. Any strong wind would tear it right off."

It was there again, his not-quite-a-smile smile. It happened when he mentioned Eden. The corner of his mouth went up just a bit higher.

He pushed his hand out at me.

"Pax."

"Pax," I said, smiling at the Latin word for peace. "Even if it is too early for Latin lessons today." I shook his hand and felt strength, and something else.

I tried not to be as obvious as he'd been, studying him in the bright sunlight. There was a tracery of scars on the back of his hand and wrist. To work on the roof, he'd pulled the long sleeves of his black T-shirt up to his elbows, exposing tanned forearms thick with muscle; a carpenter's arms were my first thought.

"Eden's right. And I was wrong. I'm sorry about your horse and sorry I was the one who had to tell you." He stopped, crossed his arms behind him, and waited.

Not sure what he wanted from me, I shrugged.

"Okay. It's okay. But I'm going to hold out a little bit of hope if it's all the same."

"Of course, and I hope you'll find the answers you need. With that in mind, I brought you a horse."

"You brought me a what?"

There it was again, that slight upward tilt at the corner of his mouth. And this time without even mentioning Eden. He nodded.

Obviously, there wasn't going to be a lot of casual chitchat from Ari Warrick. He continued to watch me with eyes that looked like two slices of blue storm, eyes lined with black lashes under the dark wings of his eyebrows. The scar tissue puckered white against the strong column of his neck.

He caught me looking, and all hints of humor disappeared. Embarrassed, I leaped to the last thing I had heard him say.

"I'm sorry; what did you say? What horse? What are you talking about?"

"In the barn, will you come?"

Turning, he marched off toward the barn, never looking to see if I was following. Chickens scattered out of his way. Open mouthed, I watched him go. Suddenly, at the barn entrance, he stopped and looked back at me over his shoulder.

"Will you come, Reed? And Reed, R-E-E-D, you do look well," he added, before starting off again.

A voice, *his* voice, ghosted through my memory again. He'd asked me to spell my name. And he'd sung to me. I remembered a man, this prickly stranger, singing nonsense words to me as I lay surrounded by painful fever and burning dreams, after I'd been attacked on the trail next to the Tannin River.

Chapter 16

Two For One

A truck horn blared behind me. It was beginning to feel like I was getting orders from everywhere. I might as well still be in the Army. Turning from Ari and waving, I recognized the sheriff's truck. Jackson looked neat, pressed, and put together when he reached me.

When I returned his handshake, he gave me one of those two-handed deals, and I watched as my grubby little hand disappeared into the cavern his big hands made. He gave me a serious once over, forgetting to let go of my hand.

"I have got to get a phone." A light breeze teased the air. I shivered inside my soaked clothes.

He laughed, "Oh, I don't know. You can learn a lot from springing a surprise visit on folks." His eyes dropped to my shirt again. I suddenly had the urge to tighten the straps on my overalls just in case. "Getting a lot done? Or just staying busy?"

"Yes, to both."

"And you have other guests, I see."

Turning, I saw Ari watching us from the barn. I pulled my hand out of Jackson's.

Jackson shot me an arched-eyebrow look and then started walking toward Ari. He was as tall as Ari, but where Ari Ben Warrick was long and lithe, Jackson had bulk and strength. Standing together, they made a girl look twice—any girl.

I watched the two men shake hands and then ignore me. Without looking back, they disappeared together into the barn. It was enough to put a girl in a bad mood, even a girl covered in chicken crap.

I came close to walking back to the house and getting a shower. But curiosity overcame my vanity.

"Okay, okay, I'm coming boys."

I was damp. I was sticky. And by the time I walked into the dark interior of the barn, I suspected I was chafing. The whole setup was starting to make me grumpy.

Then I saw the horse. What had Ari said? But he hadn't brought me any horse; he'd brought me a dream. The gelding was a black Friesian whose mane hung like a curtain down his neck. His tail dragged the ground. This horse was built like an elegant tank.

He stood cross-tied in the middle of the barn walkway. As Jackson and Ari inspected him, he arched his neck like a champion. Beyond the gelding was the horse Ari must have ridden over on, a twin to the gelding—only taller, maybe broader, if that was possible.

Jackson was the first one to notice me.

"Pretty nice neighbor you've got here, Reed. This is some horse." Ari stood next to the horse with his hands behind his back, waiting, watching me expectantly.

"What is this?"

I'd already reached out to touch the silk that was this horse's glimmering black coat, and I had to force my hand back down, curling it into a fist. I shoved both hands into my overalls' pockets.

"I brought you a horse. I raise them, and you need one. As solid as that one is." Ari jerked a shoulder in the direction of Mr. S.'s horse, Einstein, who'd managed to keep right on eating, not caring that there were two new horses in the barn. "I thought you might be able to appreciate a somewhat younger animal for your work."

Daisy, our donkey, brayed her admiration, Sid and Jeb the miniature ponies took turns saying hello and snorting their excitement. The barn rang with happy, bustling noise. And I was going to put a big, fat stop to it.

Jackson watched me with his arms crossed across his chest. Ari watched me and waited.

"Wow. Hard to know what to say, except NO. I can't risk riding your horse—if there were an accident . . . And before you say, 'That would never happen,' I'm going to stop you, because I could never replace this animal."

My palms itched to touch the animal in front of me. Ari stiffened, and I thought I heard Jackson chuckle.

I frowned at both of them.

"Thank you. Really. I'm shocked." Especially after the dismissal of last night. "But I can't risk anything that will make me more liable right now. I just don't have the money."

Ari stepped closer to me, and I resisted the urge to back up. "There's no liability; I'm giving him to you."

"No, you're not," I said, turning to Jackson. "You didn't bring me a new truck did you?"

He almost laughed, and then shook his head, inching toward the exit. "You stay there." I pointed to Ari. "I'll be right back. We'll settle this."

I trailed Jackson to his big, official sheriff's truck. He turned to me.

"So, what's that all about?" He nodded toward the barn. "What's with the horse giver back there?"

"He doesn't think that the news about Cantara is good. He has a theory, but you've known him longer than me."

"No. You'd think so, but I've only seen him around town. He comes into the feed store and the drug store and like that. An acquaintance. Hasn't lived here full time until recently," he said, flopping his hand on the hood of the truck. He drummed his fingers against the metal.

"And how about this surprise visit of yours? What's this all about, Officer?" I was pretty sure my shirt was dry by now, even if the smell probably hadn't improved.

"Honestly?" He studied me with those big, brown eyes of his.

"Sure. That'd be nice."

"One, I wanted to check on you, after your visit to my office. Two, I wanted to tell you that there has been some reported poaching activity over along the Seminole/Brevard county line, cattle mostly. Maybe it's the economy. So, be aware. And three, I was wondering when we might get together."

"Together? As in what?" I was wishing I'd bailed and taken that shower now.

"As in a date, to ride out and look for your horse, if you want. Or as in you and me, maybe a picnic, which I'll provide, of course. Or both together." The picnic part sounded so good I wanted to cry, but the mention of looking for Cantara brought it all crashing back: the odd sensation that the accident had all happened to someone else and those moments of imagining what might be left of a beautiful Arabian mare after a gator tore into her. I wasn't ready to describe possible theories from my mysterious neighbor with Jackson.

"How about Friday?" I said, choosing hope. "If the weather holds, and the Popeye's doesn't run out of chicken. Yeah, it would be nice to have some company out on the Refuge Trail. I'd like that."

He took my hand again and looked relieved, which was a pleasant surprise. I'd always thought of Jackson as a confident guy. I was hardly a big prize. He swung up into his truck and seemed pretty pleased with himself.

"Do you need any help with Greeks bearing gift horses?" He laughed when I shook my head. "And Reed, if the weather doesn't hold, we're still on. We'll go to a movie."

"Wow, that would be a date. And I promise to shower."

"Lose the overalls. Keep the shirt."

He drove away with a wave.

Yikes. I waved as the most popular boy at school drove away, and when I turned back to the barn, the burning gaze of Ari Warrick greeted me. Yikes.

Chapter 17

Breach

A ri watched me with a small smile. That smile was as disturbing and confusing as his offer of an extremely valuable horse. Jackson's offer was surprising; Ari's offer felt like a riddle.

His smile didn't waver. It was the first smile he'd directed exclusively at me. He was transformed; it was like seeing the glow of a lantern in the depth of the darkest cavern.

"Are you sure?"

At first, I thought he was talking about Jackson's invitation, and it confused me. He turned and walked away from me again, into the shadowed interior of the barn. He started to untie the beautiful gelding. It was hard to be sensible and not covet a horse like this one.

I followed Ari into the shade of the barn. This time I did reach out and stroke the velvet coat of the gelding as he snuffled my hair, probably smelling 'ode de chicken coop.'

"Why would you ever give something like this away to anyone? I hope you understand why I can't take him. I don't mean to sound like a brat."

I ran my hands down the horse's neck and over his back, admiring the perfect lines of his confirmation. Reaching his rump, I slipped my hand down his hind leg. He picked up his hoof like a champion and a perfect gentleman. His hooves were the size of salad plates. His tail swished against the clay. I came around the gentle giant and almost jumped when I saw Ari standing so close; I had gotten so lost in the beauty of his offering. He was holding the lead rope in his hand.

Einstein directed a high-pitched whinny in my direction, which made me sigh out loud. What a joy it would be to ride this horse.

Ari looked past me to where Einstein stood in all his swaybacked glory. As if reading my mind, Ari brushed the horse's forelock out of his eyes.

"Would you like to ride him?"

I did the right thing; I hesitated before I came to stand next to Ari in front of the beast.

Ari explained, "I led him here behind Vulcan, and it would be much easier to have someone ride him home if you're going to turn him down. He doesn't care for being the pack horse." I turned back to the gelding and ran my fingers through his mane. "It's the kind of thing friendly neighbors might do for one another." He made it sound like more than a favor.

Maybe it was the way he made it sound like a flirt. Maybe it was the way he'd smiled at me earlier. "Like a good neighbor, I feel I can't refuse to help out another neighbor." The horse quivered when I scratched him between the eyes. "Can you wait until I shower and change into my riding clothes? I won't be long. Do you have time? I would love to ride him."

"And I would love that, too."

"Good," I said, pulling my banged up saddle from the top rung of Einstein's paddock. Ari reached up and easily swung the saddle down. He strapped it on the horse.

And then I realized I should pretend to play at being a good hostess.

"Would you like something from the house while you wait? To drink. Or eat. Or read."

He stared. "Why don't I walk you up to the house?" He handed me the lead rope.

"Absolutely," I said, walking the gelding into the light. I waited for Ari to join me.

"What's his name?"

A shadow crossed Ari's face and then he looked at me, shrugging off whatever had bothered him at the moment.

"Hades, but don't take it literally. He's a fine fellow, and he won't drag you to the underworld anytime soon."

I started to the house.

"Good to know. Right, Hades? Besides, I don't care for pomegranates; that's how it worked, right? Persephone got stuck in the underworld when she ate six pomegranate seeds, and now we have six months of winter."

Ari fell into step beside me with the twin horse he'd called Vulcan. We led the horses up the dirt road toward the ranch house.

"That is the story. But it's the moral of the story that's important."

"What's that?" I turned to see him watching me as we walked.

"Consequences. There are always consequences to every action."

"Don't I know it; another good reason not to accept gift horses from Greeks."

He barked a laugh and then started to cough. His laugh sounded rusty, and he looked surprised when he heard it.

"Laugh much? Has it been a while?"

He took a deep breath and paused. "You have no idea."

"Really?"

I felt silly and warm at being the one to be able to make him laugh—even a little.

We tied the horses to the hitching rail and went inside. Ari waited for me in the kitchen, assuring me that he'd make himself at home while I got ready. It took me twenty minutes to wash off the worst of the chicken coop mess, throw on a pair of riding pants, and button myself into a white oxford shirt. I needed the collar to keep the sun off the back of my neck. I grabbed my riding gloves and stuffed my feet into a worn pair of boots. Ari looked pleasantly surprised when I reappeared so quickly, my hair pulled into a lumpy, damp ponytail. I gave him the one finger wait-a-minute sign and headed to the back of the house.

Mister S. sat at the kitchen table his hand around a cup of coffee and his head in a *Popular Mechanics*.

"I've got an errand to run. Will you be okay?"

He glanced up. "You're a big girl. Isn't that what you keep telling me? Out there cleaning out that coop by yourself, being the big boss, just like your uncle."

"Be thankful. I had chicken stuff in my ears."

He smiled into his magazine as I left. In the hall closet, I pulled my gun out and stuffed it in the back of my pants, planning to put it in my saddlebags.

By the time Ari and I were on the road, and I'd settled into Hade's flawless gait, I was in love. The big horse moved like a dream and responded to the slightest leg pressure. He made me lonely for Cantara. We rode in silence up to the front gate. It was the closest gate to the main road, which would be the quickest way to the river house.

The day was a golden shimmer of light and air, and it was straightforward and companionable to ride along in silence.

I tried not to smile when he finally spoke. "What do you think?"

I reached forward and stroked the silk of Hade's neck. "Don't think I don't know what you're trying to do."

Ari rode like he'd been born on top of his horse and had only come down to get a closer look at the ground occasionally. He kept his eyes straight ahead, and I noticed that he rode with his scars away from me, wondering if it was intentional.

"And what's that?"

"You wanted me to ride this horse, so I wouldn't be able to give him up." He still didn't look at me when he answered.

"Is it working?"

It was my turn to laugh. "Nope. I really can't afford to feed him. Never mind that. What I can't figure out is why. Why you would do this."

Ari's horse was a slightly bigger, broader version of Hades and it was hard not to whistle in admiration as I watched Ari and Vulcan together. The breeze lifted the dark fringe of hair off of Ari's forehead. He must have felt me staring. When he turned to look at me, I slid my eyes to Vulcan.

He said, "Trying to have a better, what was the phrase? Bedside manner."

"Can't afford it. Really can't. Nothing else needs to go wrong or break or, oh, crap." I pushed Hades into a canter towards the front gate of Gilded Oats and the gaping hole that someone had cut into the bottom corner of the wire fence next to the gate. The eight-foot-high fence that had been cut and peeled back like a tin can.

Chapter 18

Intruders

I was off Hades and at the fence before Ari could ask a question.

There was nothing on the ground in front of me but bad news. The human footprints were completely obscured by the sharp edges of addax antelope hooves. Shylock, the addax buck, had a habit of bringing his herd of lovely ladies along the perimeter fence from the big pasture to the river for water in the afternoon. The breach in the fence must have looked like a neon exit sign to the buck. From the look of the tracks, the entire addax herd had poured through the opening.

Ari walked Vulcan along the game trail that ran next to the fence on our side.

Pushing through the opening, I walked toward the main road until I found a set of expensive tennis shoe prints in the sand. Human tracks were clearly visible as soon as whoever had done this staggered off the blacktop.

It was a jumble: a blizzard of clomping big footprints—big enough to be men—and smaller shoe prints—girls—and then tiny child's footprints, walking next to the others as if someone had been holding the kid's hand.

Recognizing what that meant made my gut cramp. Whoever had cut the fence was dragging a kid out here with aggressive antelopes on the loose, and the ranch would be liable.

What were they thinking, bringing a child along on their Bill and Ted's idiot adventure? At least the antelope tracks trailed away from the highway; that was something. No one was going to get an antelope horn through their windshield at least.

Ari studied the ground. "The smaller tracks are on the property, inside the fence on the ranch, and they lead off that way, following the game trail along the fence line." He pointed.

"Great, there are people on the inside of the fence and antelope on the outside of the ranch, and I have no way to call Mr. S. to come babysit this hole. I can't afford to have more animals out wandering the neighborhood."

"Animals out? What kind?" He started rummaging in his saddlebag.

"Some of the bad ones. Shylock the addax buck is a mean piece of work. I don't see any eland tracks, but all that means is that those stupid kids are wandering around with water buffalo and eland. It's going to be a miracle if no one gets skewered."

I slipped back through the gap in the wire. Ari pulled a length of rope from his saddlebag and started to weave it through the opening.

"If you can wait here, I'll go for help. I have a few young men working for me that understand about this kind of thing."

"Why would I wait? I need to find those fool kids; they're probably the ones from the petition drive, saving the world from me or something."

He narrowed his eyes at me. His mouth turned grim.

"Those kids at the Handy Way. You remember. You came slamming up in your fancy SUV." I brushed at the tracks on the ground, trying to judge their freshness. "Oh . . . never mind. Take my word for it. I've got to get after those fools and kick some do-gooders off my property."

"Reed, wouldn't it be better to go about this systematically? I'll have my men go after the buck. Wait for me. I won't be long."

"No, someone's got to warn those kids that they are not in a Disney movie and that the lion is not going to sing for them, and I need to do it now."

This time, when he frowned, his eyebrows crashed into a V shape. "You raise lions?"

"No. Not lions. I was trying to make a joke. But there are some things worse than lions," I said, thinking about poachers. Reluctantly, he laced his fingers for my foot and gave me a leg up.

"Wait."

"No, I can't. Just hurry if you want to help."

He nodded, tension crackling from him like electricity. "You can't call your man and let him know? Mr. Stillbee?"

I didn't have time for my usual spin about our tragic financial situation. "No phone. It got turned off, and I still haven't been able to swing a new cell phone for him. So you see, I cannot afford another catastrophe. I'm hoping the antelope headed for water and cover. I don't want anyone hurt if they get out on the highway."

He handed me Hades' reins and then swung into Vulcan's saddle. Closing the gap between us, he put his hand on my shoulder and squeezed. If it was supposed to be galvanizing, it failed. It made me weak. The tenderness in his quick touch was meant to comfort, but I trembled under the weight of his hand on me, praying that he wouldn't say anything. He must have sensed how slender the thread that I was holding onto had become. He let me go.

"Reed, don't worry. I'm going for help. You go after those children. They couldn't have gotten far."

I nodded, afraid to speak.

"Go. It's going to be fine. Quickly, while there's light. They're probably sitting on a log around the bend."

He made me want to believe him.

I turned Hades down the game trail that paralleled the fence. The exotics were shorter than a rider and horse, and I was going to be doing a lot of ducking to follow the trail.

I looked back. Ari leaned down and pushed open the big main gate. It made me feel lighter, knowing he was there, going for help, that there were two of us working the problem.

"Ari, thank you," I called back to him.

He looked at me and nodded.

"And hurry. Whoever cut that fence has a little kid with them. Why would they do that? Why would anyone bring a child out here?"

"Let's not find out. Get them out of there, Reed. Surely they haven't gotten far with a small child."

As I rode away, I could still feel his strong, lean fingers on my shoulder, holding me in the saddle, holding me steady, and my stomach still fluttered. Stupid. Nice, but stupid.

Hades broke into a trot and then a canter. I stayed low in the saddle, bending over the horse's thick neck. Later, I'd think about it later—why Ari Warrick's hand on me always made me tremble.

It didn't take long. I found two girls, one sitting on a fallen tree trunk next to the river gate and the other one on her feet, her hand on her friend's back. They were crying; it was the international sound of two stupid girls who had gotten themselves in over their heads.

I threw myself out of the saddle.

"Where are the others? The little girl. Your sister?"

The standing girl nodded and pointed to the one on the stump. They were still wearing their goth war makeup. Tears flooded black rivers down their cheeks.

"I know she's here too, and I remember you both from the Handy Way. What's with the tears?"

I could tell the recognition was mutual. The girl on her feet had the pretty good start of a shiner under all the black sludge; she slumped to the ground next to her friend.

Squatting, I hoped it wouldn't take too long to get something resembling sense out of them.

"What's happened here? Do you know how many aggressive, wild animals there are around here? Stop crying. I just need you off my property. Stop it. Talk to me."

Black tears dripped into the sand.

"You've got to get Lindy back."

The girl with the shiner grabbed my hand. Hades danced away from her hysteria. I hushed him. He settled instantly.

"She had to bring Lindy. Her mom was . . ." She shook her head, gesturing toward her friend, swiping at her eyes. "A mess, and Ryder had to work. They didn't care. They were fine with it. We were going to party, you know."

I looked at her, the swollen eye almost closed. She'd taken quite a shot to the face. I needed to try and sort out the playlist.

"Okay. Start with who was with you. The little girl is Lindy, your friend here's little sister, and Ryder, the tall boy at the Handy Way . . ."

"My stepbrother." The girl on the stump replied.

I remembered the auburn-haired older boy and the little girl with big eyes under a corn silk fringe of hair.

"Are you two okay? What's your names?"

"Gretchen," the girl on the stump said. Her crying had slowed down to a dull trickle since I'd gotten there. She nodded and sniffed. She was starting to look more angry than hurt. "I'm okay. That's Jenna. It's Lindy, my little sister. They took her." Gretchen started ringing her hands.

"Stop that!" I knelt in front of her. "Who? Who was okay with you bringing a little girl out here to party?" I remembered the pierced bullies with the girls at the convenience store.

Gretchen's black cargo pants were coated to the knees in dust from walking the trail. No water. No bags or backpacks. No equipment at all.

Jenna piped up, "We weren't doing anything. Those guys, Zac and Teal, they brought us out here."

"And Mister Jones. Don't forget him." Gretchen reached up and put her fingertips to her tear-swollen eyes.

"We thought we were going to the bridge and look for the spook lights, you know, hang out."

"Not in the daylight. You weren't going to see any 'lights' in the daytime. Didn't think of that, I guess?" My patience was running thin.

Hades snorted and pawed. I wiped a trickle of sweat out of my eye. The sun cut through the overhead mat of oak leaves in laser beams of searing light. I could feel one sunbeam drilling a hole in the back of my neck.

"What about your little sister? Lindy, right? Where is she?" There were more nods, more tears.

"They took her with them. She's only four. We tried to stop them."

"Gretchen tried to stop them. They shoved me down, and I hit the log," she said, rubbing her chubby thigh. "They took Lindy. They were talking crazy. We were expecting just to hang out, drink some beer, and have fun."

"Where? Where were they going with her?"

"It was crazy, stupid stuff, about going to get the gold and a boneyard or a graveyard or a nest." The girl shook her head, worry carved lines between her eyes.

"Now I'm confused. Wasn't this supposed to be about animal abuse and the ranch? You know? The petition at the store."

Gretchen made a face while Jenna clutched at her middle.

"They were saying crazy crap—" Jenna began.

"It was supposed to be hanging out," Gretchen said, cutting her friend off. "But then they started talking about something in the woods, really crazy crap. She's right. I thought they might be drunk already."

We were going around in circles at this point, and I knew from experience that the panic was still too close to the surface for the girls to be able to give me much more help.

"It doesn't matter. I need to find them now. Which way?"

Jenna started to cry again. Gretchen hunched.

"They went through that gate," Gretchen said, pointing to a gate in the distance. A gate that led to the Refuge Trail. "And there was another guy that we didn't know, he had the craziest green eyes I've ever seen. He was here, waiting for us. He was the one. He said that they had to go along the river until they got to the old bridge, and then they'd see something big, I don't know; I didn't understand any of it. The trestle bridge, I know I heard that part."

Okay, it was a start. As long as the idiots had kept the gates shut behind them, there shouldn't be any exotic animals to terrorize them on the Refuge Trail. Still, it was no place for a four-year-old girl. The trestle bridge was a remnant of an old train track that had once crossed the river. Wooden pylons jutted up out of the water like wooden dragon's teeth. I stood up.

"Girls, walk back the way you came and stay near the fence. If you hear anything, climb that fence. You do not want to try to make friends with a grumpy eland antelope. Can you do that?"

I looked at Jenna who had started to hold her stomach with both hands again. "Can you do that?"

Jenna nodded, then reached out for Gretchen's hand.

"We can do it," Jenna said.

"Good. Friends of mine should be coming to the main gate, so stay put when you get there and wait for them. Do. Not. Wander. There are things running around here that will not be nice to you. Obviously. And I'm not just talking about the people. Tell my friends what you told me. An old man may be there, Mr. Stillbee, and a man named Ari Warrick."

"Ms. Reed," Jenna gritted out.

I hesitated.

"It was stupid crazy. The boys were talking about finding gold in a nest." Her eyes wheeled in her head.

"Okay. Maybe they were already drunk, right?"

They both nodded.

"But Lindy . . . they wanted Lindy—not us—why?"

I cut Jenna off. "Go now. Tell my friends what you told me. Go." They got up and started stumbling back to the main gate.

Leading the big horse through the arch of vines and leaves, I couldn't help but think of the last time I'd been through the river gate. The scar that somehow wasn't there ached in my thigh. I turned to make sure the girls were leaving. They kept limping in the right direction, at least that was one thing off my plate.

Reaching back, I checked the bulge in my saddlebag; the gun's bulk made me feel better, knowing how to use it made me feel empowered.

I went to find a little girl named Lindy.

Chapter 19

Found

This wasn't a prank anymore, and the farther I rode into the gloom of the up-river trail, the more ominous it all felt. The myth of the 'Taintsville lights was a fun conversation starter or an excuse to 'hang out and party' as the girls had put it, but now the joke was over.

Unfortunately, there had always been those who were attracted to the darker theories and rumors swirling around our rumored ghost lights, people playing at covens and witchcraft, or rumors of mysterious disappearances and danger. It came with the territory.

The girls had mentioned the trestle bridge. It was a part of the trail where cypress bogs along the river choked the underbrush, almost making it impossible to travel through, except for a single ribbon of the hiking trail that finished somewhere beyond the bridge.

The tangle of vines overhead grew heavier, forming a curving tunnel of gloom. Hades kept up a steady, solid pace without my having to encourage him. His smooth gait gave me confidence and helped me keep my mind on searching the trail for signs that someone had dragged a little girl this way.

The river whispered on my left this time around. The last time Cantara and I had been heading downriver. Coming this way was like swimming upstream—against the current. The air under the canopy of leaves dripped with humidity. The underbrush grew thick enough in places that I could hear the river but not see it behind the screen of bay trees.

My shirt clung to my skin. Hade's coat gleamed in the dark.

The trail dead-ended here, and only the hardcore hikers and riders pushed through to the end, only to have to turn around and hike or ride back out. The trestle bridge was beyond the trail ending, a lover's lane of sorts, a teenage party spot. It was a long way to drag a little kid—a long, hot way. And why? The only answers I could come up with made my head hurt.

Hades surged forward, sensing my worry.

I expected the trail to narrow. Instead of tightening, it widened; the scrub and palmettos on each side were crushed and flattened on both sides of a thin dirt path. I pulled Hades back to a walk.

Overhead, branches dangled broken as if someone had driven a front-end loader down the path. In places the trees had been completely ripped away, leaving gaps full of empty sky. If someone from the park's maintenance crew had used heavy equipment to widen the trail, it looked as if it had taken bites out of the canopy. It was an odd way to go about trail maintenance—sloppy, damaging. The big trees had their bark peeled back, stripped off. The pattern of wear and tear reminded me a bit of the way the whitetail bucks had to rub against tree trunks so rub off the felt on their antlers.

Hades tensed beneath me, probably wondering why I'd slowed him down when there was so much space to move around in. Surprised, I rode all the way to the trestle bridge.

The trail dumped us out at the train trestle, but we were alone. No kid. No kidnappers.

Jumping down, I strained to hear any noise over the soft, persistent murmur of the water. But there was nothing. There was just Hades and his winded breathing and the sounds of the Refuge, living and growing all around us.

At the edge of the water, I caught the flutter of a scrap of pink— little girl pink—a tiny piece of ribbon. Shoe prints and scuff marks cut into the dirt on the riverbank, disappearing into the black water. They'd gone across the river with the little girl in tow. But why?

It was tempting to sit tight and wait for Ari and anyone he could drag with him. I surely did not want to cross that black water.

I swiped at the sweat on my forehead. Hades pawed impatiently. Then a muffled sound echoed through the thick cypress stands: a little girl's scream that sent the hair crawling on my skin and made Hades rock back on his heels. He snorted and then pranced.

I hadn't imagined that scream. Lindy was out there.

"Good boy, good ears." I pulled myself up and into the saddle. Slamming my heels into the horse's sides, I pushed him over the edge of the riverbank, landing with a mini-tidal wave. It was deep, over Hades' head, and for a panicky second we went down before the big, strong horse forced himself to the surface. I let him do all the work, clinging to the saddle and a handful of thick mane. The river was wide enough here to make it a pretty good swim. The water was cold against my clammy skin.

Lindy screamed again.

On the far side of the river, the woods closed in on us. There was no room here to ride. I jumped down and pulled the horse through the underbrush. Wild potato and grape vines strangled the path. Low scrub brush gave way to the twisting roots and deadfalls of a hardwood hammock, which I knew could go on for miles or drop away into cypress bog, swamp, even a pond. I kept pushing through a stand of saw palmetto, their trunks and roots formed an ankle-breaking obstacle. Then I saw another slash of pink through the underbrush, Lindy in an oblong clearing of flattened grass the size of a football field, ringed by massive oaks and stubby clumps of scrub brush. The trees opened to a shock of cloudless sky overhead.

Whoever had taken Lindy had left her dead center in the clearing-alone. She was sucking her thumb and hiccupping.

I couldn't register anything except the little girl abandoned in the circle of that dark wall of trees.

Dropping Hades' reins, I ran toward her.

For a breath of time, the world in front of me shimmered, fell away, and I didn't see Lindy at all. I was back in Afghanistan, and it was another girl in front of me, a girl with dark hair and eyes, not blond and not blue eyed. An Afghani child was standing outside a candy store, bending down to pick up a paper bag of treats. But it was a bag full of death, not candy. My heart hammered under my ribs, adrenaline flooded my system.

Lindy looked at me with big, frightened eyes, and I saw myself in her eyes, a crazy woman yelling at her not to pick up a bag that didn't exist.

I was the one frightening her.

Stop this. Stop now. I forced myself to slow down, to control myself. I froze and called to her.

"Lindy. It's okay, sweetheart. I'm sorry." I froze and took a breath. "Gretchen wanted me to find you, and Ryder, too. Don't be afraid."

At the sound of her sister and brother's names, she took a tiny step toward me. The lace trim on her pink T-shirt was ripped. Her shorts were still wet from crossing the river, her tennis shoes were filthy, and her hair was a tangled knot, but I'd found her.

"Baby, I'm sorry if I scared you. That was pretty silly, wasn't it?"

I made myself walk as I lowered my voice. She didn't need me to be reliving some other little girl's horror. There was plenty of trauma right here, right now.

She took another step toward me, then stopped and looked up at the sky, sucking harder on her thumb.

"Careful, or you're going to suck your thumb right off and then what? You can't suck my thumb, it's way too dirty, and my horse doesn't have thumbs."

I couldn't tell if she heard me. She still didn't look at me, but then I saw her mouth smile around the curve of her thumb. I felt something soft and squishy happen in my chest.

Kneeling in the flattened grass, I waited for her to come to me. It took a few minutes, but she fixed her eyes on me, popped her thumb out of her mouth, and finished stumbling toward me.

"I have more," she said, showing me her other thumb.

Half-listening, I looked her over to make sure she was just dirty and not hurt or in shock. Reaching out, I held her by her shoulders and turned her gently side to side.

"What? Did you say something?"

She gave me a thumb's up sign with her other hand and giggled.

I smiled, relieved. She was talking and thinking and making jokes.

Whatever those idiots had planned to do to her hadn't frightened her too badly.

"Come on, sweetie, let's get you back to Gretchen."

I stood up and took her by the hand. Hades came up behind me and nibbled at my shoulder, pushing at me with his nose.

"Smart, good boy." I gave him a pat.

Lindy popped her thumb back in her mouth.

"I'm going to have this gorgeous boy here carry you all the way home." Hades dropped his head and sniffed at Lindy's white blond hair.

"Hey, he thinks you're pretty cute. Isn't that fun? Are you ready for Hades to carry you home?"

She blinked at me, and I took it as a yes.

Picking her up, I swung her into the saddle, where she huddled like a baby bird. Patting her knee, I talked nonsense and worried. I hadn't forgotten about the idiots turned kidnappers, and I took a minute to see if there was any sign of them.

"Do you know where the bad people went?"

She shrugged and took her thumb out of her mouth long enough to tell me, "No more, mean, bad boys."

"I know, baby. I know."

I turned Hades and started walking back to the river, hoping we'd be able to follow the river bank on this side of the water and not have to swim back across. It'd be nice to find a shallow spot in the river, somewhere easy to cross over.

I tried again.

"Did the bad boys say why they were leaving you alone? Maybe? Or where they were going?"

I had no desire to run into Lindy's bad men and thought about the gun in the saddle bag. Our dip in the river could not have been the best choice for the loaded gun.

Her voice was almost too soft for me to hear as we reached the center of the clearing, "They put me there. The bad one pinched me."

"He is a bad one," I agreed.

Hades' head came up, snorting. Lindy grabbed at the pommel of the saddle with two hands when the horse sidestepped to the right. He was jittery and unhappy with something I couldn't see or hear.

I wondered if we were about to get unwelcome return visitors. I scanned the tree line. Hades swung his big rump around, yanking the reins in my hand. I instinctively tightened my grip and flashed back to Cantara's panicked behavior the night of the storm.

"Hey now, Hades, settle," I murmured. "And aren't you a good girl for holding on to our handsome horse?" I looked up at the little girl, hoping to smile my encouragement, only to see her staring at the sky, along with the horse. Her fingers were bloodless, she gripped the saddle so hard. Hades snorted again and tossed his head. Shielding my eyes against the glare, I tried to see what he saw, but the sky was an empty bowl of perfect blue. Nothing. His head swung toward the tree line.

"Stop that!" I tried to break the big horse's fixation on the woods behind us.

He never blinked. I tried clicking and yanked harder on the reins.

"Lindy, look at me."

Nothing. Maybe I wasn't getting it. I let Hades turn to whatever had spooked him. Gripping the reins harder, I searched the empty blue bowl of sky. Hades shivered and started backing up.

Lindy started screaming when the creature flew up and out of the jungle, a hundred feet beyond the edge of the clearing, but it wasn't looking at us. The treetops collapsed and thrashed under the force of the animal's heaving wings. Lindy's screams bounced off the trees.

When it swung its beaked face toward the sound of Lindy's terror, names for what I saw tumbled around in my brain: accurate, technical, descriptive names from myths and legends and fantasies sculpted in stone.

"Stop. Stop. Stop."

I wasn't sure I was talking to the kid or the horse or the monster that looked at us with the hard glass eyes of an eagle.

Hades trembled and thrashed, close to bolting and not because of Lindy's screams. The big horse quivered like a dying leaf.

It, the creature, hovered over the treetops and cocked its beaked face at us. Its unblinking, marble eyes never left Lindy as it flapped its great wings effortlessly.

The girl stopped screaming long enough to take a breath, and when I looked at her, I realized that she was the highest point in the middle of the clearing—like a lightning rod or a falconer's lure. The sudden quiet was worse than the screaming.

"Terrible 'Ripton," Lindy babbled.

It was coming for us. I could see the shift of its body as it spun over the clearing. The muscles of its shoulders bunched as it reared upward exposing its furred belly and back legs.

Lindy's Terrible 'Ripton had lion's paws.

Whatever it was, it wasn't going to wait for me to come up with a name and an explanation for it. It was coming for the easiest target, the highest and closest target.

I tore the terrified little girl out of the saddle and dragged her backward. We made it as far as a clump of spidery rabbit grass when the wind from the creature's wings pushed us to the ground. The clearing filled with a raptor's roaring screech like metal gears wrapped in nightmares. I pushed myself between the explosion of sand and debris and Lindy, then looked over my shoulder.

Hades squared off against the howling horror from the sky with his teeth bared. Why wasn't he halfway to the ocean? He was lost against those talons and claws.

The tearing, screaming storm that happened next was so fast I couldn't see who moved when or how the counter move came. One minute they were facing off and the next minute the creature had its talons in the horse's massive chest. With a rippling contraction of its shoulder muscles, the wings strained upwards and then down, and suddenly the creature had pulled twelve hundred pounds of horse up and off the ground. Hades thrashed until the end.

Finally, when the big horse hung like so much meat on a meat hook seventy-five feet above the ground, the thing just retracted its claws and let Ari's majestic horse plunge to the ground.

Hades slammed to the earth. I could hear the crack of bone as the horse's legs and ribs shattered like a Jeep dropped from a Chinook, or a water buffalo dropped into a shallow creek bed.

Chapter 20

Leaving

G ryphon. The word popped into my brain like the answer to a trivia question. It was a griffin or a gryphon. A great big, mythic, paws and claws gryphon—covered in horse blood and gore. Its feathers were dripping with the remnants of poor Hades. Monster.

"Lindy, baby, we are going-now."

She made gagging noises. I could feel her body convulsing against me. I didn't try to comfort her. No time.

Grabbing Lindy around the middle, I swung her over my shoulder and headed toward the nearest thicket of twisted underbrush.

"We are leaving—like bunnies heading for home. Do you like bunnies? I like bunnies," I hissed.

Angry with myself for not already being six counties away from the bloodbath happening in that clearing, I threw myself toward the underbrush. Lindy stopped making noises.

In the clearing, there was a sudden quiet that made my heart beat faster. It flipped around in my chest hard enough to leave bruises. Internal bruising! The thought started panicked, crazy giggles bouncing around inside my head like maddened gnats.

Goofy thoughts, like rabbits darting away from a real living, flying, horse-murdering gryphon.

What a person needed at times like these was a big-A gun to make things make sense again, or a goofy image of rabbits zigzagging toward the woods.

My breath hissed out of me—loud, way too loud.

"Quiet, just like a bunny, okay, Lindy. Me too," I whispered. "I need to be quiet too."

The air around us rolled with the smell of panic and fear and sudden merciless death. It was a scent that I knew.

I glanced back. I shouldn't have, but I couldn't stop myself. I had to see, to convince myself, that what I'd seen was real. I had the impression that the gryphon had flown up and disappeared into the sun. How could any living creature fly that high?

Lindy wiggled in my arms, and I knew that she wanted to peek. Maybe it was survival instinct—locate death before you run.

"Don't look, baby, don't look because we are still running like rabbits. We're almost to that clump of bushes. See them?"

But she was determined, and struggled against me. I felt muscles straining, and it threw me off balance. I stumbled forward, too far forward, all my momentum working against me. Curving my body, I cradled Lindy as we went down, a yardstick's length away from the dark, comforting promise of the tree line.

She stiffened against me, our bodies sunk in a bare patch of sugar sand. I knew that she was looking back at a shattered nightmare. She went rigid, and I knew that the monster was back without having to look.

Lindy moaned.

"Don't look, baby. Don't. Crawl to the trees, Lindy. Crawl now."

I pushed up from the ground, shoving her away from me toward the woods. I sat up in the dirt. By the time I spun on my butt, the sky had filled with grit and sand; a bloody mini-twister. The smell of butchering got worse. If I waved my hands over my head I might be able to keep those beady bird eyes on me while Lindy crawled. Muddy tears filled my eyes. I was blind.

A raging scream tore the air around me. Was it on top of me? I kept waving, not sure if Lindy had found somewhere to hide. The shriek turned hollow and thin, slicing into my head.

The noise was everywhere. I was drowning in it. It was hard to know where it began or ended as it boomed through the woods.

Instinctively, I covered my head and crouched, ready to run back into the center of the clearing, draw the damn thing's attention, let the kid get away at least, just as something grabbed my collar and dragged me backward into a sudden cold gloom.

The shirt cut into my windpipe, and I bucked up, clawing at my neck, straight into hard arms—human arms—someone who'd dragged me out of the open clearing. Not something—a man. He pulled me backward into his chest.

The roaring stopped.

Somewhere in the darkness, I heard Lindy sucking. I ground the heels of my fists into my eyes. It had gotten so dark so fast I was blind. I couldn't make sense of it, and I panicked thinking of the little girl alone in all that dark. Had the creature swallowed the sun?

"Lindy? Lindy?" I struggled against the arms holding me. Arms pulled me down to the ground and gave me a hard, tight squeeze.

"I have to get to her."

"It's me. Quiet, be still. The gryphon can't find us as long as we're quiet. She's here." Ari said, his lips against my ear, and then he pushed the little girl into my arms.

"Lay down. Be still. It can't find us if it can't hear us."

He curved his body around mine as I spooned Lindy back into my chest. He pulled me back tighter into his chest, his arms cradling us both. A thick, misty gray had fallen over us like a blanket, as we lay on a damp mat of leaves that smelled clean and fresh and strangely comforting.

I could feel the little girl's tiny sighs as she went back to sucking her thumb. When I tried to shift my legs away from his, he squeezed me again. I froze.

"What did you say . . . what did you call it?" I whispered, turning my head toward him. Maybe if I heard someone else say the word out loud. I wanted to argue, make him say it, but a sudden sleepy fog dragged at me.

He pressed his lips to my ear, his breath a tickle against my cheek. "Quiet. Not now. Later. Rest. Be easy."

I could feel him reaching up to touch Lindy's hair, gently brushing it back from her face. She stilled under his hand. Her body relaxed into mine. I thought she might have fallen asleep; her breathing grew slow and even and measured, matching mine breath for breath.

Overhead the treetops exploded, raining leaves and twigs down on us, and Ari rolled on top of us as I jumped. Lindy never moved or gave any indication that she heard anything. Tree litter continued to pour down. Another grinding scream ripped the sky. Somewhere close, a tree trunk splintered. The shaking that had started in my hands moved into my arms and shoulders.

"Reed, don't fear. Be still."

He reached up and smoothed my hair back from my face, the way he'd done to Lindy, and like the little girl I grew still under his touch. The fear seemed a petty concern with his hand on me, his arms around me. He was here, covered by the strange milky darkness that made it impossible to see anything. I could only feel his body around me, Lindy in my arms, the damp of the leaves under my cheek. The thrashing violence above us became an unimportant nuisance as long as he held us this way, both of us cocooned in the soft safety of Ari Ben Warrick's arms.

Chapter 21

Loam

I lost track of how long we huddled there, down in the leaf mold and loam. The woods smelled of rain and wind when Ari helped us back up. Not wasting time on explanations or storytelling, he had Lindy on Vulcan's back, and the three of us headed toward the river.

By the time he had us halfway to the boundary line of the Refuge, Lindy was babbling about what had happened and what she'd seen in the clearing. Over and over, she looked up from Vulcan's back and talked about the "terrible 'ripton" and the big horsy "fallin' out of the sunshine sky."

Leading Vulcan, Ari had to keep ducking to keep the slapping branches out of his face. The big horse powered through.

It went easier for me. I walked in Ari's wake next to Lindy with my hand on her leg. I told myself it was to steady the little girl in case she slid off the big horse. Truthfully, it was probably more for me, to keep me from sliding off the edge of the known world.

I listened in silence to the little girl as she babbled of impossible things.

He never stopped or looked back at us, leading the horse through some invisible trail. Leading the horse so much like the other, like Hades. When I could hear the river again, I found my voice.

"I'm sorry about Hades. That thing, that, gryphon . . ."

He looked back at me then, the scar on his neck white with strain. The shadow and the light played over his face. The darkness that had covered us, even hidden us if I had to guess, had faded to a hazy, natural dusk. Shadows crept and crawled through the woods.

"We need to keep going, Reed. They'll be waiting. We'll be fine if we go now. Now. And we should be quiet."

He nodded at me and then glanced up at the chattering child.

"Lindy, honey. We need to be a little bit quiet so Vulcan, the horse, doesn't get nervous, okay?"

She blinked at me and obediently popped her thumb back in her mouth.

Waiting, who was waiting? Someone who knew that in this maze of jungle and rot, a nonexistent mythical creature was murdering horses? Really? If only my brain wasn't chasing the memory of impossible sights and hideous sounds.

Having listened to four-year-old Lindy's version of events made me wonder if I would ever be able to tell the story with any more clarity—probably not. I kept my eyes on the ground and concentrated on picking my feet up and putting my feet down. I knew that I could go a long way by focusing on my feet, one foot in front of another, trying not to trip as the deceptive shadows grew longer with every moment.

The woods started to fill with recognizable, ordinary sounds that I knew and understood, tiny birds twittering and lizards skittering out of our way.

When we hit the river, the trail cut away from the water and turned back on itself. I felt my heart speed up. It seemed like we were heading back, even for a moment, and it brought the bitter taste of adrenaline and panic back into my throat. Lindy felt it too and slumped in the saddle. She whimpered.

"Ari, stop! She's frightened."

He glanced back at us and then stepped so he could look up at the little girl on Vulcan's back. "As long as I'm with you, you will be protected. Do not be afraid. Don't doubt it." He reached up and took her free hand. He made it sound like the most important promise he'd ever made. Her eyes went round and dazzled by the man at her side.

I patted her leg.

"Ari, that man? The boys that took Lindy . . . What were they doing out there?" I whispered. Even now I worried the creature might hear us.

"A fool. Fools. Worse. Looking for treasure or thrills and all they found was death."

Beneath my hand, I felt Vulcan tense. His head came up as he snorted, scenting the air, and I heard Ari murmur to the animal. Then I saw the faint flash of his hand in the twilight gloom as he stroked the side of Vulcan's head.

At the place in the path where the curve turned sharply back toward the river, I smelled it too: something dead, long dead, decomposing. Vulcan snorted again and shivered. The smell dropped away as we walked.

He glanced back at me; his eyes caught a last glint of the fading light—blue fire. I needed to know what he knew, I needed answers, but the little girl above me, and the strange lethargy that gripped me since coming out of the darkness at the edge of the clearing kept me quiet.

The smell of rot came and went as we walked. Could be something as simple as a dead deer—the natural world doing what it does best, recycling itself—or it might be part of the unexplainable, the incomprehensible. I didn't want to know. Now it was my turn to consider sucking my thumb.

As soon as we turned back toward the Refuge boundary I felt it, the vice around my chest easing. I almost smiled at the relief that bloomed in my brain. When Vulcan stopped, turned his head back to the trees and whinnied, I choked on that smile, especially when an answering whinny came from the thicket, a familiar, happy, horse whinny. I knew that call. This was no mystery.

"Cantara! My horse!"

I backed away from Vulcan, who'd called out to her again.

"No, Reed, don't go to her." Ari's voice was harsh and strained. He didn't want anything to overhear him.

"I have to get her back."

Knowing he wouldn't leave Lindy, I pushed through a tangle of vines, searching.

Whistling, I got an answering whinny. She was close. Whistling again, I clicked to my horse, hidden in the overgrowth, and like a timid deer, she stepped out of the shadow of a magnolia tree, ears pricked forward.

She looked good: her coat shining even though her mane and tail were a snarl of leaves and bits of twigs. There was a cut on her flank and her hooves needed trimming, but she looked good, so good. I stretched out my hand so she could sniff me and pulled my belt off, thinking I'd be able to use it as a lead rope.

A wave of rot and stench drifted over us, making me cough. Cantara pranced at the sound: skittish, a little wild, a lot unsure of me. I reached toward her, and she bolted.

Ari called to me, but she was too close.

"I'll get her and be right there. Don't wait. Go on."

I had to try, especially with that horse-butchering monster out here. A vision of Hades being flung to the ground, shattering like a broken toy pushed me into the woods after her.

Cantara knew her way along the deer trails that crisscrossed this part of the forest. Branches slashed me in the face as I ran. She crashed through the brush in front of me into another empty clearing, just like the other clearing where I'd found Lindy, only smaller; the woods here ended in an another open, flattened space. This time it dipped in the center, and the ground sloped gently toward the hole. Cantara shot around the edge of the depression and disappeared into the woods on the far side of the clearing.

"Cantara, you idiot horse."

I looked up at the sky and saw that there was, maybe, ten minutes of light left. The stench of rot here was constant and thick. Whatever was dead was close.

The depression in the center of the clearing was a sinkhole, a newer one that hadn't filled with water. The edges crumbled when Cantara trotted by the hole in the ground. A collapsed underground limestone cavern, it was as if the earth had tried to swallow itself, pulling its skin down into the abyss.

The sun dissolved into the trees, and night came down with a thud. I walked to the edge of the sinkhole, but it was hard to see what was at the bottom, except glints of white. I kicked at the brink of the hole. Clods of dirt tumbled. Whatever was in there shifted and then settled; the smell made me gag.

Thinking of the gryphon, I squatted, staying small, getting low and staying quiet, hoping Cantara would be hungry or curious or sensible and come back. I searched the darkness, but there was no sign of my jittery horse. I'm not sure I would have even seen her if she was standing next to me.

Thinking that I'd give her up for now since she'd made it this long, I stood up and turned. The edge of the sinkhole finished falling away underneath me, and I went down in a flurry of dirt and panic and clattering noise.

Bones. The pit was full of bones, and I was drowning in them. Screaming, I began to thrash. Kicking at the death that dragged at my clothes and my hair, I scrambled up against the sensation of sinking.

Older bones layered the bottom of the pit. I could hear their hollow clanking sound as I shoved and flailed. Hints of white, dry splinters shifted beneath me. I clawed at the newer, fresher remains along the top and slid down the side of the pile in an avalanche of decay.

The fall had dragged my shirt up my back, and my skin stung where it had scraped over hard-packed clay. The pain helped, drew me back into myself, focused my panic. I forced myself to be still. Be still. Stop. Think. I unclenched my fists and let wads of dried flesh, bone, and clods of dirt drop from my hands.

Bones can't kill me. It's just bones. I might have said it out loud.

The smell was overpowering. I lay still and listened to the sound of my raggedy breathing. The woods surrounding the sinkhole filled up with night noises: bullfrogs croaked from the river, a dull thumping in the distance.

I took inventory of myself. My back stung, probably cut up pretty good, but everything else moved and flexed in pretty good order. I lay on my back, sunk to my waist in shifting, stinking bones.

The grade of the slope was gradual enough that it wouldn't be impossible for me to scramble up the side. I started up toward the rim of the sinkhole.

It should have been easy, and it was until a furious downdraft of air slammed me from above. Filth rained down on my head. I covered my face with my arm at the whirlwind of crap being flung in my face. Over my head, the sound of furious beating wings filled the sky, just as the first star winked awake in the blackness and then winked out again as the gryphon hovered.

Chapter 22

Pit

I wedged myself into the rubble of splintered bones. I only knew what I'd seen about this animal: territorial and aggressive, incredibly powerful, and Ari warning me to be quiet when it was near. I forced myself to stay still and listen.

The pit was some kind of larder, used the way an alligator would use a submerged log for its kill. Without moving, I looked up and could just make out the black outline of massive wings against a star-filled sky. It hovered above the pit and then growled low in its throat.

Across from me on the other side of the hole, the dry rattle of bones made a hollow, clattering noise as an early evening scavenger hunted for easy leftovers. I could hear the grunts of a raccoon or maybe a 'possum as it rooted around. A blasting downdraft overhead told me the gryphon was still overhead; it gave a roar of warning that made the sides of the pit tremble. Whatever had tried sneaking a bite from the pit scrambled off into the night.

Problem solved. Now just move along, nothing to see here.

Dirt tumbled down the edge of the sinkhole, and then the entire bone pile trembled under the weight of the creature landing. Feathers beat time. It dropped something, but it was too dark to see what it might be. Whatever it was, it hung on the top of the pile for a moment and then, with the force of beating wings, toppled into the hole. A big body rolled by me.

There was blood. I could feel it, smell it. The air reeked of death—old and new. The older corpses beneath me were hard and unyielding ridges of bone. The body pinned my legs and was heavy enough to make it hard to move. I reached out and touched horsehair. Hades.

Dead weight pressed harder and harder against my legs as the body settled. Revulsion and panic sent a surge of adrenaline through me, and I wriggled furiously into the softer dirt at the side of the sinkhole, to get anywhere but here. I pushed against the horse's neck and withers for leverage; I reached down and touched a slippery coil of gut.

Breath sagged out of me in a moan. "God, oh, God." The scream built in my throat.

The gryphon erupted, exploding upward in a blast of thrashing wings.

Had it heard me?

Behind my back, the sinkhole collapsed, and I wiggled into the cavity, scooting out from under the dead horse. My hand hit the leather of the saddle girth—my saddle. I reached out again and felt leather—my saddlebag, and more importantly, my gun. I pulled it free. It might be too dark to go after Cantara tonight, but if I had a chance, I was going to blow that monster out of the sky.

Another tiny avalanche of sand and dirt fell down around me, then suddenly the outline of a figure against the first stars of nighttime appeared, and I was ready to add another body to the Gryphon's collection. The gun shook in my hand.

"Reed, God's breath, Reed?" His voice was so soft it served as a painful reminder of what he'd tried to tell me earlier.

But all I could think of was Lindy. Why had he left Lindy alone?

"Ari, where's Lindy? How could you have left her alone?" I started trying to scramble up the slope of the pit after I shoved the gun in the back of my pants.

"Reed. Shut. Up." I felt the end of a rope. The night sky was a perfect black backdrop for the stars that glittered light teardrops.

There was enough light to see the bare outline of the rope, the white glint of bones, Hades' beautiful sculpted head, and, when I crawled to the rim of the pit, Ari's perfect, furious face.

"Where's—"

Instead of letting me finish, he clamped his hand over my mouth and pulled me against his side. He hustled me into the dark shadows of the woods surrounding the clearing. Without taking his hand off of my mouth, he spun me around so that I could see the moon as it peeked above the far side of the clearing. The moonlight softened the grim reality of what I'd found in that pit. It made everything beautiful. A bubble of hysterical laughter caught in my throat.

Ari held me still, his body a rigid wall behind me. He kept us close to the massive trunk of a live oak ringed with underbrush.

When a shadow cut across the lights in the sky, Ari shook me and tightened his hold on me. I could feel his heart beating against my back like before when he'd held Lindy and me, together, at the edge of another clearing. He made me watch.

"It's real, all real. Remember this."

The gryphon had brought another trophy to the bone pit and let it tumble onto the pile. It was a boneless animal body made of rags, arms and legs flopping.

I stopped breathing as Ari walked us silently back and away from the moonlight and bones. It wasn't until we were under the heaviest of the trees that he took his hand away from my mouth.

The canopy here was too thick for moonlight to penetrate. Ari grabbed me by the hand, and we ran. He kept me moving away from the clearing, quickstepping through and over the palmettos and ripping wild potato vines. Thorns snagged what was left of the sleeves of my shirt. My chest hurt from running.

I'd just gotten a whiff of the river when Ari pulled me to a full stop, face to face, and then put his arms around me. He leaned into me and put his lips against my ears again.

"I don't remember this from before," he said, running one hand under the back of my shirt. His hand was warm against my skin. I was afraid to gasp or object. Then he pulled the gun I'd retrieved from my saddlebag out of the back of my pants.

"Where's Lindy?" I demanded before he could comment.

"Safe. She is safe. I sent her with my men. Not like you, on the other hand, if you'd tried to use this on a full-grown male gryphon in rut."

He pulled away from me and put the gun in the waistband of his pants. I could feel his movements more than see what he was doing in the dark. He took my hand and moved through the darkness like he was wearing night vision goggles. I didn't fair as well, stumbling behind him because my world had gone flat. In the dark I had no depth perception, everything was a blank, except for his hand holding mine. The river tumbled and sang unseen.

I tried to tell him about following Cantara, about trying to catch her, but as soon as I opened my mouth to talk, he stopped and pulled me flush against him. He bent down to me so that my cheek was against his cheek, my lips next to his ear. This time I was aware of a hesitation in his grip, a new awareness of his hands on my body, as we waited there in the dark.

"Cantara's alive," I said. "She's out here—alone—with that thing." He needed to know. I had to tell him. I lost my train of thought and trailed off into silence.

"Reed," he whispered. "I thought . . . when I found you in that place of, the dead, I thought I would see—" His voice sounded rusty.

When he pressed his forehead to mine, the confusion stilled like the woods around us. Somewhere in the night a monster guarded its gory prize; but we were here, hidden, standing close. I reached up and touched the scars at his throat. He buried his face in the curve of my neck. It was right. It felt right to be standing here with him, feeling his breath, feeling his hands on me.

"When I watched you disappear into the jungle—"

"I heard her. I heard Cantara. Saw her. She's out there—alone."

"Not anymore. She's not alone." His lips were at my ear again. "I thought . . . you were gone."

Then his lips were on mine, and I knew what he meant, all of it. I was alive, and he had come for me, and it was right to be alive and here with him. I sank into his relief and warmth, feeling a fire begin that had nothing to do with fear.

His lips moved to my cheek as he murmured something, something I couldn't quite hear. Then I couldn't hear anything but a thundering roar out in the deep woods of the Toad's Head River Refuge.

He grabbed my hand, and I followed him quietly.

I'd felt more than heard what he'd said against my cheek.

"He's found her, and I've found you."

Chapter 23

Posse

We could hear Lindy pitching a fit before we reached the parking lot. Even from a distance, I could see that every time the paramedic tried putting a stethoscope on her chest, she smacked his hand away. The look on his face announced his belief that his patient might be fit for a psych eval and a padded cell. The rescue truck's headlights blasted to the edges of the gravel parking lot in a flood of light. A hoard of winged bugs zipped through the beams of light.

Lindy's sister, Gretchen, and the friend, Jenna, looked wilted, dark circles under their eyes that were more about exhaustion than any Goth trick created with makeup and black eyeliner.

"Come on, Lindy, the man's not going to hurt you," Gretchen said, while the little girl kicked at her.

Lindy howled.

Jackson stood near the rescue rig, in full battle regalia: bulletproof vest, crackling radio. Wow, someone had sure called in the kidnapping squad, and now we were in the middle of an official investigative whirlwind. They were going to want a statement.

I realized I smelled like a corpse and probably looked like one as reaction and exhaustion kicked in. All I wanted was a shower and some distance from the whole dramatic mess. Wasn't going to happen—not tonight.

What was I going to say? What could I possibly say without getting shoved into a rubber room, probably next to one ticked off little girl?

Lindy arched her back, jerking in her sister's arms. I watched Gretchen almost lose her grip on the little girl. When Gretchen yanked Lindy back against her chest, the child spotted me, stopped her crying, and held her arms straight out.

That needy gesture pulled at me from across the parking lot. Yeah, kid, I get it. I started to go to her, but before I could take a step, Ari grabbed my elbow.

"What will you say?" He held me by one hand, his horse's reins trailing in the other.

For a minute, I'd forgotten the blood that soaked my pants, my torn shirt, and the horror hovering somewhere behind us in the night. Shaking my head, I went blank, exhaustion hitting me like a brick.

"I don't know yet." I closed my eyes.

Still dark, the air felt damp and cool against the sheen of sweat on my skin. Headlights sliced through the darkness as the moon dipped in the sky.

"Do you know what's at stake here?" he said, his fingers tightening.

"No. But don't worry, I don't have any desire to wind up in the psych ward at Sanford Hospital either."

"Remember, keep it simple. We'll find the others. My men—"

"Right. Simple. Sure. Absolutely."

I thought about the kiss that had changed too much about the simple truth of anything that had happened to me tonight. Was anything simple now?

Jackson headed toward us before I could tell Ari what he could do with his worried advice.

It was hard not to notice the frown lines carving twin grooves between Jackson's eyes. His frown lightened when I smiled at him. I tried to get my feet underneath me before he expected answers, and pointed toward the ambulance where Gretchen wrestled her little sister. His frown snapped back in place.

Luckily, Liam Brinker, one of Jackson's officers, snagged his attention and dragged him off to handle the arrival of yet another rescue vehicle.

Who were all these people? Emergency and police lights flashed and twirled, and official types stood around waiting to protect and serve. There was fire and rescue and Jackson and several deputy sheriffs, plus a handful of younger men I didn't recognize that kept mainly to the edges of the crowd. It felt like surveillance. I imagined that their eyes followed me.

When the younger men I didn't recognize spotted Ari, they began subtly shifting to his side of the trailhead, away from the cops that congregated near the EMTs. Shaking off my disorientation, I focused on the fussy little girl and left Ari as his men circled him.

"It's okay, Gretchen. Take a break. I've got her." Gretchen handed over her little sister with a big sigh and then slumped against the ambulance.

The EMTs' relief to have a grown-up on the job was audible. One even sighed out loud. I was tempted to add my sigh to the mix.

"Hey, lady, I just need to look her over enough to be able to write something down, you know?"

I nodded. "Give me a minute," I mouthed.

I could feel the tension drain out of Lindy's body as I held her and brushed the tangle of her hair out of her face. I stepped away from the flurry of officials determined to "help."

"Hey now, Brave Girl, I'm so glad to see you," I said, trying to get her to look me in the eye. Eye contact helped, making the craziness fade a bit. I winced when she put her arms around my neck. The gesture made a cut on my neck burn, but I nuzzled her neck and made soft, safe noises and let her take her time.

"Lady, you aren't in great shape yourself," the EMT said, his voice full of professional worry. "You smell worse than a bad crash."

I ignored him. "Are you ready to go home? I know I am."

This got her attention, and she pulled back far enough to look me in the eyes.

"Yeah, but we need to let this nice guy fix us up. I'll go first, and then you can."

She burrowed back into my neck but didn't object.

"Reed," Jackson said, appearing at my elbow.

Jumping, I squeezed Lindy close.

"Sorry. I hate to bust into your checkup session here, but I need a statement of some kind tonight. We can finish it off tomorrow, but I should get something from you tonight."

He kept repeating tonight like he was afraid that I would disappear once the sun came up.

"How's she doing?"

"Good, but all this seems a little over the top." I nodded to the trail parking lot, jammed with vehicles, and officers with guns and determined attitudes.

"We've been told that you weren't alone out there and that there were armed kidnappers. That's pretty serious." He surveyed the scene. "What can you tell me about that?"

Lindy whimpered. I glanced over at Jenna and Gretchen; the mythical cat-slash-eagle-slash-beast wasn't out of the bag yet, but it wasn't going to be long if Ari's men didn't find the boys who'd helped cut a hole in my fence.

"Can you give me a minute? Please, Jackson. Then I'm all yours, okay?"

He raised his eyebrows at me but didn't argue. This time Lindy seemed less inclined to thrash in my arms when I walked with her to the back of the ambulance.

"If I get checked out by . . . what's your name?"

The EMT looked hopeful at this tactic and the fact Lindy seemed calmer. "Matt."

"Matt's going to check me out and then you, okay?"

She put her thumb back in her mouth and smiled around it. I knew we were halfway home.

By the time Jackson had me seated in his truck, I was so tired I was seeing two of him and only capable of answering his questions as narrowly as possible, with easy answers. Trying to be clever was out.

What I needed him to know was that there were two boys, no, not boys, but young men, still out there, maybe alive, probably not. I couldn't guess about the other, the man who'd been waiting for the teenagers. I'd never seen him, only heard from the girls that he'd been out there waiting.

At some point while Jackson talked to me, they took Lindy and the older girls to the hospital. I knew it was standard procedure. I hoped Ryder would be there with whatever parent was around enough to pay attention. I shook myself and tried to sit up straighter. I had let myself drift off, losing track of what Jackson was saying.

"We'll have the voluntary mounted posse out here at daybreak. The emails have gone out. Thank god for social media; we're out here after hikers all the time—wandering off into the woods, looking for the 'Tainstville lights, looking for thrills and chills."

That sounded like the worst idea I'd heard in the last twenty-four hours. There was a deadly, murdering monster roaming through six thousand acres of dense woods and jungle, and then I thought about Boxcar, and I realized that Gilded Oats had to be included in its territory.

I looked for Ari and saw him talking quietly to the young men I'd noticed earlier. It appeared like a meeting of a posse of an entirely different kind. Maybe he sensed me searching for him, because he glanced over and caught my eye. Jackson followed my stare.

"Ari Warrick," I offered, "my neighbor. You met him. We were riding the fence line. He offered to help. It was nice of him to offer."

"Where's the horse you were riding? Reed, don't tell me you've misplaced another horse?"

I looked back to the edge of the parking lot and the faint trail in the grass we'd left, coming out of the Refuge. It was faint because it wasn't on the hiking map under the wooden display board. The designated trail started at the other end of the parking lot and led to a footbridge that crossed the river and dumped hikers and riders out on the other side of the river. Where we'd come from had been off the beaten path.

Ari stared at me as if he needed a sign of some kind. Otherwise, he'd probably already be gone, I realized, back down the game trail, out into some very dark woods. I hoped he'd be able to find the missing boys before fifty men and women on horseback tried their luck at searching, for clues, evidence, bodies, a mythical gryphon. Jackson covered my hand with his.

"I'm sorry. What did you ask me? Oh, right. Sorry. We ran into a breach in the fence, our local neighborhood do-gooders. Feels like a prank gone wrong. Some kids goofing over the ghost lights, that's all."

Jackson raised a beautifully arched eyebrow over one eye.

"Your friend's hired help spoke with us earlier, and I'll catch up with your new riding buddy, Mr. Warrick, tomorrow. I've asked them to help with the search for now, and we'll look for Cantara while we're at it. It seems your friend owns all the land that isn't the Refuge or isn't Gilded Oats."

I was surprised by his knowing that, but didn't want to get into a discussion about clear title and land boundaries tonight.

"Don't bother. I have it on pretty good authority Cantara's gone."

I nodded to Ari and watched while he and his band of young men headed back into the tree line of what I could only think of as the Gryphon's territory.

Chapter 24

Cancelled

I turned down Jackson's offer to take me home or to the hospital. The idea of not knowing what was happening, of being out of the loop, horrified me. I wasn't sure what I could do if a full grown—what had Ari said—bull gryphon appeared above us in the sky, but imagining what might be happening while I paced around some emergency room would not make me feel better.

Instead, I talked Jackson into my taking a nap on the front seat of his truck. I wasn't sure what I hoped to be able to accomplish in the morning to help keep those mounted posse horses and riders out of real danger, but I knew Ari wanted me to try.

He hadn't said it, but I knew that he'd want me to try.

I wanted it too. I needed to solve the riddles for myself. Truly the word was riddles plural—the riddle of the bone pit and the riddle of Ari Warrick and the riddle of what was real and not real in my life.

After last night I wasn't going to let anyone bring Cantara out of that place but me, if she survived, if she continued to survive, and how had she survived this long? Another riddle.

Sleep came easy, even if I took the chance of adding more nightmare memories to my already tangled, overloaded dreams.

I don't know what woke me up, but I thrashed awake hard enough to bang my head against the passenger-side door of the pickup truck. It was morning, and I'd been lucky to sleep at all.

The nap had been too long to be a nap and too short to be called sleep and wasn't much help. It made me groggy and had put a crimp in my neck.

The fog had rolled in sometime in the early hours of the morning, turning everything into that gray, swirly soup that makes the world feel like it's been wrapped in a sweater. The parking lot, the flat grassland, had disappeared under a patchwork sweater of rolling mist. It ghosted over the trailers that had arrived one after another. I rolled down a window, grateful for a manual handle, and listened to the sound of jingling horse bits and the creak of saddle tack. A horse whinnied somewhere out in the fog banks. The sound bounced around in the humidity, making it impossible to pinpoint where it was coming from. It could be coming from one of the horses coming off one of the trailers or from beyond the riverbanks of the Tannin River, out there in the monster's territory.

Somehow, I knew that it was Vulcan and his master, Ari Warrick. I wanted, no needed, to talk to him before Jackson did.

I took a minute to check the damage in the truck's rearview mirror. Humidity and rolling around sinkholes full of bones had not done much for my already sketchy fashion sense. My hair was a strawberry blond snarl, wrapped in a knot, held together with twigs. My eyes were twin puddles of bleary surrounded by dark circles, and my lips were a chapped, puffy mess. And I smelled.

Swiping at the dirt on my cheek, I thought about my friends when I was a kid and their moms, the ones I'd found disgusting when they'd used spit and their fingers to "clean" a smudge on their kid's faces. I could use some spit and polish right about now.

Wondering about Lindy, I hoped someone was at the hospital getting her smudge free. Not much I could do about her now. Whatever she babbled to her family about what she'd seen would most likely be chalked up to baby talk. Hopefully.

My hair was beyond bad, and I opened the glove compartment and started rooting around, hoping for some wet wipes. Surely, one of

Jackson's girlfriends had left a hair tie or headband or something I could use to pull the wreckage of my hair back out of my face. There was an owner's manual, registration, Kleenex, a couple of receipts for tires and . . . condoms. It was the condoms I had in my hand when Jackson pulled open the driver's side door and slid in next to me. He looked down at my hand and smiled.

"Now this is a conversation I would be happy to have with you this morning."

I stuffed the condoms back and abandoned all hope for my hair.

"Don't you have any wipes or a washcloth or something? Well, the condom conversation is not the conversation I'm ready to have with you or anyone else this morning. I was looking for a comb."

Delight and relief spread across his face.

"You should be embarrassed, Sheriff Jackson," I said. Someone in the fog yelled for a flare. "Okay, maybe not now in the middle of all this. What's going on out there?"

"They're getting up a group to start searching as soon as the fog breaks. Still no boys."

Snapping the glovebox closed, I patted the dash, and he laughed. He looked tired, his uniform wrinkled; it was long past the crisp stage. There were tiny drops of water clinging to his eyelashes, and his collar was soaked through. The fog still piled up in lumpy, wet clouds hiding forms and landmarks.

His look turned speculative. I tried heading him off.

"Are you sure those boys didn't hike their way out of there and are sitting at home, picking their pimples and playing XBox?" I suggested.

"Wouldn't that be nice," he sighed. "Did you see them? The young men the girls reported out in the woods?"

I shook my head, trying to convince myself that I hadn't, not really, because I'd been too busy watching the sky and Lindy.

"Jackson, I just hope that Cantara's not on the agenda. I wouldn't want anyone hurt out there looking for my horse. I mean it. I don't want people searching for her."

Brushing at a clod of dirt on my knees, I tried to think of something to keep the riders out of those woods and out of danger.

Instead of quizzing me, he smiled. His face softened.

"Good morning, Reed." He looked at my hair and reached over to pick something out of it; a leaf.

"Okay," I said, and relaxed back against the leather seat. "Good morning and thanks for letting me crash in your truck."

"Sure, and feel free to search through my stuff anytime."

"I said I needed a hair tie or a comb . . . and a bathroom, actually, and a shower."

"And some food, I bet. If you talk me through yesterday, I'll get you food."

Keep it simple, I thought, wondering how many times I'd have to repeat the story.

Outside, I could see searchers as they led their horses back to their trailers. A few of the riders already had their horses' saddles off. I sat up and pressed my face against the window.

"Hey. What's up? Where is everyone going?"

Jackson sat up straighter. "Let me go find out." He hopped out of the truck and walked briskly over to the nearest group of riders.

Keep it simple, Reed. Keep it simple.

Jackson sauntered quickly back and hopped in the driver's seat.

"Looks like your double-riding buddy saved the day. The two boys have been found, not kids though—one is eighteen and the other is seventeen, eighteen next month. I've got two deputies taking them to my office, or I'd be taking you to breakfast and getting the rest of your statement."

I smiled. "And as nice as breakfast would be with you, Mr. Jackson, I have to go round up some loose antelopes. Those fool kids cut my fence. The whole thing is a big mess," I paused. "The search is off then," I said, pretty sure I sounded sufficiently neutral and not as relieved as I felt. "Well, I'll let you get to work then." I pulled the door lock up and looked over my shoulder to say thank you.

I thought his shoulders slumped a bit, but then he grabbed the steering wheel of the truck and pulled himself straight, more tired than I realized.

"Reed, can I ask you something?"

I hesitated and then nodded.

"The little girl's sister and her friend, they both mentioned the horse you were riding."

"And the boys? What did they have to say?"

"No mention of you or another horse, but they're telling some pretty wild stories of another man still out in the woods, and Warrick says it looks like these guys are just trying to deflect attention from themselves. They were just trying to scare the little girl. You know, one of those Blair Witch deals, trying to film something to make a splash on YouTube, hoping for spook lights and big screams from the little girl. Stupid asses."

There was more to it, of course. I had no doubt they'd hoped to film something sensational. I still needed to talk to Ari before I got into this with Jackson any deeper.

And then he was at the window of the truck. He was holding Vulcan's reins and the reins of another horse that could have been Hades' twin.

"Oh excellent, it's the horse I was riding. I was pretty embarrassed about losing another horse, I guess."

Jackson frowned at my babbling. "I guess. Didn't you tell me that you'd been doubling up?"

"Did I? Tired I guess."

I didn't have to look at him to see the disbelief and hear the suspicion in his voice, and I couldn't look at Ari, not yet.

"Thank you, again." I pushed open the truck door and turned to close it.

"It's lunch and a date. I won't let you forget. And Reed?"

I hesitated.

"You look beautiful, leaves and all. It makes me happy when you're sitting in the front seat of my truck." Smiling and nodding, I shut the door, closing his voice inside.

Chapter 25

Return

A ri Warrick had been going all night, first riding out with me, and then back out into gryphon territory after the missing boys. No doubt the plan had been to keep the Refuge woods from filling up with volunteers and their horses. He stood holding the reins to two horses; they were close to identical.

I took the second set of reins from Ari and walked with him to the edge of the parking area; the horses trailed behind. He'd been up all night, and the shadows under his eyes gave him a haunted air. The scruff of his beard made him look disreputable and a little dark and a lot dangerous.

"Nice counterfeit horse. I sounded like a nut out there explaining the missing and then not missing horse."

"I thought it best to keep the number of lost and missing horses to a minimum."

I wanted to ask the new one's name, but the image of Hades falling from the sky like a bag of garbage was too recent. Hades' twin followed behind us like a well-trained puppy.

"Sure. Absolutely. Although I would be happy to report that Cantara isn't missing, and I know exactly where she is." My voice edged up with suppressed anger.

With a hand on my elbow, he hustled me across the parking lot into the open field that bordered the north side.

"Not here."

"Fine. Okay, but I need," I said, dropping my voice to a whisper, "to know. Are these people safe here? Are we?" I looked up trying to arrange the images in my head, make sense of what I remembered, get a handle on it. "I should have told Jackson what I know."

He looked over at me. "And what do you know exactly?"

I stopped and whispered, "Nothing. Except . . ."

Several of the mounted posse members were milling around and walking their horses nearby, getting ready to load them onto trailers. I shut my mouth. We stood in ankle-high grass. The fog, wet and wispy, had begun to burn off.

"I know what I saw," I hissed.

"Please, Reed, not here. Be quiet. Sound travels in the fog. Please." It was the please that did it. I would wait to ask my questions. When, exactly, did all of this start? And how? And what? Possibilities swirled in my head, but I found I could wait.

We walked in silence through the soft creaking of saddles and bridles, the slam of car doors. When the noise of the searchers packing up to go home had become a faint backdrop behind us, Ari reached for my horse's reins, but I pulled away before he could take over.

I threw the reins over the horses' head, trying to find the energy to pull myself into the saddle. I needed to start searching for my antelopes. My worry. My responsibility. My livelihood. How could I have forgotten? He pulled the leather bridle reins back over the horse's head and out of my hands.

"Hey, give me those, I need to search for my loose animals and—"

Ignoring my protests, he pulled me into his arms and helped me up into Vulcan's saddle.

"I can talk to you better if we ride together. I don't want anyone overhearing us. And don't worry, my men are rounding up your animals," he said, tying the extra horse to the back of Vulcan's saddle. He swung up behind me, pulled me back into his arms, and headed across the open pasture toward Gilded Oats Ranch.

His arms tightened around me, but when I stiffened against him, he held me gently and whispered, "Relax, Reed. You can relax now."

We rode until the noises from the trailhead were nothing more than muted echoes.

"Jackson was happy to be able to tell the volunteer posse that they could go home," I said. "Where did you find those fool boys?"

"Just beyond the Full Moon Clearing."

"Where?"

"The open flat where I found you and the child."

The way he said "the child" made me pause.

"The clearing, that place, it has a name?" I felt him nod. I remembered Jackson telling me that Ari owned all the land surrounding the Refuge. Another question to add to the list. How had he come to own so much property beyond the state's line and, apparently, part of my ranch? Questions swirled.

"I found a set of tracks that looked like your antelope," he offered. I recognized it as his version of small talk.

The unfamiliar saddle I sat in reminded me of Hades and my tack, all now part of a macabre collection in the bone pit, along with a dead man I didn't know. Should I try to get it back? I was surprised at the flush of panic that washed over me at the thought of going back out there. I could feel a faint trembling start in my hands, and my legs suddenly felt like rubber bands underneath me. It didn't help that it had been almost twenty-four hours since I'd eaten. He gave me another squeeze. "Relax, Reed, it's going to be okay."

"Stop that. Stop treating me like Lindy; I need my gun back. Those addax antelope are a surly lot, but not as surly as that—" I couldn't bring myself to say the word. "So, is there some code word I should use for that thing?"

"No. You won't need to go back out to the refuge. I've sent my men. I told you."

I felt his legs tighten as he pushed Vulcan into an extended walk. His arms tightened around me again, holding me steady.

"The men are rounding up your game animals. They're very expert with surliness. As for a code word? Hmm, let me think about that."

Frustration at his easy dismissal of my worry was giving me a headache. "Are you teasing me?" I was shocked, turning to look at him over my shoulder. "I don't have time for this. Really. I have work to do. The fence. And what about that, that thing?"

He didn't look like he was in a teasing mood. He looked seriously focused as he watched the sky; turning back, I stared at his hands, steady and firm on the reins.

"Not today, Reed. There are things we need to talk about, like what the intrepid sheriff wanted when he looked at you that way?"

The surprises just kept coming. I struggled to even remember what Jackson had said to me and shook my head, trying to remember anything other than a wrinkled shirt and the strobe of the emergency lights.

"Looked at me? What are you talking about? He wanted to take me to breakfast and take my statement. Breakfast," I said, sighing. "It's more than you've offered."

"Would you like to go to breakfast with me?"

This time I thought I heard the hint of a smile in his voice, but when I turned to see his mouth, it was closed tight. I almost lost my balance when he pushed Vulcan into a canter.

I tried to complain about the bumpy ride. I wanted to get tough and take charge and be stubborn, but it wasn't in me—not after yesterday. I was physically exhausted. Every time I closed my eyes, I saw impossible things—beautiful, savage, impossible things, and my beautiful horse running wild through a pretty scary fairytale.

Before we'd reached the edge of the pasture to follow the tree line back to Gilded Oats, I was grateful for Ari's arms around me; I was a limp rag. If it wasn't for him steadying me, I couldn't swear to how long I'd be able to stay in the saddle. The new horse, Hades' replacement, trailed faithfully.

The fog stopped at the fence line of my home. We stepped out of the gray mist into a bright flood of sunlight; behind us, the fog formed an unnatural floating gray wall; before us, the morning gleamed with sparkling morning light.

Sun, golden clear and clean, slanted across the pastures of Gilded Oats. It sparked off the steel fencing and warmed the fluttery leaves on the trees. Invisible birds jabbered in the grass, quieting as we walked by. The sound of the horses swishing through the belly high grasses sounded like music to fall asleep to, but I refused to give in before Ari gave me something: information, answers, explanations, a reason to continue to believe in him.

"Ari, I have to know. I deserve that, and if you want me on your side, today is the day."

The world sang a gentle lullaby all around us. Maybe that's why he changed his mind? Maybe he knew that I'd demand answers and that it was better to tell me to the sound of earth music singing through tall grass. He held me tight in front of him with arms that I knew could feel like steel, but were now gentle and tender around me.

It was probably better this way, riding double, not having to look at each other. Him not having to see me roll my eyes like a fifteen-year-old and me not having to look him in the eye as he tried to explain the unexplainable.

I turned my head to watch the wall of fog behind us slip back like a wave from the sand. I shook my head, "It doesn't look real, the way it's fading."

"Still?" He chuckled. I could feel the vibration in his chest. "You still wonder at the magic of things after what you've seen, after all you've seen?"

"Magic? Magic was like games, children's games," I said, half to myself. "You have to give me some time."

I felt him inhale and exhale against my back. "Time is a luxury we don't have," he said, giving me a little shake. "To be a refugee is to live in a half world, and we are refugees living between worlds, in the breach between our two worlds. Refugees from war, a horrific war that would have killed us all. That's what I am, a refugee."

I shifted in the saddle, struggling to understand.

"What? Killed? Who?" I understood war more than he could guess at.

He tightened his arms around me. "Listen! To the magic in the sky, the birds, the wind, and believe what I say."

Vulcan's ears flicked back when Ari clicked to him. "We're alive. We're just alive in the wrong place. Dead to the other place, living here in the world above the breach. That's what we have called this place—earth above the breach."

Questions bubbled in my head.

"You said we. Who do you mean?" I said. Trees curved against the soft fringe of open grasslands. Did it all seem faintly alien now, a little wrong, knowing what hid in the shadows?

He didn't immediately answer me. We rode in silence for a while, and I tried again. I thought about fog and mist and mysteries. I had seen what I'd seen, and I knew it. The moment trailed away. I rubbed my hands on my thighs. "Is it very different, where you're from?"

Like a sigh, his body relaxed, and I would have missed it if we weren't so close, his thighs holding me in place, his hands steady in front of me, his arms cradling me. My question meant something important to him. Maybe it meant acceptance of this new reality. I wasn't sure, but I knew that something had changed when I asked the question.

"Yes and no. I've thought a lot about this: where we're from and how I remember it. The colors are purer there, more intense. But a lot is the same. The sky. The wind. But I do miss the warmth of the moon. The moon here shines cold."

"I don't even know what to ask about."

"The sun and the moon are both warm. Our world is bathed in lushness because of it. In that way, it's like the Tannin River. Lush."

He paused. His big horse gave an awkward sidestep away from a quail that shot up from the ground at the horses' feet. I settled against him.

"I noticed you didn't call it home; the place where you're from."

"No, I don't call it that, not anymore," he said, falling quiet. We turned to follow along the sandy trail, heading for the ranch's main gate.

His story, with blood and murder in it, unfolded around me as we rode home. A fairytale I struggled to accept as reality, his and now mine.

They'd dragged him to war when he was still a child, to become part of a brutal rebellion. Not just Ari, also his best friend, Luca, a smaller boy, weaker. Ari had gone to war at the tender age of thirteen suns and Luca, only twelve.

For the next dreadful march of years, they were brutalized and bullied into horror and worse by the rebel leader while Ari fought to keep them both alive. In the end, they'd been betrayed, by both the rebel leader and those they'd fought against—Ari, his sister, the gaggle of young men with him, his men. I suspected there were others, but he didn't seem ready to give me any contact list.

They'd run for their lives: from that place to our world, the earth above the breach, through the dragon's sink, a crack between the worlds, to a place called 'Taintsville, my home.

At the main gate, I swung my leg forward over the horse's neck, sliding off the side of the horse to unlock the entrance to Gilded Oats. Landing in the sand on my knees, I staggered up from the ground and walked to the gate to run my hands over the Latin words there. The copper was warm under my hands as the sun climbed. Our family motto talked about gryphons and horses and impossible love.

"Ari? Who are you?"

He didn't answer.

"Who am I?"

He still didn't answer me when he bent down to pull me back up into the saddle.

By the time we reached the ranch house, my head swirled with stress, fatigue, and unbelievable imaginings. We sat on the horse, staring at the front porch of my house. I was too tired to get down.

"Rest. Get clean. You'll feel better," he said, almost sounding kind. He dismounted and looked up at me. He put his hand on my boot.

"But the creature, that thing, that gryphon is killing—has killed."

"Eden brought it here, a gryphon's egg; she slipped through the Dragon's Teeth back to our world and stole the egg from the daughter of a gryphon keeper. That's where she was while you were at my home healing. She should never have gone back, but apparently she desperately longed to bring a piece of our world here. If I'd known, I would never have allowed it. By the time I realized, by the time I had found out what she'd done, it was too late. And now it's here and grown and someone sent those children out there, knowing. But not knowing enough to realize there is no truth to the tales about treasure in a gryphon's nest. "

"They said there could be someone else . . . out there." I couldn't stop myself from peeking up at the sky. I'd allowed the comfort and strength of his arms to seduce me away from the nightmares of yesterday. He pulled me out of the saddle and held me there.

"Why don't you kill it? How could you let this thing live and grow, not to mention let it kill? I don't understand this. I can't understand any of this."

"You aren't listening, Reed. It was too late when I discovered what she had done."

His arms tightened imperceptibly around me.

"It can't be killed, Reed, not by us. Another gryphon . . . maybe. But in this world the gryphon is as good as immortal."

Chapter 26

Dreaming

Cantara was a baby in my dream. She had long, skinny baby legs that she wasn't very good at using. I was a baby in a pink playpen. I teethed on the plastic rim of the playpen, and she was telling me what good friends we would be when we both grew up and could talk and sing and dance—and tell secrets.

And then she was grown.

But aren't you talking to me now? I wanted to know. Why don't you tell me a secret now? She tossed her head and sprouted a unicorn horn.

Voices that weren't part of the dream woke me up. I woke up in my bed wearing my Strawberry Shortcake pajamas. Great. It was hard to remember getting from my front door up the stairs and into bed; I'd been that tired. But I was clean; I'd showered. Hopefully, I'd managed under my own steam and hadn't needed help. The idea made me blush.

The voices were downstairs somewhere between the kitchen and the front door, in the foyer, and I couldn't tell if they were in the process of coming or going. Company? Not Jackson hopefully. I wasn't ready to be forthcoming about what I had seen. Did I even have words for what I'd seen? I knew one thing: I was finished with not knowing what was going on under my own roof. I kicked the bedspread off and grabbed the first thing I could find to throw on over my spaghetti strap pajama top.

Looking down at the material bunched in my hand, I almost laughed, my Army sweatshirt. I pulled it on and headed downstairs.

Halfway down, I realized that one of the voices was young, a teenager. It was Lindy's brother standing in the open front door, with Ari holding the door open; they looked annoyed with each other. I couldn't remember the kid's name. Ralph? Ranger? Ryder?

"Good morning," I called down. "Ryder? Right?"

His face brightened as he nodded.

"Hey there, do you remember me? I'm Reed. How's your little sister doing?"

The tall boy with the long hair and hazel eyes, I remembered him now from the convenience store, pale and embarrassed at the drama.

"Ms. Hunter, right? Yeah, that's my name. Ryder." I greeted that information with raised eyebrows.

He shrugged and fidgeted and then said, "Oh right. You know that. And I want to thank you for what you did for my sisters, both of 'em." He glanced over at Ari. "Lindy's fine. She's with my aunt, who's come to help me and my mother, with stuff, with everything. She's a good person, my aunt."

"Thank you for coming to tell me. I'm glad to hear all that." I tugged at the bottom of my sweatshirt, trying hard not to care that I looked frazzled. "Have you had breakfast?" I asked the boy, but I looked at Ari. He stepped back, away from the conversation.

"Thanks, but actually, I'm here for something else." Ryder's voice dragged me back to the open door.

"Sure. Sure. What can I—"

He cut me off. "I want a job, here at the ranch."

It was such a typical teenage request I almost grinned—unexpected, but every-day normal. I bit my lip to keep from smiling.

"And I'd love to hire you and five more like you. Trust me, but I don't have a way to pay my phone bill right now. No phone. No hired help."

It was unsettling when he got a belligerent set to his jaw.

"I want that job, Ms. Hunter." He stared past me, not meeting my eyes, searching the gloom of the hallway for the man behind me. "I know what Lindy saw on the refuge. I know your secret."

I had to grip the edge of the front door to stay on my feet.

"I don't know what you think you saw or heard, but you have to chalk all that up to a little girl's babble. She was upset . . ."

He stepped into the foyer, fixing his serious hazel eyes on my face. Ari quietly moved forward from the shadow of the hallway to shut the front door behind the teenager, catching my eye. He didn't look pleased.

"I know what Lindy saw. And I know that it was real."

"And what did Lindy see, Ryder?" Ari said quietly, too quietly, as he crossed his arms in front of his chest.

"A monster, Ms. Hunter," the kid said, ignoring my mysterious neighbor. "And I want that job. I can help you, and you don't have to pay me any money for now—just let me be a part of this."

He reminded me of a sad-eyed hound puppy.

Ari leaned back against the doorframe, his look speculative. "We can stand here and argue about the veracity of the eyewitness account of one frightened little girl, or we can ask you why you feel so pressured to insist on this job."

Ryder looked anxious to give the right answer. I saw him take my measure when he suddenly became hesitant.

"We," I couldn't get the sarcasm out of my voice, "aren't going to be blackmailed. Why don't you tell us what's really going on here."

"First," Ryder began, lifting his head so that he could look me in the eye and then back over his shoulder at Ari, almost as tall as the tall man behind him, six two or more. The boy hesitated, regrouping.

Ari commanded respect the way some people invite ridicule. Ryder wasn't far behind him in the height department, but light years away in the dignified respect department. Here was a boy who desperately wanted the regard of the older man, but also said what I wanted to hear, and that wasn't hard to figure out. He wanted to convince me, but he wanted Ari's approval too.

"First, how else can I thank you for Lindy? And secondly, I've believed in the 'Taintsville lights for a long time. They're real. Aren't they? She saw the ghost lights, and I think you know that they're real too. But I'm not going to call any sleazy magazine, even though I think they'd pay something for our story."

I burst out laughing and plunked down on the bottom step of the stairs. The last thing going on in the woods near the 'Taintsville bridge were ghost lights; try a real, living mythological creature with blood on its breath and flesh in its claws. My laughter sounded a little crazy, even to me. Delayed shock, maybe.

A jolt of concern for Cantara brought me up short.

"Sorry. You might as well come all the way in."

Ryder and Ari frowned down at me when they heard my stomach growl. I turned to walk down the hallway into the kitchen, letting Ari lock the door behind us.

"I'm still tired, and obviously starving. I promise I'm not laughing at you. In here." I paraded ahead of Ryder into the library where my uncle had assembled a fairly impressive collection of mystery and fantasy novels. They were jammed on the shelves next to every kind of reference book my parents could get their hands on. Scattered throughout were all of my childhood favorites, of course. Museum display cases lined one wall, stuffed with horns and antlers, wasps' nests, shells, and snake skins: bits of treasure from the dirt and air of our ranch.

Ryder walked to the middle of the room, stopped, whistled, and said, "The library, I presume."

Ari stood just inside the doorframe of the room, the same way he'd stood in the front door, leaning against the frame, not in and not out, uncommitted. It was starting to annoy me, his being here, watching me from the fringes of the room. But with Ryder wandering around the library examining book titles, I wasn't ready to confront the ever-lurking, ever-present Ari Ben Warrick. I had a vague memory of agreeing to let him crash in the library last night. A neatly folded blanket at the end of the big, brown couch was the only evidence that he'd taken me up on the offer.

"What's with the Latin everywhere?" Ryder stood in front of the massive stone fireplace with its ornate wood carving of the words *Iungeant Iam Grypes Equis*. I walked over and stood next to him.

"My uncle's work, that carving. Family motto. It's on the gates; it's a family crest kind of thing. It means 'When gryphons mate with horses.'"

The irony and the newfound reality of those words hit me as hard as a fist, the same way they had at the big front gate. I spun away from the carving, suddenly aware of Ari's electrified posture. He stood at attention, wary, watching me.

I watched his face as I explained, "It's about what can't be: impossible situations, impossible outcomes. The mythological gryphon was thought to hate horses, and it would be a kind of miracle to have them mate."

I turned back to the words curling through the cypress wood.

"It means impossible love. Is that about right, Ari? Have I got that right?"

Ryder turned, curious and expectant. "Do you know Latin then?" he asked the still silent Ari. "I'm trying Spanish out as a second language. I gave Latin a try. I failed. It's hard. I take care of my sisters a lot." His curiosity was so sincere, his confession so honest, it made me feel generous.

"Ryder, you're hired. But I haven't got any money."

I watched Ari's face go from surprise to amusement.

I decided on a practical tact. "I'm worried about Mr. Stillbee doing too much heavy work. I'd feel better just having someone to help him out, but Ryder, I can't pay you, and you really can't talk about what you think you know."

"No worries, Ms. Reed. We'll call it an internship." He picked up an antique metronome from my uncle's desk, wound it up, and started it ticking softly. "Gryphons huh? That's kind of ironic, isn't it?"

Ari walked to the desk and stopped the metronome, snapping its cover back on.

"It would be good of you to help Reed out, for now, Ryder, and I'll make sure you get something for your trouble. I can pay you, but not if you bring trouble to this place."

"About the lights . . ." the boy began. Then, seeing the thundercloud frown on Ari's face, he said, "Well, no need to blab about any of that."

"No talk about ghostly lights. If you're going to help us here, then it's just an exotic animal ranch. Isn't that right, Reed?"

I walked to the desk and pulled out a 1099 form, tempted to blow the dust off of it.

"I can take it from here. You'll have to excuse my neighbor. It is my exotic animal ranch, in't it? And I want to make sure it stays safe, stable, and anonymous. Understand. I've got enough problems with do-gooders cutting my fences. Right? I'll handle this with Mr. Stillbee, smooth it over. You'll have to figure out how to not offend his pride."

With an ironic quirk to his mouth, Ari stepped back.

All I could manage was a quick nod. "Listen, Ryder. You can start now if you have time because I've got something I need to do today, all day. Mr. S. will be down at the barn starting the daily round of chores, and I'll feed you all the Kix you can eat if you stay."

After all, he was a teenage boy, and I figured food was always good for bribes with kids his age. It had been a while since I'd been grocery shopping, but I thought I could pull off a box of cereal or two.

"Done, but I want to find out about, you know." He winked at me. "At some point. No rush." He looked serious. "You will tell me when you can, right? Please? What kind of cereal?"

"Kix. And all the sugar and milk you can stand."

"Done."

"Done on both counts," I agreed. "I don't pretend to understand all of this, but you keep my secrets, and I'll keep yours. As soon as I figure out what's going on out there on the Refuge and what those men were after, I will let you know. I've got a few things that I need to find out for myself."

Ryder pushed his big, bony hand at me. We shook. And then both of us looked over at the brooding man in the doorframe, only to find that he was gone. He'd gone so quietly we hadn't heard him, checking on his horse or, with any luck, headed home.

"Don't mind him. He's another mystery I'm working on, I'm afraid."

I sent Ryder off down to the barn while I headed upstairs to the second floor. The thought of Cantara winding up in that pile of bones and scraps was making my stomach hurt. I needed to dig out a couple of things from my service equipment and go in prepared this time. I was getting her back, I just wished I knew more about the habits and habitat of a full-grown male gryphon.

Chapter 27

Froth

My bedroom on the second floor was a pink and white froth of lacy childhood. I'd been a kid when I'd left Gilded Oats; nothing said that louder than my bedroom decor.

"I've got to get a can of paint," I sighed as I looked at a shelf full of Breyer horse models. I picked up a replica of Pegasus, letting the irony of the mythological figurine wash over me. A unicorn stood next in the line of collectables—no gryphons. Thank God.

Stubbing my toe against a pink My Little Pony trashcan, I cursed and hobbled my way into the bathroom and took another shower. I was afraid that the smell of death might still be clinging to my hair.

Hot enough to fill my bathroom with steam, I let the water wash over my aching body. The clouds of mist made me think of the fog that had billowed out and over the Refuge. Closing my eyes, I found myself wishing that I could wash away the visions in my head as easily as I could the dust from the trail.

How many people were at risk now? Too many.

I thought about the shattered body of an old water buffalo; something had changed, and it—that creature, that monster—had been able to cross whatever boundary had contained it and killed Boxcar on Gilded Oats Ranch land.

154 · LINDA L. ZERN

Or had it just grown big enough to cause that kind of destruction? Nobody was poaching my land, well, nothing human, and that was one mystery solved anyway.

I dragged riding pants and a sports bra out of the dresser and pulled them on. The shirt from yesterday was a dead loss, beyond filthy. I ignored it and started to sift through the closet. I still hadn't decided on one of the dozen, frilly, button-down shirts I'd favored in high school when my bedroom door creaked open.

"Hey, who is it?" I said, looking over my shoulder, pretending that my heart wasn't hammering its way through my ribs. I wasn't used to visitors of any kind, especially in my bedroom. "I'm pretty sure you are supposed to knock."

I yanked down a yellow-checked pile of ruffles from a hanger and held it in front of me.

Ari acted like this was how we conversed everyday—me half-dressed and him oblivious and impatient. The scars on his skin were white chalk over the muscles of his neck.

I glanced down and said, "You look like you want to hit something. I know the feeling." I turned around and pulled the silly ruffled blouse over my head.

"Reed, what about yesterday wasn't clear to you?"

He still wore the black jeans and black Henley from yesterday. I hadn't bothered to notice downstairs. Ryder had been enough of a surprise.

"You haven't changed your clothes," I said. "Why?" I narrowed my eyes at him. "You haven't been home yet. Why are you still here? I really thought you'd gone. Didn't I hear the front door smacking you in the—"

When I tried to continue, he cut me off and stepped closer. Too close.

"Don't you understand that you might have wound up on that pile of bones out there, and now you're going to let that boy get involved?" He glowered and hovered.

"Hey," I said, stumbling back into the line of shirts and hangers in the closet. "I did wind up in that pile of bones for your information. Not pleasant. Not something I could forget, believe me. And I'm not letting it happen to that boy. But that boy is involved, and so is his sister." I heard hangers banging into each other behind me, felt clothes slipping to the ground. "And what about my horse? She's out there, Ari. I saw her, and I'm going after her."

"No, you're not."

"Hey! Again, you are so wrong. She's mine. She's my responsibility, and if you think I'm going to leave her out there alone to wind up dinner for that, that, creature . . . No way, I'm going. Forget it." I fumbled with the buttons on the shirt.

"No, you're not." He punctuated this statement by grabbing my shoulders. His big hands on my arms made me feel small and fragile, and that had me steaming mad. I realized I needed mad. I could use it to get me to go back out there—face the demons—do what needed to be done.

"An adult, male gryphon in rut is the most territorial creature alive. It will tear you apart. You don't know anything about this."

"Maybe, but this is my home. I grew up here. And it can't find me, not if I'm in and out before it knows I'm there. Please let me go." I felt him tighten his grip on me for a second and then he let go, taking a step back. I flinched when he put his hands on my shirt.

"Sorry, but you're all buttoned wrong."

I looked down and saw the crazy way I'd jammed buttons into button holes. "Well, jeez, I'm not used to strange men standing around watching me dress." He dropped his hands, looking unsure for the first time. He didn't seem to know where to put his hands; his embarrassment cheered me up.

"Thanks. But I've been dressing myself for a long time." I started to walk by him, find my socks, my boots. "You really shouldn't be up here. What will my uncle think?" I'd said it as a joke, but it hit too close to home, and I pulled open the sock drawer in silence. He turned his back to me.

"Reed, I can't let you go."

I started to root around in the sock drawer. "Okay, you have concerns. So do I, and we should talk about what happened out there, and I don't mean just mean that—gryphon, but—" I hesitated, and blushed. Oh, for God's sake. I was a grown woman, and this was getting ridiculous. I swung around to face him and found him standing close enough to touch.

"I can't let you go." This time when he touched me, there was nothing but wanting and tenderness in it. His eyes flashed fire and heat over my face, my lips. "I can't," he repeated.

My hands found their way to the front of his shirt.

He pulled me against him and looked down at me, searching my face for the answer to some grand puzzle. He smiled faintly.

"What else happened that we should talk about, Reed?"

Looking into the flashing blue of his eyes was like staring into a deep well made of sky. I felt myself drifting, forgetting what I was about. How easy would it be to let him keep me safe?

"You can't go."

And there it was. Another order? It wasn't going to work. I pushed away from him.

"I'm going. It will kill Cantara." I tried to square my shoulders, suddenly desperate, feeling the heat rise in my neck and face. "It's killing everything in sight. It killed Boxcar. He's going to kill her."

He frowned at me, his eyes studying me, and then I watched him notice the rest of me. The muscles of his face softened, and the blue of his eyes turned darker to some mysterious color I had no name for. I felt cradled, protected by his concern, his need to convince me of the danger. He brought his hand up to touch me again. My hair. I waited. His fingers hovered next to my cheek, touching but not quite. It felt like a storm of static electricity swirled between his hand and my face. I tripped back into my closet. "Don't. Don't touch me."

"No, he won't," Ari said. He shook his head.

"Excuse me?"

He made it so hard to concentrate.

"He, I mean the gryphon. He won't hurt Cantara."

"You can't know that."

His voice dropped to a whisper.

"Iungeant Iam Grypes Equis. What does it mean, Reed?"

The moment spun away from me as he waited. The words, so familiar, flitted in my brain like moths.

I whispered, "Impossible things. Impossible love."

The blue of his eyes filled the room. He had a beautiful face, all hard lines and planes, beautiful the way a bird of prey is beautiful, yet dangerous and fierce.

"Impossible."

A shadow passed across his face, some memory that brought a moment of uncertainty. It faded when he smiled at me and stroked a finger down the line of my jaw.

"Beautiful and impossible things," he said. "One blue and one green, your eyes, and I'm a man that understands the price of miracles. He won't hurt her. He wants her." He ran his hands down the length of my arms to my clenched fists. He gently pried them open.

"He wants her." He pressed his lips to mine. "He loves her."

Chapter 28

Sixteen Again

His kiss, soft and incessant, ended before it began as he stepped back. I was confused, disappointed, and a little bit dizzy. But I hadn't eaten, since, I couldn't remember.

He lifted my chin with his finger. If I kept my eyes closed and waited, maybe I'd let him talk me into . . .

"Reed. Downstairs. I believe Mr. Stillbee is calling you."

He confused me, in more ways than one. I tipped my head at him and shook the cobwebs out of my mind. "What? Are you trying to distract me?"

I heard Mr. Stillbee start thumping up the stairs.

"Oh great, you can't be here, not in my bedroom. I can't, I don't want to explain right now, and Mr. S. will not be happy about you being up here." I finished buttoning the shirt over my bra. "This is too ridiculous, good grief. I feel sixteen again. You stay. Here."

I started to head off Mr. S. before he could catch me making out in my bedroom, half dressed.

Ari caught my hand as I reached the door. "Cantara. We'll go together. Promise that you won't try to approach her without me. I've been tracking her. I may know where she'll be, tonight." He kept his voice low. "Meet me at the barn. Around six o'clock. Swear it. That. You. Will. Not. Go. Alone."

I heard Mr. Stillbee call my name, more impatient now, "Come on, Reedy-Girl. I've been worried."

Suddenly, I remembered that there was more to worry about than a boy kissing me. I squeezed Ari's hand. "Does he know? Did my uncle? And my family?" I thought about the curling words of our family motto. "Did my father and mother know about you? The others?"

Feet stomped up the stairs. Ari pointed to the door, put his finger to his lips.

"I'm coming down," I called, and then whispered, "Okay, okay. But there's more to talk about. You know that and soon."

He brought my hand to his lips. "Promise me."

"Yes, I promise I won't go alone, but not because of a couple of kisses. Don't you dare think you can kiss me into submission or hypnotize me or whatever it is you do. I need to find Cantara as soon as possible. Today. It has to be today or tonight, Ari. It has to be."

"Tonight. We'll go tonight. There'll be a full moon."

I could hear huffing and puffing coming down the hallway.

"He's probably worried that I'm losing my mind having Ryder help out. I'm broke after all."

I poked my head out of the bedroom door. Ari grabbed my hand and pulled me back inside my bedroom.

"Reed, it wasn't distraction."

"Reedy-Girl?"

I pulled my hand free and finished tucking my shirt into my pants just as Mr. Stillbee knocked. I stepped through the door. "So, what's kept you busy since I saw you last?" I tried keeping my voice light, the whole time wondering if I looked like I'd just wanted to have the stuffing kissed out of me.

"Haven't felt chirpy for a couple of days. Stayed close to the bunkhouse. Thought you'd be around to check but then that young Mr. Eager Beaver showed up."

I pulled my bedroom door closed. "Ryder?" I asked. He nodded and grumped.

"Come on, I'll explain."

I offered to make him hot chocolate while I told him what I could. Escorting him down the stairs, I took a chance on looking back one more time. The hallway stayed empty. Ari had already found a way to avoid the situation entirely, hopefully. I did my best to play it cool, fumbling around in the kitchen while I made the cocoa.

"Reedy-Girl, it's not just that gawky kid, Ryder, not sure how much work he'll be able to do; but it's those others."

I pushed a mug of hot chocolate across the kitchen island at him. It wasn't cold enough for hot chocolate, but it was one of Mr. S.'s few indulgences and one of the few things I could make.

"What others? Who do you mean?"

"Those others. Those tall fellows that don't talk much come over from the River House. Are they staying, going? They rode in on a matched set of black horses the size of Clydesdales. What am I supposed to be doing with those boys? The Ryder kid is one thing, but those others are just strange."

When Mr. S. mentioned the "others" I had a sinking feeling I knew who we had to thank for the extra help. If Ari thought he was going to mount a guard without my permission, he was going to have to think again. How was I supposed to explain this and not talk about the real threat?

Mr. S. looked at me while he sipped chocolate and waited for an explanation and instructions.

I told him about kids cutting the fence and gave him a vague version of finding Lindy and the rest. I took comfort in letting a pattern of logic and reason settle over me. A bad dream, it was all starting to feel like a bad, bad dream. I'd found the little girl, and they'd found those boys trespassing, and that was that. Fences mended.

"For now, just put them in the bunkhouse. The sheets are clean, and there's soap."

He raised an eyebrow over the mug.

"For now. Mr. Warrick is just trying to help out a neighbor. He's worried about kids cutting his fences, causing more trouble."

"I don't know why he'd want to help. He and your uncle never much ran into each other. Some legal mumbo jumbo or other."

"They knew each other? I thought I knew everyone Uncle Rulan knew," I said. "At least at one time. I figured I knew how it all worked around here but that was yesterday. How about you? What's your take on our mysterious benefactor?"

I watched Mr. S. frown over his hot chocolate and maybe some memories.

"Acts like the king of the county, if you ask me, stuck on himself . . . the way he insisted on taking care of you when you were sick." There was more than a little bitterness in his observation. He shook off my startled surprise. "I think Mr. Warrick is more interested in being your neighbor than he was in being your uncle's neighbor."

I ignored his smirk. Sure, okay, let him think this was about a flirty neighbor—safer that way. We finished our hot chocolate in silence.

Chapter 29

Rings

Mr. Stillbee insisted on going back to the barn to monitor the sudden influx of farm help. He didn't trust them as far as he could throw them. I knew it for a fact because he'd muttered, "I don't trust them as far as I can throw them," all the way across the front yard.

When he was gone, I closed the door and pressed my back against it. The house settled around me. I'd grown up here. My parents had lived here before their deaths. Their things surrounded me, all the curiosities they'd collected. I had no actual memory of them, but it sometimes felt like I did because of the pictures: the yellowing, fading photographs of an average, happy family.

They called to me, those pictures, after what I'd learned. I had to see them again, my blue-eyed mother and my father with his wire-rimmed glasses and soft grin. In the library, I avoided the words over the fireplace. Instead, I turned to the museum case where the photo albums waited.

I'd been a child in a world of grown-ups. My mother. My father. Me. There I was a baby in a pink blanket. My father holding a three-month-old me on the back of my mother's horse. My mother, pregnant, standing near the front gate. There was fresh black paint on the gate; the trees were smaller, younger. I picked the picture up and studied her face as she squinted into the sun and the small smile that seemed a little sad. Her black hair glistened where it caught the sunlight. She held her hands over the rounded lump that was me, her elegant fingers resting carefully, protectively, on the bulge of her belly. I traced a finger over her hands, thinking how women had that way of touching themselves when they were pregnant, already protective.

Then I saw it. Her fingers. Bare. She wore no wedding ring. I grabbed up a stack of snapshots; in all the pictures with my father, she wore a band, a braided band of three metals: gold, silver, and rose gold. I knew that ring. I kept it on a silver chain in my dresser.

But my mother was not wearing a wedding ring in the gate picture, not when the trees were saplings.

Chapter 30

The Miracle

"How can she have survived out here?" I might as well have been talking to myself. I decided against bringing up the false report he'd given me about Cantara being dead. It didn't take a detective to figure out he'd been trying to keep me clear of the Refuge.

A storm of questions flew through my head: Who were they? My mother, my father, Ari Ben Warrick, me, and Eden who'd brought a nightmare with her? Was my mother pregnant before the ring in my dresser drawer went on her finger? And why not? People were hardly embarrassed anymore by surprise baby news. I clung to that thought like a woman sinking in quicksand, scratching at the end of a rope.

Ari had barely spoken to me since we'd ridden out.

I'd spent the afternoon down at the barn, trying to figure out what Ari's orders had been to his men—all three of them—but only managed to get a lot of polite non-answers. Scrambling, I put them to work on everything from putting another coat of paint on the chicken coop to replacing the door latch on the tack room door. That would teach them for lurking around Gilded Oats. When Ari showed up at six o'clock, I had his little army slaving away mucking out stalls.

I told Mr. S. that if they insisted on staying, they were welcome to make themselves at home in the bunkhouse. It was pretty close to a direct order, and he hadn't been happy about it.

And then Ari showed up riding Vulcan with a new big, black horse in tow. I'd known a few horse breeders, but this man had a gift for raising beautiful animals. I thought about asking him to see his stables, something mundane and ordinary and safe. I let the notion drift away.

One of his men, a guy with soft blue eyes under a fringe of black hair and a shy smile, handed the reins to me and told me the horse's name: Apollo.

Ari didn't give me a chance to complain about the new work arrangements or the invasion of his men before we were riding out toward the Refuge. In front of the others he ignored me. And now I'd watched his hard, unyielding backside all the way to the border gate. No smiles. No welcome. Just a quick, "Let's go."

I gave him a chance. I did, all the way to the river gate.

"Hey, Mister, hold up. I need a minute of your time."

I didn't have to see his face to know he was in no-nonsense mode. One minute he was trying to kiss me into submission and the next he was the brooding, silent escort type. He pulled Vulcan up short and waited for me to bring Apollo up next to him. "How far?"

"His area is about five thousand acres east to west, but the mare won't be allowed to go that far. He won't allow it. Territorial, remember?"

"What are you talking about? I watched that thing kill Hades. What's going to keep him from picking her up and dropping her in a heap?"

"The same thing that's kept her safe this far."

He didn't look at me as he bent down from the saddle to push open the river gate.

"Sure. Okay. But maybe it's because she's just smart and quick!" Night noises began to replace the lazy chirp of afternoon crickets.

"No. She's alive because he allowed it." His horse sidestepped away from the creaking gate.

He dismounted and waited for me. Shadows started to creep and lengthen as the sun dipped. He held the gate open for me, and I rode through onto refuge land.

Ari stopped me with a hand on my knee and finally looked me in the face. He stood in the damp litter of fallen leaves looking up. Shadows grew around him. My stomach jittered. His hand on me made me jittery.

"You need to follow my instructions if you want her back. I mean it. I won't take you to her without your promise." He waited for my response.

"What did you mean, 'he wants her'? You said that when you were—in my bedroom. I'll promise if you tell me."

I wanted to be cool, controlled, rational, but even the casual touch of his hand on my knee made me nervous: a few kisses under duress I told myself, nothing special, but it was hopeless. I dropped my eyes under that burning blue gaze. Heat crept into my cheeks and neck. He shook his head at me.

"It's better if I show you. He's kept her close. He's kept her alive," he said.

"But why?"

"We're about to find out, aren't we? This is not a game. This is life and death, and I need your promise." He patted my knee and then swung into his saddle. "Promise me." He blocked my path, grave, and stern. "I won't take you if you don't. I mean it."

I nodded and said, "Promise."

His shoulders relaxed a fraction, and I thought I saw the corner of his mouth curve up. This was as close to pleased as he was going to get.

"The real danger is on the opposite side of the river. We'll cross near the train trestle. There's a shallow crossing near there. This side is safe enough."

Once he had the gate closed, he pushed Vulcan into a bruising trot along the twisting trail.

The sun disappeared, hidden by the jungle canopy, and pockets of gloom marked the twists and turns as we traveled. I was breathing hard after a half hour of trotting, but refused to ask Ari to slow down. Time for a break. Sitting back in the saddle, I pulled the big horse into a one-rein stop and waited to see how well trained Ari Warrick's horses were. Apollo, agile and lithe, spun into the circle like a champion. He backed and stood like a bronze statue—waiting, ears back, anticipating my next request.

I stroked his thick neck and thanked him. Ari disappeared down the trail ahead of us. He did not look back. He didn't seem all that worried.

"Well." I stroked Apollo's neck. The air smelled like green perfume, bright and clean and intoxicating. I took a moment to catch my breath and settle my pounding heart, trying not to fixate over the last time I'd ridden the trail as twilight fell.

"I wonder if your master will even notice." He didn't. It was the best evidence I had that he wasn't worried about the gryphon on this side of the river. Probably more worried about being hammered by my questions. He was right to worry.

I pushed the big horse into a walk while I adjusted my stirrups and settled into the unfamiliar saddle.

"Apollo, how about we try a nice, steady, even, walk?"

He responded without a twitch.

The trail began to feel oddly familiar: thoughts of another ride, another night that had turned to haunted thundering and turmoil; it had not been that long ago that I'd lost Cantara in the first place.

The hush of dusk fell across the open pine scrub that I glimpsed between the heaviest undergrowth. The little birds began to slow their twittering movements, going silent for the evening. I kept Apollo in a steady walk as the world around us grew quieter and slower. The trail that Ari and his horse had taken did not fork for the longest time, and when it did I let Apollo pick the path. I knew that horses had a way of finding other horses even in the dark. I believed Ari when he said we'd be safe on this side of the river, and if we were very lucky we would find Cantara here and be able to lead her home—soon.

The path became a serpentine track of twists and turns, finally becoming impossible to navigate as night locked the trail in the dark. A knotted tangle of palmettos and Spanish moss closed in around me.

Ari appeared at a curve in the trail up ahead. He'd come back for me, holding a sphere of blue-green fire in his hand. The light fell on the sharp lines of his face, the scars on his neck, giving him a hollow look. His eyes glittered like cat's eyes in the strange light.

It was the noise first. The woods across the river filled with the muted sound of a lion's deep, huffing roar, not an eagle's screech this time. The call was followed by what could only be Cantara's whinny. She sounded excited. Except for Ari's strange light, the darkness was total, and the sounds of roaring echoed. Every time the gryphon called out my heart jumped.

I pushed Apollo harder along the trail when I felt him tighten up beneath me, wanting to bolt. Each roar made Apollo shift and squirm. I kicked him harder toward the sounds of lion and horse. He reluctantly obeyed.

The trail narrowed at the water's edge, fading away into the river. I remembered the place where I'd crossed with Hades; we'd had to swim. Ari waited at the water's edge, the light in his hand glowing softly. The current trickled across a shallow crossing of sand. I couldn't remember the water ever being so low. He led the way across, the water barely wetting his horse's hooves. Glimpses of something that looked like flecks of blue mica floated just below the surface. I quit trying to make sense of this night as I crossed and let my horse carry me into an enchanted place.

My thigh muscles burned by the time we came to the end of the trail and the clearing. Ari's light winked out. I was momentarily night blind. The lion's song ended.

Apollo tensed and quivered beneath me, wanting to be anywhere but here. I didn't immediately see Ari or his horse; without his globe of light, night had slammed down across the woods around the clearing. I heard the squeak of leather, smelled the horses' nervous sweat. A shadow moved near me. Ari was on the ground, tying his horse.

A faint gleam came up over the clearing. Moonlight glowed just above the tree line, still climbing.

"Stay out of sight, and you'll be fine," Ari whispered to me.

Shocked, I saw his horse yank backward, fighting its tether. It took Ari by surprise. The horse's snort sounded like a cannon shot.

"Stay," he ordered, and then backed his horse farther into the woods. Too many smells. Too close to the predator. We were lucky the horses hadn't answered Cantara's high-pitched calls.

Ari must have expected me to follow him into the thicket bordering the clearing. I didn't. I couldn't tear my eyes away from the clearing in front of me, the sounds that still rang in my ears.

The gryphon's voice, hidden and secret, roared again from the darkness. I shivered, the hair on my neck creeping. My body recognized the danger even if my mind still wasn't convinced that the world had become a dream, and dreams had become flesh—flesh that roared and clawed and moved on eagle's wings.

Enough of the moon peeped over the tree line to cast a pale, slicing glimmer across the clearing, winning the battle against the night.

Cantara pranced into the field in front of me—I could just make out the gleam of her dark coat, flanks slick and wet. She picked her way delicately to the center of the clearing. Her head came up as she sniffed the air and then pawed at the ground nervously. Her tail flew like a banner as a soft breeze picked up, and every muscle in her body vibrated. She spun in a circle, elegant neck arched, her attention staying focused like a laser on the far side of the clearing where the shadows hung as thick as a black blanket.

She was here, within reach, within the sound of my voice. I wanted her safe. I dropped to the ground and pulled a lead rope out of the saddlebag.

I took a step into the clearing, forgetting about the eagle that roared like a lion or what that might mean for my safety or my horse. The gryphon screeched. I stumbled when Apollo spooked and jerked the reins through my fingers. Panicked, Apollo came close to falling as he spun away from me, away from the clearing. Leather burned through my fingers and then snapped with the force of the horse's panic.

I hardly blinked when Apollo ran. Forget him. Let Ari worry about a runaway horse; I was going after mine.

Cantara barely registered our arrival or Apollo's sudden departure; she was pre-occupied. She pranced and watched and snorted—not frightened, I realized—flirting. I called to her from the edge of the clearing. Her ears barely rocked back. I called again--this time whistling. Cantara spun like a top in my direction. Her ears pricked forward. If I could get her out of this open space and into the protection of the tree line, we'd be safe.

Smiling, I started toward her, my hand out. Ari came scrambling out of the thicket, but a moment too late.

Out of the underbrush on the far side of the clearing, the nightmare creature Ari called gryphon exploded from the brush. It bellowed: part eagle, part lion. The sound pounding through the air.

Instinctively I put my hands over my ears, trying to block the tidal wave of noise. It made the ground tremble under my feet, and the light evening breeze became a gale as the impossible creature with a lion's roar and an eagle's hooked face began to flap its massive wings. Dirt and leaves swirled into a dirt devil that moved across the clearing.

Instead of retreating in the face of this winged horror, Cantara lifted her head and answered its roaring with another happy whinny. Incredibly, she took a step toward the creature, away from me, head dipping in submission.

"Cantara, no!" Why wasn't she terrified? Why wasn't she running for her life?

The creature lunged into the clearing and crouched low in the puddle of moonlight. At the sound of my voice, a hooked beak and eyes like glass swung toward me, and the sound that followed threatened to bring down the trees, the moon, the sky.

I screamed, but no one heard me. The sound was swallowed up in a fury of more roaring. Cantara resumed her nervous dancing in place, now suddenly nervous and unsure. The gryphon measured my threat. The muscles of its body coiled and bunched beneath a smooth, tawny coat, while the feathers of its head and wings glowed candle bright in the moonlight.

Horror and panic and adrenaline filled my mouth with the acid of terror just as hard hands dragged me back into the shelter of the tree line. He pressed a calloused hand over my lips.

"God's moon! Are you trying to get yourself killed?" he hissed, spinning me around, holding me against his chest. Ari stared into my face. I had to twist my head as far as I could to see what was happening behind us in the clearing. "I had to tie my horse away from here. I didn't think I would have to tell you not to try to bring her back." He shook me.

"It's going to kill her," I choked out.

His hands tightened on me. "No. He won't. And he won't kill us either. He has other things on his mind this night."

I froze. The gryphon hopped toward the sound of my voice. My heart pounded in reaction; it had heard us clear across the clearing. It took another step toward us and shook its hooked beak. Raising his head, it sniffed at the air, suddenly distracted by the mare's closeness. It padded in a circle, stepping across itself, focusing on my horse—its massive head first lowered, then lifted.

Beak to the sky, it tipped its head back and forth and made a noise that sounded faintly like the cooing of a dove. Folding its wings against its body, it lost all interest in us. The cooing sound got louder.

I stiffened in horror. Ari's whisper in my ear was savage. "Watch. Be quiet. Be perfectly quiet, you little fool." He turned me in his arms so that I faced the clearing.

The moon hung in the sky and light bathed the open space now. Cantara stood frozen in the center of the golden glow as the creature continued its soothing noises. Instead of turning its claws and beak on the defenseless horse, the creature padded closer to Cantara, its movements slow and deliberate, even patient.

When it reached my horse, the creature moved close to her side. She played at bolting, but then snorted her interest. The beast stretched out its feathered head to nuzzle at her neck. She quivered under its gentle attention.

I gasped, knowing that what was happening now was beyond experience or nature or imagination, and what would happen next would be something beyond fantasy.

Cantara allowed the great beast to circle her. It breathed in her scent like she'd become the air that it required in its lungs. Occasionally that high-beaked head would lift to the sky, producing a muffled huffing noise. Cantara began to swing herself into position as the beast circled her. Keeping her rump to the creature's head, she signaled her readiness. The mare raised her tail as she swayed in rhythm to some ancient religion that called to her from beyond the reality of this place.

When the fantastical animal finally moved to mount the horse, its movements were strangely elegant and languid. Cantara staggered under the creature's weight. It grabbed for her mane with its beak and spread its wings to lift itself slightly off of her much smaller body. Cantara braced her legs wide as she submitted to the larger, stronger animal.

Instead of frenzy, the gryphon moved with her in a slow, gentle mating.

Realizing that the only thing holding me up were Ari's arms, I spun around and buried my face in his shirt. His arms came around me as he dragged me back into the safety of the trees and underbrush.

As the sounds from the clearing faded into night rustles that I recognized—tree frogs and crickets, the hoot of an owl hunting along the river—I realized I was crying. Ari's horse stood sentinel in a thicket back from the threat in the clearing. Ari tossed me into the saddle, and when he threw his leg over the horse behind me, I slumped against him. He gathered up the reins and pushed his horse out of the brush and back onto the trail.

I wasn't sure when Ari started talking. I know it was after we'd crossed the river. Maybe it was somewhere between the curve near the live oak and the murky ditch that ran along the fence line of Eagle Rock. His breath stirred against my hair as he spoke softly—almost to himself.

"I never thought I'd see it. You can't know what a miracle we saw tonight, which is . . .," he paused, readjusting his hands on the reins. "I know why you cried."

I hung my head, appalled and embarrassed. I couldn't imagine what he wanted me to say, apparently nothing, because he didn't wait for an answer. "I hardly think that it's the first time you've seen animals mate, living as you do." I wriggled uncomfortably in the saddle. He tightened his arms around me and whispered into my ear, "Not animals such as these, though."

I tried to protest, but he chuckled and said, "You cried because the world you know is well and truly gone. All the illusions, all the shreds that kept you anchored to what is real died tonight under the moonlight in that clearing."

I remembered his mouth on mine back at the ranch house, and a crush of images made me blush, and I was suddenly grateful for the total darkness the canopy created over our head. Occasional shafts of moonlight speared through the leaves to light our way.

"I've constantly been amazed at how completely the people of this world can be so blind to magic and the fantastic."

That was an observation that stung, and I said, "Is it self-delusion to, to, want—no, need—normal?"

"It can be when it puts you in mortal danger."

"I just wanted to get her back."

"Do you always head toward what can only be absolute mortal peril?" I pretended not to understand the particular mortal danger he was referring to.

"What do you mean?"

"I have never seen anyone in this world or any other world run toward a courting gryphon."

"I thought you'd never seen a gryphon 'courting' before." He ignored me.

"Courting or not, this is the second time you've ignored the danger. What did you think you were going to do to a full-grown male gryphon?"

I shrugged. "I'm self-delusional, remember?"

He laughed and said, "Or you have more courage than is healthy for any average female. Normal, now there's a thought and a discussion I'd like to have with you—in front of the fire in your uncle's excellent library."

I turned my head to see if he was serious. Starlight glinted in his eye. "Sounds like a date," I said, and saw his mouth turn up. Something skipped through my chest, a small stone across a troubled lake. The night fell like a blanket over us as we rode back to the farmhouse. We finished the ride in companionable silence; I ran over the scene in the clearing again and again before we finally reached the end of the trail. The moon was high in the sky, making it easy for Ari's horse to pick its way across the open pasture. Whatever had become of Apollo was anyone's guess.

"You were right about the crying," I said.

He didn't say anything.

"Ari, what if all the bedtime stories are real?" My chest felt tight. "Okay, there's nothing I can do about getting Cantara back—tonight anyway. But what if that's true of everything? My uncle. My parents. Gone. The day-to-day world, gone, like a dream within a dream."

Maybe if I'd been there to see my uncle buried, maybe then the normal balance of things wouldn't be feeling like the fantasy, and what I'd seen tonight in the clearing would be just another story to tell the children around the campfire. I wanted to wake up, then everything would be back to the way it had been when I'd woken up every other morning in my pink and white bedroom full of lace.

And the things I'd seen in the war, the insanity I'd witnessed overseas. That had been a reality that resembled a nightmare, and now this. I was losing my grasp on what counted as real.

He wrapped his arms around me and kicked Vulcan into a canter. By the time we reached the barn at the ranch, I should have been tired enough to fall off the horse rather than dismount. Either way it didn't matter, because Ari made sure I made it to the ground in one piece. Dismounting first, he reached up to lift me down, letting me slide down his body in a way that should have shocked me. It didn't. It felt like an invitation that he was waiting for me to answer.

I stepped back when one of his men walked into the barn, murmuring something to Ari that I couldn't hear. He briefly introduced the young man I remembered from the convenience store as Rand.

Apollo waited, exhausted, at the entrance of the barn, still fully tacked up. While Ari unsaddled Vulcan, he had Rand take care of Apollo while I wandered to the entrance of the barn to watch the moon finish its journey through the stars.

I closed my eyes and listened to the sound of men speaking in a language I had never heard before.

"Will she be all right?" I whispered. I knew he was behind me, close. I glanced back, saw him cross his arms over his chest.

I looked at Ari and repeated, "Will she be all right?"

"She'll be fine." He looked at the full moon. "She'll be gone for another week or so, I'm guessing. She'll come back. The gryphon will stay distracted for at least that long."

"What does it mean?"

"Cantara and the gryphon?"

I nodded.

He looked at the sky again, sighed, and said, "It means that a year from now something impossible will be born here at your home."

Skinny Dipping

Ari gave Rand the assignment of walking me back to the farmhouse. I wasn't sure whether to be disappointed or relieved. Rand proved to be polite, quiet, and if I didn't miss my guess, shy. It seemed to be a job requirement with these guys. When I asked him what he thought of the bunkhouse, he just smiled a sweet smile and mumbled something about being glad there was a roof. When I asked him how Mr. Stillbee was behaving he shrugged big shoulders and stayed silent.

He seemed relieved when he was able to deposit me at the front door of the house and then disappear back down the way we had walked. I stood on the front porch, watching Rand's figure grow smaller on the soft glow of sugar sand barn road. The night rolled out in front of me: hot, humid, and thick. The big, empty house loomed around me.

I didn't realize I'd been white knuckling the porch railing until the ache in my fingers made me look down. It was a relief when I finally let go. Flexing my fingers, I opened and closed the door behind me. Climbing the stairs was too much. I made it to the worn couch in the library, grateful for the feel of cool leather under my cheek, happy for the chance to collapse. The house settled over my head, and I let myself be comforted by the creaks and thumps I'd been listening to all my life. Tomorrow I'd try to make sense of the new rules, but for tonight, at least tonight, I'd listen to my childhood home talking to me in the language of gravity as it worked its magic on earth's wood and stone.

In the morning, there was a crick in my neck and a pounding on the front door. I shot to my feet, pretty sure that my hair was a nest and my breath smelled lethal, but the knocking was pretty insistent. Staggering to the front door, I threw it open.

"Yikes." Ryder didn't try to hide his bad manners. "You. . .You look . . .Yikes."

"Ha. Very funny." I raked a hand through my knots. "You compliment your mother with that mouth?"

He looked pained and uncomfortable, and I remembered, too late, the look on his face when he'd talked about his mother. Trouble there; he didn't like talking about.

"Oh, forget it. Come on. Have some breakfast."

He followed me down the hall to the kitchen.

"Coffee? Or aren't you old enough?"

His face brightened. "Sure, I'd love some. I learned to make coffee when I was seven."

Coffee was already brewing. Another bit of familiar, Mr. S. liked to start the day with a cup of comfort and familiarity, not to mention a nice jolt of caffeine. Ryder blew on his cup and wolfed the corn pops I put in front of him. Sugary cereal, it was as American as, well, sugary cereal, and it was a relief to watch him eat with such enthusiasm.

"So how was your night?" Ryder looked through the steam of his coffee cup.

Shocked, I felt my mouth drop open. What could I possibly tell him? Saw some interspecies animal sex under a full moon. No. I shook my head and realized he was only being polite, making conversation, and I needed to relax.

"It was okay after a long day. I crashed downstairs." I waved my hand vaguely around my crazy hair.

"Sure." He looked sheepish. "Sorry about that 'yikes' comment. But you were looking pretty rough." He took a swallow of his coffee.

He made me laugh. In contrast to the swirly jumble of memories from the night before, his clueless rudeness felt good.

The front door creaked open. Mr. Stillbee was right on time for his first cup of coffee.

Instead of the old farmhand, Jackson Rogers strolled into my kitchen like he'd been doing it all his life. "Hey there! How about some of what he's drinking?" He looked at Ryder and then me. "This is good luck. I can interview you both at the same time."

Ryder jumped to his feet; his big hands braced on the back of the kitchen chair. "I don't know what I can tell you?"

Jackson smiled at me and then studied the nervous boy. "I wouldn't mind knowing what you know about what your sisters were doing on Ms. Hunter's property."

Ryder jerked his shoulders and then shot a look at me.

"Go ahead. Tell Sheriff Rogers about the protest. It'll help."

And he did: the convenience store, his sister's idea of justice, the other boys that had been with the girls when they were soliciting signatures, and how I'd signed against my own family's ranch.

After telling his story, Ryder scurried off to help Mr. S., seeming more than relieved to escape from Jackson's questions and hard looks.

When the sheriff turned his piercing brown eyes on me, I was pretty sure I understood how Ryder felt, skipping away from this early morning interrogation.

"Want some more?" I pointed to his cup and then made a show of going to fetch it and wash out my cup. I was still tired and hardly sure of what I'd seen. It was a matter of time before I slipped up and blurted out some ridiculous version of the story I'd already told him. "Jackson, maybe we could do this on our date? If it's still on? Wasn't it breakfast?"

"You slept in your clothes." He hadn't answered any of my questions. "Bad night?"

When I turned around, he was studying me with raised eyebrows.

"It's been how long since your horse went missing?"

I couldn't tell him that I was worried. I couldn't risk anyone else going out there and becoming prey. "Those kids are pretty sure I'm the devil's daughter and that I belong in Hades." I said it before I thought. Hades, Ari's beautiful horse being dropped by that creature like so much garbage. "I mean, hell. I raise animals for wealthy CEOs to blast into oblivion. They cut my fence, let the antelopes loose, but I don't want to press charges. And then they went goofing off, hunting 'Taintsville lights just like everyone was saying. You know how kids do around here."

"But you found her."

I didn't want to talk about what else I'd found. "Listen." I held out my hands. "The ranch has been keeping me pretty busy. I really—" I hesitated before I added, "I need a shower."

He stood up to bring his cup to the sink and gave me that sweet half-smile of his. "Reed, I hear you." His eyes roved over me. He didn't seem to be distracted by my rumpled clothes, my lack of good grooming.

He reached out and pulled me into his arms. "I liked that you remembered we had a date."

I put my hand on his chest. This was not happening. "Hey . . ."

"Reed, I need you," Ari said, standing in the entrance to the kitchen. "If you aren't too busy."

Jackson frowned down at me and then stepped back.

"What is it?"

"There's some difficulty at the barn. You're needed."

"Well now, Mister Warrick, you're someone who I absolutely wouldn't mind chatting with. Right now would be a perfect time. The coffee's drinkable."

Ari walked into the room. Jackson turned to stand with him—toe to toe. I'd had enough of this. I felt grubby, embarrassed, and off balance. I was done.

"Fine. You two help yourselves to the drinkable coffee. I'm going to get cleaned up." I stormed passed them. Neither one acknowledged my leaving.

When I came back downstairs, my hair still wet, the front door was shut, the house still. I almost sighed. Ahhhh . . . A moment of peace, I thought, and then walked into the library intending to straighten up. I picked up the throw I'd used the night before and went to toss it on the couch. I discovered Ari watching me from the corner of the room. He sat like a king surveying his kingdom from the overstuffed throne of my uncle's easy chair.

"Sorry. I thought everyone had gone." I held up the brown material in my hand like some kind of explanation. "I was trying to be normal. Is that what we do now? Act normal? Because I don't know what I'm supposed to be doing or telling the local authorities."

He watched me with steel in his eyes, unblinking.

I kept talking. "Did you and the good sheriff have a pleasant conversation? We should probably coordinate our stories." I turned away from him. "I'm pretty sure I don't know how to keep hiding from—"

Spinning me around, he towered over me, glaring down.

"You will not be with that man."

Stunned, I stared up at him. "What?"

He reached out and grabbed my shoulders. "That man wants more from you than a retelling of what happened on the Refuge. You will not."

"Get your hands off of me." I was getting pretty tired of men standing too close, looking down at me.

He tightened his grip, inched closer. "You. Last night. What we saw was beyond magic. I know you felt it. He, the 'good' sheriff," he scoffed. He would never be able to feel the magic of it. Reed, you felt it."

Horror. Shock. Confusion. If that's what he meant, I had certainly felt those things. Yet, underneath the strangeness, there had been the sensation of wild delight like velvet cobwebs over my skin, in my mind, and a kind of breathless recognition; it was a familiarity I couldn't explain. But I couldn't tell him that. I wasn't even sure I understood it.

I looked down at his hands on my shoulders and then up at him. "You are hurting me." Now it was his turn to feel shocked, judging from the look on his face.

He loosened his grip, but did not let me go.

"And I know that you don't want to hurt me. I know that."

He raised his hand to my hair and pulled one of my curls forward. It felt cold against my cheek, but where his finger trailed the curve of my skin, there was fire.

His voice grew careful and low. "You asked me how the mare could have survived for so long. Do you remember?"

I nodded.

"Because he would never hurt her."

Overhead the first tap, tap, taps of rain hit the metal roof. It was one of the things I loved most about the ranch house, the music of raindrops on that roof.

"It's raining," I said.

"Thank you. I hear that." He smiled and ran his finger along the edge of one of my ears. "Where I'm from, when the rains come there are waterfalls that come over the cliffs. The water fills the lagoon and the Blue Pool in front of the Commons. The water is a blue like no other blue in our world, and where the cliffs meet the sky, it looks as if the heavens melt. Blue is the color of our place and everyone born there is born with the sky in their eyes."

I stared into the deep well of his own eyes. He touched the corner of my blue eye.

"So what does it mean when you're born with the sky and the earth in your eyes?" I asked.

A shadow crossed his face. He stepped back, suddenly serious, suddenly distant. I shivered.

"It means you're not like anyone else."

A slash of lightning lit up the hallway. Something in his voice chilled me.

"I should go. There's work to do. I wanted to tell you that the gryphon will not be able to come onto ranch land. He's contained. Your property will be safe. The lights we use, the lights you saw last night, we call them—"

"Limits. I remember. When Eden came in that night at the River House, I remember."

"Yes. Our limits, your famous ghost lights."

The rain thudded.

I hugged myself and rubbed the chill from my arms.

"He will keep her, and I will keep him. The sheriff cannot help."

He didn't give me a chance to comment. I heard the front door shut quietly before I could ask my next question. "But the myth, the ghost lights . . . they've been around for a hundred years."

Evidence

A nswers. I needed them like I needed air. The man I had called my uncle was gone, and his absence weighed on me now in a way that it hadn't before. Of course, I'd mourned, but now I felt the emptiness of his connection to my parents. Who else had been in my life from the beginning? Who else would be able to answer my questions? Explain?

I tucked the photograph of my mother into the back pocket of my jeans. Stuffing my wild curls under a black ball cap, I headed out, needing to find Mr. Stillbee.

Rain still dripped from the nodding heads of my uncle's hydrangea hedge along the fence that bordered our yard. It didn't do much to keep the wandering deer from snacking on the spring flowers, but the white wooden pickets gave the illusion of separation from the big pastures of the ranch. The storm had cooled and cleaned the air, and I decided to walk.

Water pooled in the ruts of the road, shrinking as the sun inched toward its zenith. Our small herd of Watusi cattle rested in the shade of the tree line, their calves tucked in the center of the group: protected and cherished, it was a behavior called "glumming." All the members of the group watched over all the babies. It was their way. Mr. S. had taught me that. Animals lived by an instinctual set of laws written in their blood and bones. But now? Who wrote the rules for the world now?

A shadow from above drifted over the open pasture land in front of the cattle. I stopped, trying to keep my heart from skipping into a faster rhythm. Shading my eyes, I looked up and saw a bald eagle glide away. Was this how it was going to be? Heart-stopping fear every time a shadow appeared from the sky?

Shaking off my unease, I hurried toward the bunkhouse.

They were all there, Ari's men. They jumped to their feet when I slammed the front door. The place was neat as a pin: cots that lined the wall were made up; floor free of sand and swept; no one's gear laying around. I saw it now for what it was—military discipline. They watched me with calm blue eyes in faces that ranged in shades from white to rich, brown coffee. But their eyes? All blue, startling and clear, even icy. Ari's people.

I turned to Rand. "What? Day off from running the register?"

He shrugged. "I just fill in when people take time off, kind of a part-time thing. I came out here to help with your antelope problem." A few heads nodded. "Which we did? Right?" He waved a hand at his companions. They murmured their agreement. "And we're happy to fix fence, ride the line."

I thought about arguing, but the phrase "beggars can't be choosers" jumped into my head.

It was my turn to shrug. "Okay," I sighed. "And thanks. I just don't want you to neglect the work at your own place." I raised my eyebrows, wondering if they would volunteer any information about their boss's operation. Nothing. I braced my hands on my hips and tried not to scoff openly. "How about Mr. Stillbee? He know about all these big plans?"

Rand looked relieved when he had an answer for me, "Oh yes. He was the one who suggested we ride the perimeter and check the boundary fence."

"And where would he be?"

"He said that he would be at the Eagle Rock. There were repairs he had to do."

And that was going to be a hike; the park was almost to the highway and the entrance to the access road. When I turned to leave, the relief on their faces almost made me laugh.

"Shall we saddle a horse for you, mistress?" One of the younger men stepped forward, ready to serve. His blue eyes gleamed in his dark face.

I did laugh then. "No. I'll walk, but thank you. And don't ever call me mistress again. Ever."

Rand tipped his head. He said something under his breath as I walked out, but I couldn't quite catch it—not sure that it was a language I would have even recognized.

It took me a little over an hour to walk from the bunkhouse to the tiny park where the heap of rocks forming a hundred-and-twenty-foot-long eagle shape bore witness to the need of the earliest inhabitants of this land to build monuments to the Gods of earth and sky. They'd dragged enough chunks of coquina fifty miles from the coast to create the tribute, if that's what it was.

A stone observation tower donated by the Kiwanis Club made it possible to see the heap of stones from above as it was designed to be seen.

I opened the gate to the park. The picnic table was empty. The tiny spot of grass needed cutting and someone had left their fast food garbage on the ground; picking it up, I shoved it in the garbage can.

"Mr. Stillbee?" But I knew he wasn't there.

The eagle was hard to make out from ground level, and theories about the mound of stones and their purpose varied: a grave, a place of worship, a gathering spot. The archeologists loved to come out and scrape away at the pile and then write complicated papers outlining their theories, but no one knew, not for sure.

Out of habit, I climbed the tower.

The bird's wings stretched a hundred feet, tip to tip, and from the tower's height, the animal's shape was easy to make out. What had the people used to see the giant bird before the Kiwanis?

After what I'd discovered about my neighborhood, I looked with new eyes at the mound of stones.

An eagle? The bird's head faced east and the rising sun. Its beak was hooked and ended in a vicious point. The animal's tail fanned out in a frilled pattern. Feathers? A ruff of fur? Was it all the power of suggestion?

I leaned out of the observation window.

"Be careful there. You'll lose your balance, Reedy-Girl."

Yikes. I spun around, biting back a scream.

Mr. S.'s cheeks were unnaturally red, the skin around his mouth white and bloodless.

"Are you okay?" I made a move to brace him up.

He held me off with a raised hand. "Fine. Don't fret over me, girl. It's hot, and I walked."

"Well, at least sit down." I waved him to the concrete bench that lined one wall of the tower. He did.

I sat next to him, let the moment settle in silence before I spoke. "Those boys said you'd be here. I, I wanted, no needed, to find out about something."

He leaned forward a bit, his head drooping between his shoulders.

"Seriously, are you okay? Should I go for hel—"

"No. Give me a minute."

I reached out and patted his arm. Pulling the photograph out of my back pocket, I looked at my mother again, seeing myself in her face: its heart shape, the point of her chin. My mother.

Someone called my name from outside. Mr. Stillbee didn't react. Maybe he hadn't heard. I stood up and went to the observation window.

A woman looked up at me. She stood in the curve of the eagle's beak. Her black hair streamed softly away from her face—her heart-shaped face. I only knew her from pictures because I'd been a baby when she'd died, but I knew her. I held the picture of her in my hand.

"Mother?" It was too quiet. The woman could not have heard me, but, still, she smiled.

Behind me, a moan broke my concentration. I turned and watched Mr. S. slump forward onto the floor of the tower. The picture, forgotten, slid free. I rushed to his side and pulled him into my arms. "Mr. S., I don't have a phone. I can't . . ." He faded out. "Hey. Hey!" I slapped his face. "Come back. Please come back to me. You can't leave me alone, not with monsters in the dark."

I pressed my hand against his chest, feeling his heart beating stubborn and steady.

His hand came up, covered mine.

I gasped.

"Oh now, girlie, don't fret so. It's just a touch of the heat. Sure. Sure." He patted my hand. A bubble of fear and tension popped and I felt tears slide over my cheeks, watched them splash and break against our clasped hands. He asked me to help him up, and we did our best to stagger down the steep steps and back to the house. He refused to let me go for help, but we took it slow.

It wasn't until much later that I remembered the woman, and the picture, and the questions I had wanted to ask.

I let him sleep it off in my uncle's bedroom while I thought about what the future might look like without my old friend. The ranch still hung in the balance by a financial thread—my life was still happening in what I thought of as "the real world." The fantasy did nothing to get my bills paid, my stock fed. What would the National Enquirer pay for pics of a real, live gryphon and the story of another world beyond ours? I laughed and listened to the clock tick on my uncle's desk, afraid to leave Mr. S. alone. I started work on a new and improved To-Do list. Number one: Be able to afford a cell phone. Number two: Try to embrace the new normal.

I checked on Mr. S. at dusk, and he reassured me that he was fine, tired but fine. His color was good, and I determined to relax. He insisted I leave him be.

Standing in the kitchen thinking about trying to eat, I suddenly remembered the photograph of my mother at the gate. I reached into my pants pocket, knowing before I touched it that it would be empty. The photo was gone, forgotten when Mr. S. had collapsed. Daylight winked out. In the backyard, lightning bugs bounced along, busy and cheerful, going about their happy lives.

I should have put an end to the night right there and then, but I knew that I'd never be able to stop my brain from spinning if I tried to sleep now. The more I thought about everything, the more I wanted to blame someone for what felt like a life of lies, but I didn't know who to blame: Ari for not being here to answer my endless questions or myself for wanting to ask them. And the woman at the monument—a vision, a dream, a hallucination?

Humid night air hung over the woods and pastures like a dewy cloak. I needed, what? The thought of the Clear Bottom Spring popped into my mind like an ice cube bobbing to the top of a glass. I started walking.

It was a trip I'd made a hundred times before: down the path past the hollow cypress surrounded by a green carpet of deer moss, across the big stock pasture, and then along the blackberry path close to the river where Boxcar and his cows called home. It was a natural spring that formed a crystal-clear pool, fringed in water hyacinths. The moon rose, so walking was easy. I promised myself a quick swim and then home again, then to sleep without dreams—I hoped.

The water felt like satin against my bare skin. The burn scars I'd gotten in Iraq were finally beginning to soften, and nothing helped like swimming. I'd been so busy. An occasional twinge in my hip reminded me of the beginning of all this, but the spring worked on the invisible wound Ari had treated me for all those days ago. Swimming helped to tire out my brain. Closing my eyes, I allowed myself to drift to the sand bottom of the pool, letting the water silence the night noises and night memories. I held my breath until I couldn't anymore and then pushed to the surface of the pool.

The soft whine of mosquitoes greeted me as soon as I came up for air, but I was one of the lucky ones the mosquitoes didn't bother with too much. "Bad blood," Uncle Rulan used to say. Bad blood. I stood on the sandy bottom looking up to the stars.

The sky overhead was so thick with stars that it looked bejeweled. Floating on my back, I tried counting stars to keep from thinking about my beautiful horse or, on a more mundane plane, clear titles to property and my next-door neighbor in question, Ari Warrick.

The spring stayed a perfect seventy-two degrees year-round, springing out of the bowels of the earth, answering to the demands of physics and nature. Natural laws. Natural behavior. Rules I understood. All the rain from the watershed poured across Eagle Rock seeking low ground, on its way to the Tannin River. The spring stayed independent of the watershed but even it was required to follow the laws of water dynamics, flowing toward the insistent river. Mr. S. made a habit of watching the spring for wandering gators or the like, so I didn't worry.

I thought about Boxcar and his cows and how happy they'd been to wallow in the shallows and muck produced from the gush of water from beneath the ground. Boxcar. Dropped from the air by a monster created by myth, legend, and magic. He'd been left for dead, like a Raggedy Andy doll, downstream, on Gilded Oats Ranch property— outside the protection of some kind of magical boundary that kept the gryphon under control—contained. I looked up at the sky again and realized that something was very wrong with the system that was supposed to keep Ari and Eden Warrick's secrets; what had Ari been holding before we'd gone to the clearing—a ball of light? How did it work? Spook lights, ghost lights, the 'Taintsville lights; the names tumbled into my head. What had Eden said? What was the word? Limits. My brain spun in ever-spinning circles.

I sighed. I'd made the walk to go swimming, hoping to turn off my questions.

Starlight sparkled across the surface of the spring as I stood waist deep in the perfect water. A dark cloud skittered across the face of the moon, like the eagle's shadow across the pasture. I shivered in the night air, realizing that my sky (day or night) had changed forever and that a shadow across the face of the moon could not be dismissed. I thought of the way the chickens worried when the shadows of eagles skittered by. The shadows meant danger for them, and now for me.

Ari had told me that the gryphon would be distracted, and I believed him, or I wouldn't be out here in the open. I must believe him, right? But what happens when the gryphon wasn't distracted anymore?

I pulled my clothes on without drying off, too anxious to bother— more keyed up than before.

Chapter 32

Moon

I was close to a dogtrot by the time I'd reached the old, hollow cypress when the moon slipped below the tree line, and the trail turned to murk. He was a man made of night when he grabbed me from behind. Instinctively I jammed an elbow into his gut, and heard a grunt. The attacker spun me around. Ari Ben Warrick held me tight.

"Oh my God." I slapped at his hands on me. "You scared me to death. How did you know . . .," I tried to catch my breath, "where to find me? I needed—" I was going to say "to talk to you," but the urgency of his arms around me made me pause.

"I was there when you left the house." His voice sounded hoarse. "I thought you were going to do something . . ." His breath came fast. Had he been running?

"You thought I was going to do something . . . stupid? What? Were you watching me? I just came to get cool and try to—" I felt his arms tighten around me. "To try and turn off my brain after everything that's happened and—"

He cut me off. "I was afraid for you when I saw you leaving."

"You said it wasn't going to be interested in us. I believed you." It was a whisper. "Isn't that true?"

If only I didn't have a nagging feeling that there was going to be more to worry about than Eden's monster. Why else would he be afraid for me to go out on my own property?

But the way he held me in the shadowy dark made it hard to remember why it mattered. I felt his breath slow. The darkness felt as comforting as a caress.

"I've been afraid for you since the night I found you on the trail that first night. When you were in my home, in my bed, I remember Eden asking me why I watched you the way I did."

"I don't remember it." But I did. His voice, the music of his voice.

"I didn't want you to remember it. You were so sick. A gryphon's poison is like a monitor lizard's, slow, but I watched you and smiled because you were so strong, and I knew you would live. I can't remember when, but I came to like knowing you were safe in my house. And then you went home, and I tried to forget that you'd ever been in my life. I had more than enough to worry about. That's what I told myself."

"I don't remember any of it," I whispered. "Just slivers of memories that I'm having a harder and harder time holding onto."

It had gotten too dark to see clearly under the ceiling of branches that covered this part of the trail. The hollow cypress rose out of the forest behind me like ancient pillar of some pagan temple. His face was lost in shadows. I tried to remember the questions I wanted to ask, the answers I needed him to give me, but like on the trail when he'd talked to me about what had happened in the moonlit clearing, I was content to be comforted by the sound of his voice.

"Reed." It wasn't a question. "Reed, I like knowing that you're safe. I like knowing that you're here, home, back from that war so far away. You were injured, but you're better. I could tell."

"How did you?" I asked, but I knew. "When you took care of me. And tonight. Were you watching me?"

He didn't answer me with words. I could feel his fingertips trailing down the length of my throat.

"I wanted to forget that you'd ever been there. And the other night, when we saw them . . . together."

I thought about the clearing, the sound of the gryphon cooing to his beloved, the horse and beast coming together in a way that would bring a miracle to our lives. Our. Together. Reaction started to set in, after the adrenaline and the worry. I felt light-headed. I lifted my face to the sound of his voice. His fingers stroked lower, over my collarbone. I wondered how much of me he could see in the dark. "Tonight, watching over you again, I felt . . . I'm sorry you were hurt once. Ever." His lips brushed my hair.

"I should be telling you that I don't need you to take care of me or that I don't need anyone else or help of any kind. Isn't that how it's supposed to go these days?" He grew still. I fisted my hands in the softness of his cotton shirt. "But I don't want that to be the way this goes."

His hand stroked up under my shirt, his fingers tracing a ridge of scar tissue on my back. "You've been wounded."

I lifted my hand to the scars on his neck. "So have you."

He turned his head, kissed the palm of my hand.

"Reed." It wasn't a question. "Like the slim water reeds that grow at the edge of the Verdant Inlet."

"Earlier, when you said, 'He wants her.'" I shivered when the night air hit my bare shoulder where his hand pushed at the loose neckline of my shirt. "What did you mean?"

"It was true, wasn't it?"

"Tell me something else," I said, feeling the heat of his lips a breath from my own. There was a sudden chill on my neck and lower when he pulled off my shirt. "Were you only talking about the clearing?"

"No," he said.

"Can I tell you a secret? I'm pretty sure she wanted him too." And then I kissed him.

That kiss.

My kiss. It was like the first rumble of an avalanche between us. Moonlight slipped and slid through the canopy of leaves, first in one dazzling stream of light and then another, searching for any opening. Light teased over us. One minute it was shrouding him in darkness and all I knew was the touch of his hands on my face, my bare skin. And then the light would find some way through the leaves to us, and I could see his face: the hard, intense lines of his jaw, the spark of fire in his eyes, his scar stretched tight over hard muscles.

"Reed, I . . .," His hands dropped to my waist, feather light, gentle. He suddenly sounded unsure. "I'm not a casual man. I don't come from a casual world."

"Casual? No . . . not that."

The moon's light slipped away again, and it was all sensation, hands on skin, his muscles solid and warm beneath my hands. I covered his hand with mine, giving him permission and encouragement.

"You were right," I said. "He didn't want to hurt her at all."

I heard him groan in the dark as my own breath quickened.

"Reed, he will protect her for all her life. He will. It's his nature. I will." A sudden flare of light punctuated the end of his sentence, and I could see that he meant it: the truth of it was in his eyes.

My body grew warm under his hands and then when he found my neck with his lips, I forgot that I'd ever been cold. I forgot everything but the feel of this man as he pressed me down into the moss next to the hollow cypress under the teasing light of a waning moon.

Where his mouth touched me, flame ignited and radiated. When the darkness covered us like a blanket, it was easy to close my eyes and concentrate on the flames that licked through my body, pleasure became the universe, blooming inside me like tiny explosions.

He took control, and I let him.

For a moment he was gone, and I felt abandoned to this aching need he'd started in me. I reached for him in the night, desolate without his body on mine. He murmured something I didn't understand, and then my name.

"Reed, I'm here, sweet love. I'm here." And then more that I couldn't understand.

I pushed up on my elbows, searching. When his body met mine in the dark a sudden hesitation gripped me. I felt him pause in response, only for a moment, one long lonely moment, and then his lips were at my ear. He said things that reminded me of the cooing of the gryphon, soft, calming, gentle. When he kissed me again I was lost to whatever he wanted from me.

I wrapped my arms around him as he pressed me into the soil and loam of Gilded Oats. He grew still.

"Reed."

Anything. He could have anything that was mine to give.

"Please, Ari, please or—"

He ground his mouth against mine and then pressed into me, fully. If I cried out it was into his mouth, against his lips. He stilled. After a moment, I realized he was waiting for something from me.

"Reed, I hurt you. Why didn't you tell me?"

"And now you know," I said, breathing him in. "That I'm not . . . I'm not a casual woman."

Light glowed softly on my face, and I smiled. I hoped he could see me. I moved against him, to try to tell him with my smile, with my body that the pain was nothing, and that his body inside mine was all that I could ever have wished for, now or ever.

"Please," I whispered. "Please, Ari. Don't stop."

It was his turn to smile before the moon winked away again and we were blanketed in night and each other.

It was easy to believe that I could have stayed that way forever, cradled in his arms, forgetful of the way the day began to bleed into the night. I think we may have slept there on the moss that grew near the cypress tree for a while. Forgetful.

I woke up to the sounds of a fox squirrel barking at us from a slash pine at the edge of the clearing. I could count on one hand the number of times I'd slept under the stars without the benefit of at least a tarp. We should be drenched with dew, but we were covered in a semi-circle of gauzy light. As the light grew brighter the covering over us faded. Ari had waved it away. The gryphon wasn't the only curiosity I needed to know more about. I turned my head and found him smiling down at me.

I heard the fox squirrel before he did, and he heard the men searching for us before I did. With a hand on my shoulder, he shook me.

"I'm awake."

"I see that. But you should know that someone's coming. I'll go and meet them," he said, pushing himself to his feet. Sometime during the night, we'd pulled our jeans back on, curling into each other without our shirts. I remember he'd pulled my bare back to his chest and covered us both with his shirt.

Since I'd come to swim alone in the dark, all I'd worn was my jeans and a T-shirt. He touched my bare shoulder.

"I'll send them back. Okay?"

I felt too shy to answer him suddenly.

"Reed, meet me at the house." He stroked my hair until I looked at him. His eyes were full of concern.

I touched his face. When I nodded, he exhaled. He'd been worried a little bit, too.

"Fine. Go." I pulled on my shirt. "I'm right behind you."

And I was right behind him, filled with a fresh tenderness and delight I wasn't ready to examine too closely. Later, I'd replay it later. It was a promise.

Dressed in jeans and my white T-shirt and not much else, including shoes, I hustled through the backyard garden gate, hoping to slip past any witnesses to my lack of clothes. And hoping that Ari had timed his arrival far enough ahead of mine so that no one would be able to add one and one and get their nose in my business. No, not my, ours, our business. It was something else to think about.

The police lights on Jackson's truck were flashing like the beacon from a lighthouse, warning of killing rocks and reefs. The front yard of the house looked like the scene of a crime spree.

"What's happened? So much for a moment of quiet time," I muttered to myself, realizing that Jackson's light flashed over a group of men crowded around the open door of his truck. I saw Ryder and some of the young men that followed Ari around like puppies, but no Mr. S. and no Ari. I wasn't sure whose absence upset me more.

"Jackson, what . . . is . . . this?"

The group of men turned at the sound of my voice like one person. "Jackson," I called, but still couldn't see him. "What's happened?"

A couple of Ari's men dropped their eyes and had the good manners to try not to stare at me.

Ryder had no such concern. His eyes dropped to my shirt, my bare feet.

"Ryder, it's not nice to stare." I plucked at the front of my thin T-shirt.

I pushed my way through the group to stand next to Jackson. There was blood on the hand he had braced against the roof of the cab of his truck.

"What? Are you hurt?" I grabbed for his bloody hand.

"Reed, it's good you're here. Tell this old fool he needs to get checked out and not just by me."

Mr. Stillbee sat on the passenger side of the truck holding his hand over a bloody patch of wadded up T-shirt against the side of his face. I pushed closer.

"I ain't going nowhere, Reedy-Girl."

"Mr. S., what's happened to you? Why aren't you listening to Jackson? If he says you should go to the hospital, you need to go."

"Don't you start in on me. I'm not going anywhere. Who called the police in the first place? Who was it? I've been managing this ranch for forty years plus more and now there's so many Indians running around without chiefs that I can't keep it straight, or Native Americans I should say. Don't want to be a bore."

For all his bluster, I could see that he was in pain.

"What happened? Who called?"

I searched the group of faces watching the drama. It was Ryder who lifted his hand like a kid in a classroom. I nodded at him.

"Miss Reed, I showed up to work this morning early, and I found Mr. Stillbee at the front gate. He was propped up against the fence, but he was more out of it than he is now."

"Mr. S., what happened?" I was tempted to pull the cloth away from his face, but he was giving me a look that said "enough" and that he didn't need to speak. I knew to go easy in front of the other guys. "You're not going to let Jackson take you to town, are you?" I looked up at Jackson and saw my answer.

He mouthed the words, "Tough old bird."

I glanced back to Mr. Stillbee, who didn't bother to even shake his head at me. He did glare pretty effectively though. It made me laugh.

"Okay, no hospital. How about you come into the big house, and let me feel useful?"

I saw his shoulders relax a bit and knew he must be feeling bad, bad enough to let me make him hot chocolate and doctor him up a bit. He narrowed his eyes at me, taking in my top and bare feet. He tried to glare, but it hurt him.

"I was swimming."

"Nice swimsuit."

"Didn't wear one."

He let me take his arm as I helped him out of the truck. I glanced at the ring of faces and knew that they'd seen the scars on my back, the scar shaped like fire licking its way up my back and out of my shirt. I saw it in their faces, but instead of pity, I thought I saw surprise and not a little admiration. It made me uncomfortable, almost as uncomfortable as Ryder trying not to check out my chest.

"Hey, all of you, I'll be back to let you know how it's going here, but, in the meantime, I could use some help with the fence line. We had some silly kids cut the fence. I need to know they did it only once. I need help riding the line to check for other breaches. There'll be some cutting of the line up around the green swamp area. It's pretty grown up over there, so you'll need machetes. Okay?"

They looked relieved to be given a task.

"I don't know if you need to check with Ari, I mean Mr. Warrick."

"We were told to follow your instructions, Mistress," the tallest one said, Rand I reminded myself, the guy Ari had asked to walk me home yesterday. "Rand, thank you. And what did I tell you about that word?"

He nodded.

"Be sure to give Ryder something to do, please."

He nodded again, and the crew started off like they had a purpose other than having to see me stumble in from skinny-dipping and more.

"Mistress," I burst out, laughing. "Well, that's pretty darn Victorian. Jackson, will you stay for a while?" I braced Mr. S., drawing his arm over my shoulder. Jackson nodded and eased up under his opposite arm. Mr. S. started to splutter and object, but Jackson headed him off.

"Hush, old man. I'm helping, and if you give me any trouble about it, I'll hit you with my flashlight."

Mr. Stillbee stopped glaring, shivered, and stumbled. It frightened me and made me think that he was feeling worse than he was letting on.

"No, no flashlights. No more lights," he said, muttering. "Flashing or otherwise."

I looked over his grizzled head at Jackson, who shrugged.

"Are you ready for me to look at that cheek?"

"I feel like a fool. I must have fallen. I can't remember what happened, and that fool boy had to call you out, Sheriff. I'm very sorry for that. Okay, Reed?"

"Did you give him the T-shirt for his face?"

"Yes, I usually keep clean towels in the cab of my truck, but after this weekend I was fresh out. I'd been handing them out like tissues. It's all I had."

We got him to the bathroom in the front hall. He grumbled that he still knew how to use a toilet. He closed the door in our faces.

I looked at Jackson. He frowned as he stared at the closed door.

"Can you tell me what's going on? He says that he can't remember. That can't be good."

"No, I was hoping you could tell me something." Jackson scratched at a smear of blood on his hand. "All I know is that there was a lot of blood."

We gave him time and then knocked. All I got was a simple "yeah" and "come on" in return.

"Ready?" I said to Jackson.

"Why do I feel like I'm opening the chute for a bull rider?"

"Because you kind of are," I laughed. We stepped into the bathroom. Jackson watched as I started to pull the soaked shirt away from Mr. S's cheek. It stuck at the edges. Jackson handed me a wet hand towel and then asked me where to find the first aid kit. Nothing out of the ordinary about that. Ranch work came with a lot of cuts and scrapes and splinters to dig out. The T-shirt had soaked through with dried blood.

"So, all those boys are out riding around the ranch," Mr. S. snorted. "They know to be careful, I hope. Shylock is still pretty pissed off."

"They'll be fine." I hope I sounded confident.

Jackson put the first aid kit on the back of the toilet. "It's pretty nice of that Warrick fellow to loan you a gaggle of rough riders out there to help out," he said. I looked at him and saw that he was staring at my bare feet.

"Yeah, that Warrick, he's a helpful type." Mr. S. didn't sound grateful.

I didn't add to the conversation, hoping the heat I felt in my cheeks didn't show. What could I say? I focused and loosened the stuck-on cloth and carefully pulled it free. "Could you have fallen, maybe?"

Mr. S. shrugged. "Maybe. Don't know. Can't remember."

He flinched when I started to clean his cheek with an antiseptic wipe. The wound had bled a lot, but it was smaller than I expected.

"And yes," I said, using my bossy nurse voice. "Ari has been kind to offer the extra help."

Jackson caught my eye.

"Ari is it? Mr. Helpful Warrick. Huh. Don't know why he wouldn't be helpful with ranch property." He looked down his nose at me. "He's been fist fighting over the title of Gilded Oats with your uncle for as long as I can remember."

I stopped cleaning Mr. Stillbee's face and wadded up one of the hand towels.

"I know he's the one who's keeping me from being able to subdivide my ranch." I wondered what difference that made now, knowing that there were dreams and visions and nightmares to be dealt with first. Taxes and phone bills hardly mattered, except that they did—in my lawyer's world.

I went back to cleaning his face, wondering why it was that faces bled so badly. I finished with the cleaning and pressed a clean gauze pad to the wound before it could start up again.

"Hold that," I said, looking at Jackson.

"Money trouble. Horse trouble. Now, maybe man trouble." Jackson's eyes roamed over me. "Careful, Reed, you might wind up with a lot more drama."

I rolled my shoulders, suddenly aware of the tension in my muscles. I snorted, "Drama, I already got. Here, let me see if you're going to need butterfly bandages." I pulled the gauze back and realized that there was more than one cut. I looked closer. A series of razor fine slashes and curls covered his left cheek.

"Drama, we've got," I repeated, pulling the gauze back. "Jackson, what do you see?"

Jackson Rogers shifted so he could stand closer to me. He leaned forward.

"It's just . . . No, wait. There are letters. S. t. a. . . . Starlyn. It says Starlyn. But that's—"

"My mother's name . . . Someone scratched my mother's name into your face. How can you not remember that happening?"

My hand shook as I put another strip of tape across his face. The three of us looked at each other in the bathroom mirror.

A warning? What was I supposed to think of something so cruel? Maybe it was some cosmic coincidence that the wound looked like letters that happened to spell my mother's name. Yeah. Maybe. I focused on Mr. S. and getting him settled.

He continued to refuse to go to an emergency room. I knew that he would. The wounds were more like scratches than cuts—deep enough, but hardly life threatening. I tried to scare him by saying that if he didn't get some medical assistance, he was going to court infection and then watch out. He hadn't bought it. I knew that he wouldn't.

When he'd promised me that he would go back to the bunkhouse and rest, I let him leave. I knew he was lying, and he knew that I knew. He would head to the barn and back to fussing around.

"I'm going to take bets that old man is not going to go rest," I said as I watched him walk out the door. "And he's going right back to his ranch chores and checking up on those boys."

"About those 'boys,' Reed?" Jackson sounded tired all of a sudden. "They show up, then someone assaults Mr. Stillbee. Does that strike you odd?"

"Of course it does, but are you saying that those guys did this to him? Why? How?" Annoyance warred with exhaustion. I did my best to brush it off. "I can't worry about this right now. I need a shower, and I need to—" I'd almost said find Ari, to tell him, to talk to him about how out of control my world had suddenly become, but I didn't want to have that conversation with Jackson Rogers, not now.

"I just need to re-group." I stared at the bloody T-shirt in my hand. Jackson put his hand over mine on the shirt.

"Okay. I'm going up to the big gate to see if there's anything that will help explain how this could have happened, and I'm coming back as soon as I can."

"It was so cruel—to him, to me. Who's wandering around leaving notes in people's faces? What's happening?"

He turned to leave, suddenly looking as tired as I felt; at the door he stopped, turned around, and put his hands on my arms, pulling me close. He wrapped me in his arms. We didn't speak. It was nice to lean on him, my high school friend.

"Don't forget, Reed; I am going to need to talk to you about the Lindy situation."

"I know. Okay." I tried to catch his eye. "Jackson?"

Pushing me away, he walked through the back door and down the porch steps. The door creaked as I opened it to follow him out, resting my foot on the first step of the stairs. I hesitated. I needed to make sure he understood.

"Wait. Just let me say something." I walked down the stairs, then balanced on the bottom step, my hand on the banister. "Thank you, for bringing him to the house. He would have hated to be fussed over at a hospital."

He smiled. "I know how he feels."

Ahhhhh! The accident that had not only sidelined him from football and West Point but had almost killed him.

"Jackson, we're lucky, you know."

"How so?"

"To have you here. We're lucky. You could be off saving the free world, but I'm glad you're not."

He flashed that dazzling smile of his at me and shrugged.

"You too," he said, checking me out again. The look he gave me was appreciative and not a little interested. I wondered if there were twigs in my hair. It felt like there could be twigs in my hair after my night under the stars, lying next to Ari Warrick, listening to him breathe, listening to the earth sleep beneath us.

"I know that you were hurt, and I don't mean just in Iraq. Mr. Stillbee told me something of the time after Cantara went missing."

I hadn't thought about the wounds I got from the gryphon for a while. The pain had faded so quickly that I hardly thought about it. It never hurt now. Not the way my burn scar hurt, pulling and stiff when I moved certain ways. I'd never felt self-conscious about my hip, not the way my burn scar made me self-conscious, even under my clothes.

"Just an accident. It's how I met the Warricks."

"Right. He told me that, too." He looked at me again, but this time he was in serious mode. "Warrick, you were at his home for a while. Doctor Warrick, huh?"

"Right again."

He leaned on the edge of the banister. "Except I can't seem to find any record of Ari Warrick's medical credentials, and believe me I've tried, being the sheriff and all."

What was I supposed to do with that bit of information? What was he trying to accomplish? "I'm not sure what you want from me. He helped me when I needed help. Mr. Stillbee called him a doctor. That's all I know." Almost.

Maybe thanking Jackson Rogers hadn't been the best idea right now. I was starting to regret the way the conversation was going. He frowned and I thought that maybe he was regretting it too.

"Okay, don't get peeved. I just want you to know that Warrick may not be what he says he is, and he and those 'boys' of his may be the common denominator in all the trouble around here."

It felt right to protest his paranoia. I opened my mouth to object.

He stopped me with a raised hand.

"I'm just saying, Reed. Just saying."

"Believe me, I understand. Mr. S. has my mother's name carved in his cheek. I think I know that there's," I stuttered, "trouble or problems or I don't even know what word works here."

He stepped up close to me again. Standing on the bottom step of the stairs brought me up to eye level with Jackson. He did it again, flashed that impossibly beautiful smile.

"Sometimes I think you use that smile of yours like C-4."

"Just . . . You know, be careful. And don't get all offended when I say that. I know you can take care of yourself. I get that. Just let me worry a little, okay? It's my job," he said, lifting my chin with his finger so that I had to look him straight in the eye. "And I like it. Let me."

"Jackson," I began, shaking my head, wondering how I was going to break the news to him about our date.

A breeze of cool air gusted through the door when Ari pushed his way onto the back porch. When he saw Jackson and me together at the foot of the stairs, his face became a blank. There was no emotion, no hint of what he thought, and that felt like a message all by itself. Jackson held his position. I was the coward here.

"Reed, there's something important you should see," Ari said, ignoring the sheriff.

My weariness must have shown.

"But I'm sure Sheriff Jackson will be able to assist me, and then," he said, glancing at Jackson, "I'll be back for you when you're done changing."

"Good. Okay," I nodded. "And Jackson, thank you again for your help."

He tipped an invisible hat to me and left. Ari stood in the doorway, his blue eyes trained on my face like lasers. "Soon," he said.

It was all he said.

Chapter 33

Revenue

Steam rolled from the shower. I took stock. I couldn't get my horse back. I couldn't subdivide the ranch and raise some much-needed revenue. I couldn't tell Jackson much of anything about what I knew about Lindy's kidnapping, and he was certainly going to ask.

"Shit," I said, letting the water pour over me in the shower. Couldn't. Wouldn't. Shouldn't. Could not. I scrubbed the evidence of the night before from my body, the damning evidence. Not a dream, even if it had felt like one. That was the only way to think about it. And what was I going to do about Ari Warrick, a wounded man trapped in a world not his own, trapped in my world, or was it even *my* world?

The gryphon's existence was a kind of coloring outside the lines that could get us all in massively complicated trouble. I thought about my beautiful horse submitting to that murderous beast. Maybe everyone would get lucky and Ari was wrong about what the future held.

"Let nothing out of nightmares be born on the ranch a year from now." I said it like a prayer.

Couldn't Ari be wrong? He had to be wrong. Wasn't the possibility of Cantara's being pregnant by that thing without precedent?

I'd been so seduced by the hot water and the feeling of being clean that I didn't hear the door to the bathroom open.

"Shit," I yelled again when I saw the figure standing in the bathroom through the steam on the glass of the shower enclosure.

I went into modesty overload and tried to cover myself with a washcloth in one hand while I wiped away the steam on the glass.

"Eden! What are doing in here?" Ari's sister whipped around, putting her back to me. Seeing me huddled behind a washcloth must have tipped her off that I might be a little shocked at having someone watch me shower. Childlike? Isn't that the word Ari used about his sister? It made me wonder if it was her remarkable history that made her that way, or if Eden was just one of those individuals destined to be unique in whatever world she found herself in.

"I'm so sorry. Sometimes I don't think things through, that's what Ari says, you know, but I jus . . . just needed to give you a message."

I finally exhaled.

"Okay, no worries. Just hand me that towel; I'm pretty done." An understatement for sure.

Eden flipped the towel over the top of the shower, and I managed a quick exit from what had turned out to be a pretty stressful shower after all.

She kept her back to me.

"I'm so sorry, Reed. I'm always doing stupid things."

She sounded so distressed that I found myself comforting her for barging in on me.

"Stop now. We're all girls here. It's hardly the end of my world, kiddo. Come on into my bedroom, and I'll throw some clothes on, and then you can give me your message. Come on." I took her hand and pulled her into my room, making sure she sat on the edge of the bed.

"Sit. Stay."

When I turned away from her, I heard her gasp and remembered my burn scar, a little late.

"Did the salamander fire burn you?"

I didn't turn around or make a fuss. I kept my surprised confusion to myself. I hadn't understood what Eden had said to me, but I was pretty sure I was going to have to add it to my new found lexicon of the unbelievable. Ari Warrick might have held back a few bits of information about what might or might not be prowling the Refuge.

"Like a lizard?"

She nodded.

I decided to try to steer the conversation back to familiar pain and bad dreams. "No, I was burned in the war. Just regular old people fire." I searched around for clean socks.

"I'm not sure that's better. Are you? The salamander only burns the air to warn people away from the gryphon's nest. There's a relationship. We learned about it in school. It's two things needing each other, a kind of give and take, symbiotic." She sounded proud for remembering. "Yes, that's it. Symbiotic."

"Did you bring the salamander fire with you when you came? Is it protecting anything specific in that nest?"

"No, it was only the gryphon egg that I was responsible for bringing, no matter what Ari thinks. We may be from another world, but we are still people with our memories, our beliefs. He doesn't understand. My brother still wants to forget everything that we were. But what we were made us what we are, don't you think? But you didn't ask about any of that, did you? The salamanders were already here. They became what the gryphon needed them to be to protect and watch over what is his. But they aren't protecting anything silly like gold, no matter what the silly stories here say. The salamander's sweat becomes balls of fire. It scares people. We use it."

Turning to stare at her, I added it up. "Scares people away. Balls of light in the swamp, you mean like the ghost lights?"

"Yes." She smiled, shrugged, and looked sheepish. "Some of the time. Sometimes it's the mage who commands the controlling fire. We call them limits." She began to pace around the room. "Never mind. He wouldn't want all our secrets told too soon."

I watched her run the tip of her finger over my jewelry box. "Sure." I could sympathize with Ari's concern. Urban legends that were real, that tended to draw attention. The Gryphon of the Refuge—that's how I'd started to think about the creature I'd seen—was a danger to us all, a real danger, but more so to Ari and his people than I'd realized. It could be the ruin of their safe existence in their world.

But I understood Eden's need to hold on to what she knew, to honor her past in her present. At that moment, she seemed very young and very, very normal.

I pulled a thick, soft Henley T-shirt over my head and gathered a pretty heavy-duty pair of walking shoes from my closet; being prepared felt right. Better to be ready for fire-breathing amphibians or lusting magicians. Now it was my turn to feel sheepish. I glanced back over my shoulder at the young woman sitting on my pink ruffled bedspread, a bedspread that I'd had since I was about her age. Her age. There was another paradox, I thought.

"Eden, how old are you?"

She looked confused.

"Okay, how about this: How old were you when you traveled through the breach between our worlds?"

"This old. I've always been this age, since before you were born, because you were born here. Otherwise, time seems to pass differently for those that came through the breach. How many do you have?"

Her strange syntax made it a struggle to follow her meaning at times. "Years. How many years? I'm twenty-seven."

"Yes, I've been here for twenty-seven years."

She looked no more than fifteen. That would make her forty. This time I could not keep the shock from my face.

"Eden, what do you mean, 'because I was born here time is different'?"

"Because you were not born when you came to this place. Your mother brought you here inside her body. Time seems to pass for you as it passes for these others."

"My mother." There'd been a photograph of my mother standing in front of a gate and wearing no ring. I'd held it in my hand.

We are refugees.

I dropped the walking shoe I'd been holding. My hands felt stiff and numb. I rubbed them against my jeans.

"Eden," I said, my voice cracking. "What's the message you have for me?"

Eden chirped, "Oh, it's a meeting at the 'Taintsville Community Center, and you need to be there. Ari told me to ask you."

"Wha . . . what? A meeting?" I couldn't have been more surprised if she'd offered me a free ride on a llama. "What? Why?"

"My brother asked if you would please come." She waited like a puppy for a treat.

"I guess so. Sure."

She gave me one of her happy Eden smiles. I couldn't help but smile back and nod my head like it was the most normal thing in the world to be heading out to a meeting today.

"When?"

"We should get going."

Stunned, I couldn't think of a reason not to go. Mr. Stillbee had assured me that he was fine for now, and I knew that it would take a backhoe to dig him off the ranch and in to see any kind of a medical professional. I should have given Ryder the chore of following Mr. S. around until I could figure out something more for him to do than ride the fence line with Ari's men. The teenager seemed to be good about taking orders at least, and I gave a silent sigh of gratitude.

"Eden, I have a ranch to run here. I can't . . ."

"Our friends are here to help you, Ari's friends and mine, and they will help you. It's important that you come with me."

"And where is your brother? Oh right, down at the community center, doing what? Planning the Fourth of July parade?"

When she didn't correct me, my mouth dropped open.

"What is he thinking?"

Eden's lovely face crumpled up with real concern.

"Ari had to go and needs me to bring you. Please, Reed. I need you to come with me."

I grabbed my Jeep keys.

"Let's go. It might be nice to go to a town hall meeting in the middle of a crisis of attempted kidnapping and assault."

The lines between her doe eyes deepened.

"And that, Eden, is an example of sarcasm."

And so we went to a town hall meeting.

It was a meeting, an actual meeting.

It was a meeting of the 'Taintsville Holiday Parade Committee. I walked into the community center and wondered if I'd ever be able to get my mouth closed. Ari sat in the center of the head table, hands folded neatly in front of him, eyes on an eight-and-a-half-by-eleven piece of white paper in front of him. An agenda?

The sound of our feet booming on the elevated wooden floor as we walked in drew the attention of several members of the committee.

Mrs. Newton, my casserole-slinging friend from the Handy Way parking lot, smiled and waved us over.

The 'Taintsville Community Center, one of the first buildings built when the town was established, had settled into a comfortable collection of crooked lines and squeaky boards. It was one big room that smelled like wax, lemon Pledge, and cobwebs. I'd attended my first dance at the community center. A kitchen and set of bathrooms flanked the back wall, accessible by a long hallway, and that was it.

There was no place to go except to the kitchen to wash dishes or the bathroom to wash your hands or the folding table to stand in front of the Village Parade Committee.

"Eden, dear, would you mind bringing out the cookies and punch from the kitchen?" Miss Lockard, the school librarian, asked.

Eden looked relieved to be on to her next duty after delivering me to the meeting. "Mr. Warrick. Mrs. Newton," I said, nodding to a few of the others, whose faces were familiar. I was a little shakier on names, so I didn't attempt them. "A Thursday afternoon meeting of . . ." I paused and waited.

"The Holiday Parade Committee, of course." Mrs. Newton sounded shocked by my lack of community awareness.

"That would have been my first guess." I looked at Ari, who acted as if he sat behind that folding table every day of his life, instead of monitoring the whereabouts of a bloodthirsty gryphon, organizing his little militia of boy soldiers, and fighting with my uncle over ownership of Gilded Oats.

"Miss Hunter, it's a scheduled monthly meeting, the third Thursday morning of every month. If you were receiving our community newsletter, you'd probably know that. I can be sure that you get added to the mailing list if you'd like," Ari informed me. He looked up from his paper, searing me with his eyes. My heart flip-flopped with remembered sensations. The glint in his eye was enough of a challenge to make me want to smack him or kiss him.

"I was under the impression that you were practically a shut-in, Doctor Warrick. I had no idea you were so civically engaged."

"Don't be silly, Reed. Ari has been committee chairman for as long as—"

He stopped Miss Lockard with a hand on her arm.

Putting my hands on the table, I leaned toward him.

"No, don't stop. I'd like to hear this. I'm filling in a kind of timeline of various events in my life, like my birthday and other important days. The day you became the chairman of the Holiday Parade Committee would be an excellent addition to my timeline. And how about the day you and my uncle started arm wrestling over clear title to my ranch? Or maybe I should double check with the committee on the accuracy of the trail markers out on the Toad's Head Nature Trail."

He was up, on his feet, around the table, and escorting me from the meeting before I was able to ask for any more clarification. He dragged me toward the screen doors of the community center while Eden started to pass out cookies.

"Just a minute, I need to let the newsletter committee that I don't have a phone number at present due to financial constraints brought on by my inability to pay my bills."

And then we were on the porch.

"Hush, you'll upset them. They think they can trust you."

"Trust me? Why wouldn't they be able to trust me? They'll just be full of tasty gossip for the village grapevine. Don't you mean that you'll be upset because people will be talking about your business?" I seized on something he'd said. "Wait, trust me with what? Are you telling me that those people in there know something I don't know?" I walked to the squeaky screen door and watched people I'd known all my life with new eyes. Miss Lockard turned, saw me staring, and smiled—her wild nest of gray hair was piled on top of her head the way I remembered it from school, the same, always the same. Miss Newton hadn't aged a day in twenty-five years. Mr. Bart, the local realtor, was round and red and as stern as the day he'd marched at the front of the first parade my uncle had ever brought me to. "Ari? Who are these people?"

"You know who they are. They're your friends and neighbors."

I turned to look at him. A storm cloud covered the sun, plunging the day into a swollen gloom. The rain was coming, the way it did here—hard and fast, full of lightning and danger—the way it had on that night on the trail. Shaking my head, I took a breath and remembered that I wasn't sure why I was here in the first place. "Why am I here? Eden said I needed to be at a meeting. A meeting? After last night? This is not how it was supposed to go. None of it. She said things about me, about my mother I didn't know. Ari, who am I to you, to these people?" It was annoying to be able to hear the breathlessness in my voice.

He'd stood perfectly still during my mini-rampage, watching me with that look in his eye that let me know that although he might be hearing me, he wasn't worrying too much about anything I was saying. When he took my hand I had to catch my breath. When he touched me all I could think about was waking up in his arms today before the sun had even come up.

"Reed, I know how strange this must feel. I do know." He reached up and ran his fingertips over my cheek. "I don't want you to be sorry, you may find this hard to believe, but the committee was hoping to ask you to be the Grand Marshall of the Harvest Parade."

I felt my mouth assume its initial open-mouthed status. I had the sudden urge to laugh hysterically.

"Since you're a hometown hero, back from the war." This time there was the spark of irony in his words.

He stepped closer to me. I recognized what he was doing: using his body, his presence, to distract me from my anger and frustration.

"A parade? What are we talking about here? Two days ago a little girl was used as bait for a monster within riding distance of my home."

"We're talking about the fact that going about our normal lives is the best way not to unleash that monster into a very unsuspecting world." He reached out and took me by the shoulders. "Reed, we've got to go about our lives. That's what we do. That's what we've always done."

I didn't figure him for an uncaring son of a . . . "I'm not sure that's going to work anymore. Mr. Stillbee was attacked by someone who carved a name into his face."

He finally looked worried. Now he was hearing me. This wasn't something that he could normal away.

"When?"

"Today, that's why your men and Jackson were there in my front yard this morning. They'd been worried about him, looking for me. How could you not know? Where did you disappear to after last . . . after they found . . . us?" I thought I detected a hint of something close to a smile on his beautiful mouth; I think he liked it when I got embarrassed or flustered.

"I wanted to make sure," he said.

I waited. Finally, maybe, here was Ari Warrick offering up some of the precious details of his mysterious life, even if it did lead me right back here to a meeting of the Holiday Parade Committee.

"Sure of what?" I snapped, stepping closer to him so I could lower my voice.

There was a popping sound, and I felt him punch my shoulder—hard.

"Hey!" I opened my mouth to tell him what I thought of his friendly shoulder punch, but it was getting harder and harder to hold him up, even though he was standing close. Close enough for me to see the bits of glittery blue in his eyes.

"Hey, again. You're crushing me. And that . . . hurt. Why did you hit me?" My voice sounded strange. When I was supposed to sound like the Grand Marshall of the Harvest Parade. I sounded silly. Did he hear it too? "Why did you hit me? That was not necessary."

I heard my name, but it seemed so far away.

"Reed! Reed! My sweetling. Reed, I didn't hit you."

His arms enveloped me.

"Ari, did you hear something?" I said. And then he was saying my name over and over again. I could tell he was saying my name because his lips, his clever lips, moved, but there was no sound. Why was he trying so hard? I slumped against him and reached up to rub the spot where he'd hit me. My hand came away slick with blood.

Chapter 34

Hospital

This time it was a hospital—a real one—and I was pretty sure that I'd be adding new scars to my growing collection of old ones, actual or magical.

The blinking and beeping were too familiar. It was depressing.

I tried to lift my hand.

"Hey, Slick, slow down there."

One of those foam cups with a bendy straw appeared at the corner of my eye. I made a face.

"Come on Reed, the faster you do all the human stuff, the faster you'll be getting better and out of here. We still have a date. We seriously need to get you out of here." Jackson said this last part almost to himself, and he looked worried.

"They just took you off the ventilator, and so drinking is the order of the day."

Good grief, a ventilator. When had I stopped breathing?

I gave talking a try. It came out close to a growl.

"Drink," he ordered.

I tried again. The result wasn't much better. "Whaaat," I said, and then cleared my throat, "hhhappened?"

"Drink."

I took a sip to satisfy him. "Tell me."

"Someone took a pot shot at you at the community center."

"Shot? I was shot. But why?"

A memory of Ari's voice calling to me, telling me to hold on filtered through some of the noise and beeping. It didn't feel like water was going to do the trick. It felt like I was waiting for some kind of transplant.

"Jackson," I said, but it came out like a croak. "How bad? "

"You were shot on the front porch of the 'Taintsville Community Center. Sniper. Luckily not a very good one. Don't worry. I'm right here, and I'm staying."

"A guard?"

I tried to lift my head when he touched my hand, but the thundering in my head discouraged me.

"Reedy, it's okay. I'm your friend." He squeezed my hand when his voice cracked. He was choked up.

"Okay." I felt a tear leak down my cheek.

"Hey now! Where's your game face, soldier?"

We waited through one of those moments where it was hard to decide who had the bigger lump in their throat. I kept my eyes on the acoustic tiles over my head, trying to ignore the throbbing in my shoulder and the tendency that it had to synchronize to the beating of the monitors next to my bed.

"Okay, Ms. Hunter, let's do this right. I want you to try. The doctors are saying that you are going to be out of here soon."

I looked over at him out of the corner of my eye. I discovered that if I kept my eyes half closed my head hurt less. He pulled a small spiral-bound notebook out of his pocket.

"A notebook, Sheriff?"

"Walgreens. Five for a dollar."

I started to snort, but that made a sledgehammer-sized pain jolt through my shoulder. Reflexively I reached up to touch my head and touched bandage.

"Jackson?" I wondered if I looked as worried as I felt.

"You were lucky," he said, squeezing my shoulder. "The bullet hit your collarbone and then bounced around a bit, but there shouldn't be any permanent damage. And that's the official diagnosis."

"But my head."

"You fell and hit the porch railing, apparently."

That made no sense, Ari had caught me, had been holding me. I couldn't remember falling.

Closing my eyes again, I said, "Okay, Officer, but I'm not sure how long I can give you."

"Ms. Hunter, you were on the front porch of the community center arguing with one Ari Warrick?" He waited for me to fill in the blanks.

"Yes, I was on the porch, and I was telling him off, not arguing. I wouldn't even say that, I was just telling Ari, Mr. Warrick, about the assault on Mr. Stillbee, and I was hoping for some ideas of who would do that to him."

"Why would you think Mr. Warrick would have any answer for you on that?"

And that quickly I was in over my head. I didn't know what to tell him. I thought Ari might know because, well, he's a political refugee from a supernatural world under the river and swamp that runs along the border of my property. You know, I thought, the river, the one that borders the wildlife refuge where an adult male gryphon was making time with my full-blooded Arabian mare.

"He's been here for a while and, and he seems to know about stuff."

The medication was making me feel too slow for any battle of wits with the good officer. "You know. Stuff." I sounded like a school kid without a ready excuse. I slipped under the weight of drugs and pain.

Sometime later, I heard him whisper, "Reed, don't worry. I'm going to go and get that horse of yours back. No waiting."

The thought of Jackson riding into the gryphon's territory unwarned brought me back, dragging me up out of my sleepy funk.

"No, no, you can't go out there. It'll be mad. It'll drop you on top of the Vulcan. It will. I need you to be quiet. It'll be mad. It has to protect its gold." The drugs. Some place in my drugged-out mind, I knew I shouldn't be talking about any of this to him. Be quiet. Be quiet. "Don't make it mad," I slurred.

My Jeep looked dusty, rusty, banged up, and pretty darn great waiting for me at the pick-up curb of the hospital.

"You stay still until I can shuffle over there and open that door."

I wanted to laugh at the pair of us: Mr. S. stiff and limping about and me with my arm taped against my chest.

His face had healed while I'd been in the hospital. He claimed the wrinkles had won out over what had looked like graffiti. There was nothing written on his face now. He blamed my silly imagination. It was my imagination that had me seeing my mother's name, must have been. Except I knew that it wasn't.

My cracked collarbone and my taped-up arm kept me from talking myself out of believing that I'd imagined any of it.

I'd had to talk both my surgeon and Jackson into letting me go home as soon as I could stagger away from a wheelchair. Gilded Oats needed me, and I just wanted to go home. Mr. S. assured me that Ari's ranch hands were still helping out. He seemed resigned to it. I think he felt better with more hands and eyes on deck.

Jackson wasn't sure about the new help, wanting to blame them for all manner of evils, but there was no reason I could think of that one of Ari's quiet, steady farmhands would have followed me to a public gathering to shoot me.

Jackson had wanted me out of the hospital even more than I did it seemed. At least he'd come to visit me, tried to interview me. Mr. Stillbee had come too, along with a few people from the community center, but no one from the Warrick contingency. Maybe real hospitals made Dr. Warrick nervous. Maybe spook light damage control was keeping everyone moving lively. Maybe.

The last I'd seen of Ari, his face had been a thundercloud complete with a smear of my blood slashing across his cheek, and then nothing. Just foggy memories of three days in the hospital.

When we finally pulled into our front yard, my car door creaked open like an old gate hinge. I let Mr. S. help me out, trying not to put too much of my weight on the arm he offered me. As I slid from the Jeep seat to my feet, the sky turned an unhappy gray. A raincloud drifted in front of the sun. I swayed.

"Whoa, you'd better watch out. I might take us both down." I closed my eyes and waited for the nausea to pass.

"Oh no, Reedy-Girl, I'm wiry. Always have been. You lean on me."

I swallowed hard after my stomach settled and my vision quit spinning.

"Too soon? I was wondering about that." His face collapsed into a worried frown.

I harrumphed. "Long enough, that's what I say."

We shuffled to the front door. "The doctor was amazed by my recuperative powers. Didn't you hear?" And he had been, too. The good doctor pronounced my shoulder halfway to healed by day three. "If you're tough and wiry, then I'm tough and stubborn. We just might make it."

We took it slow and steady, and I felt like we'd crossed the line of a marathon when we walked into the cool, stale air of the foyer. I sighed loud enough to have the sound bounce around like an echo in a cave. It was the first time I had felt comfortable since the community center.

"Up or down?" Mr. S. offered.

"The library sounds great. There's a perfectly good couch. And not a nurse in sight to wake me up in the middle of the night to see if I need a sleeping pill."

He grunted his agreement.

Being in the hospital had made me realize how dear the two-story ranch house had become to me since my uncle's death; it was home. Big and rambling, rooms and additions added over the years, randomly it seemed, it had a comfortable weathered feel, and now I would be trying to hang on to the ranch and pay off some fairly steep medical bills, hoping that the skies over my home stayed empty and safe. I pushed the worries away: back taxes, my sweet horse, someone trying to shoot me, and someone else carving letters into Mr. Stillbee's cheek. I concentrated on the feel of smooth leather under my fist as I sank into my uncle's worn couch, curling into his favorite spot.

The perfume of old books and leather filled me. If I closed my eyes, I could imagine that I could still smell the faint scent of Uncle Rulan's aftershave. The leather sagged under me, and I closed my eyes and saw him there—reading—always reading. My shoulder was sore, and it was making me feel sorry for myself. It made me wish for my uncle to be here to tell me that everything would be all right.

Mr. S. made me promise that I'd stay put until he could bring dinner back from the bunkhouse, and I didn't argue too much. Instead, I let myself settle into the comfort of the couch and the contentment of being home. Tomorrow, I'd worry about how to hang on to it all, tomorrow.

For right now, I'd probably fall asleep to the same thing I'd been obsessing over since I woke up in a hospital. Where had Ari Ben Warrick disappeared to since I last saw him on the porch of the 'Taintsville community center? He'd never come to the hospital; I tried hard not to let that reality hurt me, but it did.

I ran over the possibilities the same way people count sheep or write novels in their heads before they drift off.

Ari was gone. That was my first theory. I'd brought too much heat down on them, given up too many secrets, and he'd led his people back through the crack between our worlds.

Or maybe Eden had run away to join a less strange cult than the family she was already a part of.

There was always the theory that the gryphon had eaten Ari or Eden or all of them.

On it went, the worries spinning through my head over and over again, until the smell of sandalwood aftershave and aged leather lulled me into the first real nap I'd had since I'd showed up at the meeting of the 'Taintsville Holiday Parade Committee. The first sleep where I didn't dream strange, sad, drug-fueled images of flying eagle-headed horses made of green hospital Jell-O.

Chapter 35

After the Hospital

"Reed, wake up."

Eden? Eden's voice felt like a trick. She hadn't come to the hospital, none of them had, not Ari or Eden or Ryder, just Jackson and Mr. S. That fact made it hard not to be pretty shocked and shaken, but I would have rather taken another bullet than admit how much that hurt me.

Someone touched my good shoulder.

"Reed, are you awake? Mr. Stillbee needs you outside. If you can come?" She shook me again. I bit my lip against the ache.

"Eden, what time is it?"

"Morning."

I'd slept the entire day and night on the couch. The whole world could have collapsed into a pit of hospital Jell-O while I was asleep. Good pills. The thought of the world ending made me sit up too fast, and that made me instantly dizzy. I clutched at the arm of the couch, putting my head between my knees and curling around my suddenly throbbing arm and shoulder. The good pills had worn off.

"Eden, this had better be worth my keeling over on the floor."

"Oh, I think that you'll be delighted. That is if you don't faint, I mean."

Eden was the master of understatement. Somebody was banging pots and pans in the kitchen at the back of the house. I thought I smelled bacon. When I glanced at Eden, I realized she was practically vibrating with excitement. I thought about telling her to give me a minute to find my medication and figure out the source of the bacon frying, but the look on her face was a giant push to get off the couch, and see what Mr. Stillbee had to show me.

"Come on. If you help me, I should be okay."

She trotted to my side like an Irish setter, and I draped my arm around her bony shoulders, grateful for the help.

We made it through the front door with a minimum of bumping around, and I hated to admit it, but the fresh air made me feel better—my head clearer. It was good to be home I thought, and took a deep breath of fresh ranch air.

I expected Mr. Stillbee with a banner or the ranch hands with a hip, hip, hooray, but instead it was a stranger, a man with hair the color of old straw. He stood squinting into the sun. It didn't seem important at that moment anyway, because in his hands he held a lead rope. At the end of it was my beautiful Cantara. Seeing that horse felt like having my best friend back.

Forgetting about my shoulder, I pulled away from Eden and hurried to throw my good arm around her neck. She'd been bathed and groomed and shone like a diamond in the early morning light. It was stupid, the immediate prick of tears I felt with my face in her mane, smelling her familiar scent, feeling the velvet of her muzzle.

I realized that I'd been muttering thank you over and over again, and I might be sounding unhinged.

Gulping back the flood of tears that choked me, I started running my hand over her neck and back, down her legs.

"She's perfect, beautiful. How did you catch her? I can't believe it." I walked around the back of my mare, running my hand over her rump. She hopped away from my hand a bit. "I thought she was gone forever." Cantara snorted. "Still a little bit skittish. She's been gone for ages."

He looked at me with a funny half-smile. It reminded me of the way a fond uncle might admire the antics of a toddler.

Time to get my dignity back by acting like an adult. I stuck my hand out, thinking to shake his hand. Instead, he handed me the lead rope.

"I'm so sorry. I'm acting crazy. My name is Reed, Reed Hunter, and I can't thank you enough for bringing her back to me."

He reached for my injured arm. It hurt when he pulled my hand into both of his, but I was so grateful I tried to keep the grimacing to a minimum. He didn't seem to notice that he was hurting me.

"Your Mr. Stillbee helped me find you," he said, not looking at her. His voice had that deep, rich timber of someone confident in their statements, their demands. I liked the sound of it. "She, I mean the horse, walked right up to me on the hiking trail, and I'd seen the flyer around."

"Oh Eden, you're a wonder," I said, meaning it. I looked over at her, but she had retreated away from the happy reunion scene. She stayed in the doorway, half in and half out, almost lurking, watching us carefully.

"Thank you again. Mister?" I let the question hang. "I wish I could give you the ransom that got posted on the flyers, but that was a practical joke. At least I'd like to know your name and thank you properly." I couldn't be sure, but I thought he hesitated as if I confused him. Why wouldn't I want to know who'd brought my horse home?

I didn't have time to wonder about it. Cantara arched her neck, snorted, and then sniffed at my hair. I reached up and scratched between her eyes. I raised my eyebrows at him and waited. He stared at me with beautiful green eyes.

"My name?" He studied me quietly and then said, "No. No. I'm fine. I don't need any thanks, and I'm pretty sure that having your beautiful horse walk up to me at the beginning of the trail was no great feat. Mr. Stillbee, I know him. He's the one you should thank."

"How lucky that you knew him." It was lucky. Something pricked at my brain about the stranger who'd brought my mare home. Cantara snorted again, and I could feel her getting antsy—ready for some real food for a change, and her stall. I shook off the nagging itch of worry between my shoulder blades. Count your blessings, Reed. It was a good reminder to quit looking for trouble.

"Would you like me to walk with you to the barn? I see that you've been hurt." He pointed to my sling.

"Accident. And I'd appreciate the help a lot. Thanks, I would like to get her home before she decides that her wild adventure in the unknown wilderness was better than the dull old barn."

When I turned to wave to Eden, she'd disappeared into the house.

I looked at the sky, trying to remember details about the gryphon's territory and behavior, hoping that it was over: the gryphon's interest in my horse or my water buffalo or anything else that was mine. I smiled my thanks at the stranger, but still felt uneasy as I started walking my mare down the barn road. He fell into step beside me. He didn't seem anxious to pick up the conversation.

He was tall, as tall as Jackson and Ari, and walked with a long-legged stride reserved for ranchers or hunters. Before we'd reached the first curve, I was out of breath and grateful for his presence. I didn't need to pass out and have Cantara running loose again. As we walked, I couldn't keep myself from touching her neck, partly to assure myself that she was back, and partly to brace myself in case I stumbled.

"I'm sorry. I need to stop for a moment. I'm not usually this wimpy. I've just come home."

He looked at me and frowned.

"From the hospital," I said, trying to explain. He didn't comment.

"It's not far—the barn. This is probably ambitious for my first day back, and when Mr. S. sees me wandering around, I'm probably going to get my first lecture of the day." I gave him my best hey-let's-be-friends effort. He didn't smile back. Okay. Whatever.

I told him a little bit about the day-to-day world of running an exotic animal ranch. It seemed a natural enough subject to talk about with a stranger visiting Gilded Oats, especially someone who'd brought my missing horse home from the deadly woods.

Chapter 36

Stranger

Before we got to the barn my curiosity kicked in, and it was his turn to answer some questions. But instead of being full of the charming tale of how he'd found and rescued my horse, he asked about the number of men it took to run the ranch. He never mentioned my arm, but I saw him glance at me as if assessing and measuring. I slowed my pace, partly out of necessity and partly to give myself time to think and maybe make some assessments of my own. Something about this man felt wrong.

"So, you like the Toad's Head Trail for hiking?" I asked. "It's pretty isn't it?"

He looked at me and smiled. I hadn't thought of myself as being that transparent, but he had a way of making me feel like a five-year-old. Oh well, in for a penny—I pressed the point.

"Or were you riding the trail? A lot of people like to ride it."

"Hiking. I enjoy that, walking the land, getting a feel for," he said, hesitating while he slid another look at me, "where I am."

I hadn't noticed before in the excitement of having Cantara back how green his eyes were, a stunning emerald color with flecks of gold. His look seemed to see more than my lost Arabian mare or me. He looked at me again, searching my face. "Your eyes are quite unusual."

Not everyone noticed—he had. I tipped my face up to the sun.

"Heterochromia. A fancy word for I got them from my parents."
He didn't comment. "You're not from around here," I said.

"No, not from here."

And as if to prove it, he slowed his steps, dropping back behind the
horse to follow. Talk was over. I glanced back to find him watching
the sky. A pair of sandhill cranes speared through the blue above us,
and a family of doves flushed from a clump of saw palmettos on our
left. Half expecting my horse to shy or jig away from the birds, I
tightened my hand on her lead rope. Cantara walked on, steady and
straight.

"I guess it takes more than a couple of birds in the bushes to shake
you up these days." As if to reassure me she stretched out her muzzle
and snuffled at my hand on the lead rope.

She was back and alive but I couldn't keep the feeling that trouble
was following close behind. Unease grew in my gut like a malignant
mushroom.

We'd almost reached the barn when Cantara whinnied a happy
hello. Several horses whinnied back. We only had one other horse,
poor old Einstein. I assumed the new horses belonged to Ari's men.
More of the beautiful black horses I assumed Ari bred. I was feeling
weak as a kitten by the time I saw the barn. There was a hushed
stillness to everything that added to my unease: no one working
outside and no sounds from inside. Quiet, except for the horses' happy
talk.

"Funny, I thought there'd be more going on around here. A few
days in the hospital and the whole place goes to sleep."

I started to call out to any of the ranch hands, but the stranger
stopped me from behind and reached up to pull Cantara's lead rope
out of my hands. He grabbed my bad shoulder and squeezed. It made
me sick to my stomach, and I retched.

"Stillbee, she's here," the man called out. "You should come now,
and we'll be done with this."

He turned on me and held me with those eyes of his—unblinking pools of green.

"Your mother," the stranger began, watching the barn but talking to me. He yanked on the lead rope when Cantara started to prance, kicking up the dust on the road outside the barn entrance. He made no attempt to go any closer to the barn. "Your mother," repeated. "I met her once. "

Before I could say anything, men I didn't recognize led Ari Warrick from the barn. They were armed with short, curving daggers. Ari's wrists and hands were wrapped in leather hobbles, the scales on the leather visible from where I stood. Behind them, walking stronger and straighter than I could remember, was my childhood friend and caretaker, Garland Stillbee.

I forgot the horse, forgot the man who threatened me. I tried to bolt and go to Ari and Mr. S. The stranger tripped me. It was easy; I was unsteady and tired and terrified.

Ari elbowed the men holding him.

The green-eyed man jerked at Cantara's lead rope. She snorted and scrambled backward, dust spewing up from her hooves.

I rolled away from the choking dust. "Stop! You're scaring her!"

"Reed, be still. Don't speak." Ari was a dark angel in the hands of the two men. They had a look of sameness that made me think they could be related to each other.

"What is happening, Mr. S.?" I pulled myself to my knees and tried to push up with my good arm.

The green-eyed man kicked me down again.

"That's enough. It isn't necessary to break your prize or there won't be a reward. Use what brain you have." Mr. Stillbee sounded like he was talking to a rebellious teenager. "I told you this would go easier if we acted quickly and cleanly."

"Mr. S.?" I choked. What was happening?

"She's only a bit like the mother, don't you think?" The stranger looked to Mr. S. "But Master wants her. You took too much when you ran, Ari Ben Warrick. Did you think our master wouldn't come for what you took?"

Cantara started prancing again, this time in earnest. I scooted up to my knees and tried to keep my head from spinning, needing to move. I didn't feel like being horse stomped. With the loose end of the lead rope, the stranger thumped her nose. She pulled back, sinking onto her haunches, squealing.

I tried to yell at him to stop, but all that came out was a grunt.

"Ari!" I finally managed.

The man beating my horse looked down at me.

"Reed. Stay down." Ari struggled again. "Stay down, please. Be still. Stop this. What are you called? Hear me."

The green-eyed man snorted. "Do you think I would give you power over me by giving you knowledge? Think again, Dark Mage."

Mr. S. shook his head. "Enough. If you want to limit his power, don't talk to him or about anything. Shut up. The longer we wait the harder it will be to return below."

Why was Stillbee pretending to be one of them? Why would my oldest friend do that?

Cantara lifted her head and squealed.

"The mare, you must not hurt her." Ari wrenched against his bonds, ignoring Mr. S. "Look at me. Listen. The horse. The horse is a miracle. Don't hurt it." When Ari made a move toward me, the men on both sides of him closed in like dogs. Mr. S. smirked and rolled his eyes.

"The gryphon has mated with this one. He's marked her as his own. She's pregnant." Ari's words were brittle and sharp like dry bones under a bleaching sun.

Chapter 37

History

L aughter burst out of the men: an oily, ugly explosion. Cantara's captor tipped his head considering the idea. "Not even in our world is that kind of magic possible. I've seen the war gryphons pick a horse up and disembowel it in midflight." He stopped talking, considering the possibilities. "What have you been about? You and my master were brothers in arms, once. Do you not remember when you were children, teaching other children how to slaughter even more children?"

Horrified, I looked up into Ari's face. He avoided looking at me.

"Really? Ashamed of your past now that Reed knows more of the story." Mr. S. folded his arms, making no attempt to approach me or even look at me. "How interesting. Reed, he isn't what you think: none of them are. I'm sure he's told you of their epic struggle, their heroic escape. Remember, history is written by the winners and they, he and his *friends*, were not the winners." He walked to stand and stare into Ari's face. "I thought the loss of one beloved would be enough. I'm amazed you had the courage to love again. My master told me to look for the unseen, unhealed wounds, but he did not mention a living weakness." He turned a bland, heartless look on me.

"I can't understand this. You've been part of our lives, my life. What does this mean? You've been my friend since I was born."

"It means I'm done being the good and faithful servant. It means that I'm ready to be on the winning side of this history. It means that I have been a good and faithful servant, but not to the Hunter family. My master, your real father, will reward me handsomely for your return. Your wretch of a mother deserved what she got. That pathetic lump of a stepfather of yours, too."

The foundation I had built my life on fell away in an avalanche of betrayal. Tears hit the back of my hands. I couldn't say when I'd started crying.

The man holding Cantara laughed again, and just for good measure slammed the end of the lead rope into the mare's face.

Cantara screamed, reared, and pawed the air. While he wrestled with the unhappy animal, Ari caught my eye, gave me a brief headshake.

I'd heard the words but couldn't make sense of them: beloved, shame, unhealed wounds, betrayal.

"Think what a treasure the mare is, producing the rarest of creatures: A hippogriff. You know the stories: the gold of a gryphon's nest. But not the gold people on this planet imagine. Just go. Take the treasure and go." Ari relaxed in the middle of his captors, ignoring me, looking both at Mr. S. and then the green-eyed man.

The green-eyed man started to laugh in earnest. "Ari, I've known of you since I was a child, living among the dunes of crystal sand. Are you trying to convince me that you don't care if I take this animal and what may be growing inside her? A miracle worthy of an emperor." He paused, considering. "And you." He towered over me while Cantara snorted and stamped. "You with eyes of blue and green. Your mother's daughter. But your father's too, I think. Another prize. The prize your father has craved for years and has finally found."

The reptilian flatness in his face had me trying to scuttle away from him. I instantly regretted putting weight on my bad shoulder.

I babbled, "Ari? My mother? My father? What's he saying? What is happening here? And why are you standing in front of my barn being held at sword point? Holy hell." I flashed a look at Ari, who stopped me with a desperate look. The throbbing in my shoulder and arm filled me up with misery. I plopped onto my butt and cradled my arm against my chest as gently as I could.

"Look at me, gnat," Ari shouted. "Don't look at her! Tell me, tell me that you aren't a filthy, scat-eating mercenary. Even scum have names."

But the man's eyes never wavered, staying fixed on me.

Stillbee—not Mister, never again would I use the word Mister—walked to Ari, bound and trapped, and spit in his face.

"Now!" Ari's command filled the air like a gale. "Name. I demand it." The two men holding Ari looked confused, as if they'd forgotten their assignment. Stillbee staggered back.

The man near me turned to Ari. A glaze filled his eyes. His hands relaxed on the rope. Even as he shook his head, I heard him say, "Holtzer. I am Holtzer."

"Idiot," Stillbee muttered, sidestepping Cantara when she pranced his way.

Holtzer yanked again on the lead rope, and I rolled toward my horse, determined to take her from him.

"Stay down," Ari howled. There might be magic in Ari's voice, but I seemed to have some magic of my own—stubbornness.

"If I weren't hurt, I'd get up and kick your teeth in, mister, horse or no horse."

"Reed, shut up." Ari concentrated on Holtzer, but watched me out of the corner of his eye. "There's no point in this, Stillbee. I'll go with you—back—would that satisfy him? Not her. She would never survive it. Take the gryphon's seed. Let that satisfy your master's greed."

"Satisfaction?" Stillbee scoffed. "He won't be satisfied until what is his is returned to him, his offspring. I, on the other hand, will be satisfied to take back the gryphon's seed. There is reward enough in that."

I took the time to search the faces of the men holding Ari. They were a type. Hard, converted, dedicated. I'd seen men like them in Iraq, followers of some despot warlord, probably related in some way to the boss man. I looked again at Holtzer, his body tense as a piano wire as he watched Ari. I couldn't bring myself to look at my childhood friend. I studied their faces, trying to put the pieces of information together.

Maybe it was the pain, the fear, my own denial, but I felt slow and stupid trying to make sense of what was happening.

They spoke of my mother. My mother had blue eyes, and me with one blue eye and one green eye; then I remembered Eden's nonsensical reminiscences, talking about my mother, from another world with me inside her.

Stillbee drew up to his full height, made his voice important, when he said, "Ari Ben Warrick, you are found in full-fledged tribal default for abandoning your command. You are hereby also charged with the kidnapping of Starlyn of the Blue Sky People, and her daughter, Reed Baye."

"And I will go with you and satisfy the full extent of the default, no one else need be involved in this," Ari paused and looked at me, "this thing that is between me and . . . your master."

I knew the moment Ari saw that I had put it together. He heaved his shoulder into one of his captors, elbowing another in the jaw.

Stillbee screamed, "I told you. I warned you."

I shoved up to my feet, pitching sand into Holtzer's face and blocked the kick he aimed at my face. My shoulder screamed louder than any warning. Ari spun, slamming his head into the gut of the guy beside him, and they all went down in a heap. I focused on the man threatening my horse. He'd stumbled back with a face full of dirt. Launching, I landed on his chest, ignoring my arm and praying that I wouldn't collapse. Hands grabbed the collar of my shirt, dragging me off the man on the ground. Someone threw me up against the side of the barn. The last thing I remembered was the sound of rushing wings.

"Reed, can you get up by yourself? My dearling, you need to get up now and look." Ari stood alone. There was blood on his forehead, his mouth, but he was too focused on trying to tell me something. "Reed, get up, now." He reached down to pull me to my feet. I looked up at the sky, the sun burning a hole of fire in the emptiness over my head. I saw a dark shadow pass across the face of that furious light. Limits or no limits, the gryphon had come for Cantara.

I looked at Ari, who calmly held a hand out to me. He curled his fingers at me when the gryphon's scream shattered the angry tableau in front of the barn. No one had to be told to take cover. Death had arrived. I heard my mare whinny. Cantara was safe if what Ari had said was true, that she'd been impregnated already.

"Where are the others?" Ari's captors and Stillbee were gone, but Holtzer was still there, hanging on to Cantara's rope with a stubborn determination amidst his fear.

"Broke and ran when they heard the gryphon. Hiding in the barn."

"Where's Stillbee? Where has he gone?"

Ari focused on the gryphon. "The barn."

Holtzer looked from the sky to the horse thrashing at the end of the lead rope. She dragged him further out into the open.

"Was that the hope, to breed yourself a hippogriff all along, Ari? A weapon of mass destruction, isn't that what they call it here?" Holtzer started to laugh again.

"Reed, I need to get to Stillbee, to find him."

"Go. I'm right behind you. Get that traitor."

A quivery shadow passed over us again, larger now, closer. We pressed hard into the side of the barn. Ari bolted into the barn.

Holtzer darted in to grab me, yanking me back against his chest by my bad arm. I bit my lip to keep from crying out. Everything in my body and my mind demanded quiet, knowing that we were now prey to that thing flying overhead and that it was always listening.

A black shadow stroked over the ground again.

"Holtzer, you don't want to be here when that gets here," I warned. Cantara lifted her head to the sky and called to the gryphon. I felt his answering shriek in my bones. Holtzer shoved me against Cantara's left flank.

"What are you doing? I don't have anything you want. And your fearless leader, Stillbee, left you to the monster."

He started backing me, still shoved against my horse, into the opening in the barn.

"Don't you?" Holtzer grunted as he shoved Cantara backward. He didn't even look at the sky. I could barely take my eyes off of it.

"Seriously, why aren't you worried? If you are from where you say then you understand what that creature can do. And believe me, if he wants this mare he's going to take her."

At just that moment, Cantara had finished being pushed around by this stranger. I could feel her hindquarters tensing, her body going rigid with panic. She was surely going to bolt. I couldn't let her disappear again, and I wasn't going anywhere this Holtzer wanted me to go. I scrambled under her belly, stood, wrapped my right hand in her mane, and threw myself onto her back. I felt stitches tear and almost went back off the way I had gotten up. Thankfully, it worked for me to slump forward, bury my face in her mane, and hang on for dear life.

She exploded past Holtzer, and I hung on, knowing that I wouldn't be able to survive hitting the ground without turning into a Raggedy Anne doll.

It had been a long time since I'd ridden bareback, but once upon a time during the long lazy summers, it had been the only way I'd ridden my horse: no bridle, no saddle—just my legs on the horse, my hand in her mane, and speed.

I hoped for Ari's sake she'd remember that I was still the boss and that those bareback summers weren't all that long ago. I needed to get her back to the rear entrance of the barn before the gryphon got there. I gulped down the fear and nausea, telling myself that I'd vomit later.

Driving my heel into her right flank, I released as much pressure as I dared on the left. I whispered a quick thank you when I felt her start the bend that would bring us back around to the rear of the barn.

At the back entrance, Ari stepped out into the light. Blood soaked the front of his shirt. There was no sign of Holtzer or Stillbee. She spooked away from Ari, and then there was no stopping her. We flew away from the barn.

A tearing sound ripped the air apart with a rush of hot wind. I stayed low over Cantara's neck and felt tears burn my eyes as we tore across the north pasture. A blast of hot breath washed over me, and I turned my head and looked into the eyes of the gryphon of the Tannin River Refuge. He flew low to the ground, paralleling Cantara's every movement.

For a moment, I thought there was an almost joyous delight in our wild ride across Gilded Oats Ranch.

Cantara ran for her life. Not away from the gryphon or Stillbee or even me. She ran because she could, and the beast at her side anchored her to the sky and to life. We circled the big north pasture. I looked over and watched, stunned, as the gryphon did a loop-the-loop. It was all a grand lark for the horse and the creature.

Her speed brought us around to the back end of the barn faster than I'd expected, and without any real plan, it was my turn to want to bolt. My heart hammered in my chest with the thought of being caught between the gryphon and Holtzer or Stillbee, the men who were claiming knowledge of an entire part of my life that I hadn't known existed. But the memory of blood on Ari's shirt and the threat of enemies, known and unknown, focused my plan.

I realized that the gryphon wasn't worried about me at all, he was just staying with Cantara. I knew what to do.

I kicked her and pushed her into another circuit of the big pasture, out and around a stand of cypress that would be a screen between us and the barn; hoping that I wouldn't get plucked off her back like a tick by her devoted companion. I leaned back to slow her down, pressing my weight down into her hips. Forward meant speed and leaning back across the horse's backside meant the opposite. It worked. She slowed.

I congratulated myself on my good riding, ignoring the fact that Cantara was winded from her wild sprint away from the men who'd frightened her. I urged her deeper into the cypress stand. The presence of the gryphon felt like an ax waiting to fall.

Whispering as much to calm Cantara as to take my mind off the fact that I could feel blood sheeting down my side from my stitches, I said, "Baby, I need one more burst of speed from you, and if I know your boyfriend up there, you'd better be fast."

I looked up and saw curved claws balancing on one of the massive limbs of a lightning-blasted live oak, which branched out into the cypress stand. His huge body blotted out the sun. I tried not to let primal fear and instinct take over. When Cantara snorted, the gryphon shifted, tipping its oddly elegant eagle's head at the sound. I tried to swallow around the dry lump in my throat. "Loverboy up there is going to help me with a little standoff."

I didn't dare dismount. I knew I wouldn't be getting back up, or I would have jumped down and used the lead rope to have a little more control over the situation. Ari was in that barn. The bad guy was in there with him.

"So, if you don't mind, we're going to do a little bit of barnstorming. Like the good old days, right?"

She tossed her mane. I would have liked to believe she did it to reassure me, but I realized it was probably more for the gryphon's benefit. "Okay, Big Boy; it's time to make yourself useful."

I leaned forward and prayed to stay conscious long enough to distract Holtzer, Stillbee and the others. It was going to be close. I could feel my strength dripping away underneath my shirt. Just one more push, one more.

Cantara was getting harder to control with the gryphon so close. I couldn't tell if she was excited he was here or frightened; either way she was tearing around the cypress knees like a mad thing. Overhead I heard branches snapping as the gryphon tracked her every move with his body.

"Come on, Buddy. Come and get her."

I knotted my hand in Cantara's mane, prayed for the power of pheromones and lust, and kicked her into a headlong gallop back to the barn, hoping there was enough cover to keep Holtzer from putting it together. I wasn't even sure why he hadn't come after us when we'd taken off, except that the sky belonged to the gryphon. His frustrated shriek boomed through the air, but all I could do was hang on for the ride.

Cantara flattened out to the ground and ran. I let her. I'm pretty sure I couldn't have done anything to slow her down anyway.

The world shrank to a blast of wind in my face and the pounding of muscle and hooves beneath me. I trusted the gryphon to follow, but was too weak to check. We rolled across the back pasture like an out of control ball of lightning straight into the back opening of the big barn. With a final shrieking scream, the gryphon followed us in.

There was an explosion of squawking chickens, flying hay, the pounding of fists on the flesh of men in the middle of killing each other and the frightened whinnying of one Arabian mare. The smell of blood caught in the back of my throat. The gryphon slid into the barn, claws tearing up the clay floor. Fascinated, exhausted, barely conscious, I watched the monster snatch one of the men close to Ari in its beak. The vision disappeared as hands reached up in the struggle and tore me from Cantara's back. My last thought before blackness filled my vision was that I hoped they turned out to be friendly hands.

Chapter 38

Nest

I t was hard to know how long I'd been unconscious, but it had to have been long enough for someone to manage digging out a pretty decent nest of sorts in a pile of hay in the corner of the barn. They'd dumped me into it. It was long enough to wonder where everyone had gone. It was quiet. Too quiet. Curled in my nest, I was afraid to move. I couldn't feel wet blood anymore. I had the vague worry that if I moved it would start up again. My arm and collarbone should be throbbing, but I couldn't feel anything. Carefully, I began an inventory, curling my fingers around the hay, pointing my toes, stretching my legs. It was silly. I felt fine, but I knew that I was procrastinating the moment I might be discovered, or that I had to face a reality I wasn't ready to see.

Slowly, I rolled to my back and stared up at the rafters. Spiders were busy spinning away their lives. I almost envied them. Hay trickled into my eyes. I brushed it off my face and turned my head to stare up into the eyes of the gryphon, its head cocked to one side as it watched me. It balanced elegantly on a beam overhead among the spiders and dust.

"Reed, don't move. Please stay as still as you can."

At first, I wasn't sure who was talking to me. Not Ari. Not a bad guy. Not even Mr. S., and then I realized it wasn't a man. It was

Eden's voice. Somewhere behind me, hidden I hoped, Eden was talking to me.

"And don't try to talk to me or it will be drawn to you. The winged lions are quite curious. It's here for its mate, I think."

She didn't offer up any information as to what had happened to the men who had been holding her brother at the point of a sword or the man whom she'd cheerfully brought to my doorstep. I wanted to explode out of my hiding place and slap that silly giddiness out of her voice, but the gryphon looking down at me convinced me to listen to her.

The beast's glassy eyes did not blink. I waited for Eden to continue.

Somewhere in the barn, I heard a whirring sound like a rope being twirled. The gryphon's head pivoted toward the noise. There was eagerness and excitement in its body language at hearing the sound. Its shoulders squared, and its claws curled and uncurled around the rafter beam. The twirling sound grew louder and faster. The gryphon's claws peeled wood from the beam as it turned to the source of the sound. It dove after it, thumping to the ground.

Not seeing the gryphon was way worse than seeing it; I sat up expecting to be in pain. Nothing. I felt fine. My arm and shoulder were perfect. I shook my head. Later, I would worry about that later. I peeked over the side of the hayloft.

Eden stood at the entrance to the barn, twirling something that looked like a giant slingshot—something like a falconer's lure, but instead of a hunk of meat or a bait, there was a lump of fire: round, glowing, and hot, like a chunk of sunlight.

Eden extended her arm as she twirled it faster and faster. I had the absurd notion that she had a giant firefly tied to the end of a string. In the middle of the barn, the gryphon watched the firefly lure like a fascinated cat. Its tail twitched and thrashed. Eden finally let the ball of fire go, flinging it into the sky. The gryphon gave two silly hops and then flew up, dipping down and out of the barn, going after the ball of fire.

On my feet now, I expected to see Eden flat on the ground. Instead, she stood her ground, watching the gryphon's lure do its job. She'd done this before. That was obvious.

I waited for the pain, a twinge, something, but it was if I'd never been shot. I tore the arm sling off and went to shake some answers out of Eden Warrick.

Chapter 39

Eden

"Eden, where is he? Where's your brother?" I shouted, grabbing her shoulders. "Where's Ari?"

Her glazed eyes jittered with a strange inner light as if a fire burned somewhere down in her core and the sparks were flaring up, searching for a way out. I shook her.

"Eden, where is everyone? That horrible Stillbee," I said, trying to get her to focus. But it was like she was listening to the sound of her heart beating as if it was a fine symphony. "Holtzer, did you know?"

I checked the sky for shadows. It was becoming a habit, a paranoid, obsessive habit, but it was a day created for picnics and rowboats. I felt the bubble of a hysterical giggle boil up at the thought of how innocent it all seemed, including Eden.

She looked clueless and vacant—close to empty.

"Eden, you have to talk to me."

Her eyes snapped open as she searched my face. For some reason, the order had gotten through to her.

"Of course, Reed, what would you like to talk about?"

I gripped her arm and started dragging her down the road to the farmhouse.

"I need to know that your brother and Ari's men and Ryder and all the others are not lying in a heap of bones someplace because of my bringing that monster down on them." She stumbled over a rut, our feet tangling in the dirt. I stopped, took a breath, and helped her catch her balance. She frowned and closed her eyes. When she opened them again, she was shaking her head.

"No, of course, they're fine. I sent the gryphon after the limit. You were there. You saw. It'll lead him back to the refuge. I made sure. He'll be busy for a while and forget about the mare, for now, for long enough." She stumbled over another rut when I dragged her into the middle of the dirt road.

"Long enough?" I rounded on her. "Long enough for what?"

She smiled a dreamy smile, eyes drifting. "Long enough to get them all home, back where they belong. Mr. Stillbee promised that he'd come back for you and me. You are the most important part of this equation, after all. I just want to go back, Reed. We don't belong here, where no one's eyes mean anything, blue and green and brown and all mixed together in a mush. A nonsense place." She turned her clear blue eyes up to the sky. "I want my people, the people of the blue."

I reached up and touched the corner of my one blue eye.

She looked at me. "All mixed up like mush. It was simple . . . before. Everything here is pain and . . ." She looked down at her feet, coated in dust. She scraped one tennis shoe over the other. "So much filth. When we came here, it was up through the mud—the place between—the Dragon's Sink, its teeth."

"Eden! Ari, Cantara, Stillbee?

Her eyes cleared. "What? Stillbee has the horse and what it carries, the gryphon's baby: a hippogriff. A miracle and a treasure more precious than gold. I gave him that so he would give me what I want, to go home."

"That man thinks he's going to take Ari and my horse . . . where? Sink? Dragons? What are you talking about? And Mr. S.?"

She shrugged, unconcerned. "A sick old man. At least, he was. Isn't Luca's magic amazing?"

"But your own brother?" A sensation of freezing cold settled in my blood when I thought about Ari's connection to this other world that called to Eden this way.

"My brother? Ari Warrick," she spit his name at me. "Ari Warrick is nothing more than a kidnapper. Brother or not, he took me here, to this awful place. He took you away from your illustrious father and birthright. Your father wants revenge. The man they call Master is your father. Don't you want to know why you heal so fast? Why you aren't like others?"

I didn't even bother to argue. "Why doesn't this amazing father of mine come to do his own dirty work? Why would he send spies?"

"Because he's a king. Because he can. He's been teaching me the truth in my dreams. I know everything now."

The more she told me, the faster I walked until I was jogging, dragging her in my wake. Whether possessed, brainwashed, or deranged, Eden was not the girl I'd met at the River House just a short time ago. Sand kicked up as we moved down the road, soft clouds of dust marking our steps. I had to make her hurry before the gryphon came back from whatever game it was playing, before Ari disappeared through some kind of mystical wormhole to a world where he was considered a kidnapper and worse. She stumbled and went down to one knee. I yanked her up.

"Eden, you better start picking up your feet, because you're going to show me where they've gone."

I dragged her with me into the house, not wanting to take a chance that she was going to fade away again, slipping into the background and then showing up as the girl with the gryphon's lure. She watched me pull the fifty-caliber pistol out of my uncle's desk. The smell of gun oil and the sound of the mantle clock were the first comforting sensations I'd experienced that day.

"That isn't going to work. You can't fight a magi's war magic with bullets."

"I'm not sure I even care. It makes me feel better." I slammed a drawer shut and grabbed my backpack, the one I carried when I was out on the ranch, and then I snatched the keys to the Jeep from the hooks in the hallway and gave her a shove toward the front door.

"We can't drive where they're going to be. If I take you there at all."

"No, doesn't sound like somewhere you drive. What a shock. But we're going to go in as far as we can and then we walk."

Pushing through the front door, Eden practically knocked Ryder off the top step of the porch. He reached out and steadied himself on the porch railing.

"Whoa there, Ms. Hunter, I heard you were coming home yesterday. I thought I'd come and find out if there's something I can do—" He stopped and then looked more closely at Eden. His eyes glanced over her to me. "Is there something I can do?"

"Yeah, you can come with us. Now." I tossed my pack at him. "Get in the Jeep."

"I couldn't find anyone at the bunkhouse or the barn. Or . . ." He paused. "I thought you were shot up and stuff." He hopped in the Jeep and pushed my bag out of the way and into the backseat, next to Eden.

"Sit with her, would you? She doesn't go anywhere, got it? No matter what crazy crap she says. Got it?"

"Got it."

I slid in behind the wheel, turned the key, and sped down the dirt road, leaving a dust devil behind us.

"Yeah, about my injury. I was shot, and still was shot this morning, now that I think about it. But it seems I'm a quick healer. It runs in my family."

I was taking the ranch road too fast, and the Jeep kept bottoming out, making me glad that I wasn't still hurting. Magic. Just like magic.

I started to laugh, thinking about being in the hospital and begging to be let out, but then I remembered that it was Jackson who'd been there, arguing for early release. Jackson who should have wanted me to stay where it was easier to keep a guard on me, or at least until the investigation was finished. "Ryder, get the gate. And Eden, you're going to tell me where we're headed. When you said dragon's sink, what did you mean? Tell me." I stared at her in the rearview mirror. She seemed completely unconcerned. Her eyes looked blue-green in the shadows of the car. There was a soft pink flush to her cheeks. Like a doll or a puppet, she looked beautiful and untouchable.

"You aren't going to be able to stop them, Reed. Ari is going back and the horse too, and Stillbee will come back for you and me when he's done with them."

"Eden, why? Why would this 'master of magic' use you to hurt Ari this way?"

"Because of your mother, because of Starlyn. And Ari's first love, Janalyn. Because of them."

It was starting to sound like gibberish. She spoke of a place and people with no context.

The Jeep rattled like a piece of rusty chain as we bounced over the main road.

"What's the plan?" Ryder wanted to know.

I stared at him in the rearview mirror sitting next to the doll with the answers that made no sense.

Chapter 40

And Then There Were Two

I hardly saw the road in front of me. Eden's words kept rolling around in my head, "Because of Starlyn's sister. Because of Starlyn." The mysterious Ari Warrick and the mysterious Eden were somehow connected to my mother. Had my mother been one of them, the exiled, a stranger in a strange land?

"Miss Reed, Reed, Miss Hunter!"

I jerked back to reality. Ryder sounded more than worried; he sounded desperate. It took desperation to cut through the fog that filled my brain.

I glanced back at Ryder's pale face, and then at Eden. I was shocked by her still calm perfection. She might have been carved from wax.

"Ryder, what's wrong with her?"

He shook his head, meeting my eyes in the rearview mirror. I tightened my grip on the steering wheel.

"Eden, where are we heading?" I barked in my best staff sergeant voice. "Where are they?"

I caught Ryder's eye in the mirror again and nodded.

"Find out," I ordered.

He put his hand on Eden's shoulder and tried to jolt her out of her stupor.

"Hey! Girl!" he shouted. "Are you in there? Wake up and tell us where we need to go."

She turned to him and smiled a beautiful, icy smile, but something about her distance must have made him uneasy. I watched him slide away from her and hug the Jeep door, shaking his head.

"Miss Reed? I'm not so sure she can tell us much."

I cursed creatively under my breath and headed to the main highway, but I was driving blind. I had no idea where Stillbee, Ari, and the others might be headed.

I tried again. "Do the words *Dragon's Sink* mean anything to you?"

He sat up straight in his seat, looming behind me.

"Sink. Like a sinkhole, maybe?"

"Maybe. But where?"

"Did she say that?" He glanced at her. "Or something like that?"

I turned right and headed to the trailhead and the bridge.

"Yeah. She said something like that and then she threw fire at the gryphon with a slingshot. That's it. That's what I know. Don't ask me for the detailed workings of the mysterious Warrick clan and companions. And she said something else, something that sounded like eagle's teeth or dragon's teeth or—"

"So what Lindy told me is true? There is a monster out there."

"Ryder, I haven't got time for this. Didn't you tell me that you knew what we knew? Are you sitting there telling me you bluffed your way onto Gilded Oats?"

I pinned him with a look in the rearview mirror. He had the good manners to look guilty. Great.

"Yes, it's all real. Now where could they be heading? Could it be somewhere near the River House, Ari's place? They're pretty far out there along the river all by themselves."

"Wicked," he whispered.

I slammed on the brakes of the Jeep and pulled into the parking lot of the Refuge trailhead. I whipped around on my knees and reached over the Jeep seat to grab Eden. She looked at me with vacant eyes. It was like watching water out of a cup through a slow drip.

All of a sudden, I became very afraid for her. "What did they do to you? Eden, sweetheart. Answer me." I wanted to shake her until her head snapped on her neck, but an odd feeling of tenderness came over me, and I reached out to stroke her hair. "Eden?" I let my voice soften. "Eden, sweetheart? What did they do to you? Was it Stillbee, or Holtzer?"

His name, that name seemed to give her a small jolt of concern. I watched her blink for the first time, maybe since we'd gotten in the Jeep. I could feel Ryder's tension as he sat beside the beautiful girl next to him. He knew something was very wrong.

"He gave me the gryphon keeper's fire," she said, frowning, "to use. He wants me to keep the gryphon until he gets back. He," she paused. Her cheeks had taken on a pink tinge that made her look lit from within. "He said that he would come back and take me home." Longing filled her words. Her face stayed blank and calm and still but her voice—

"Back to . . . How will he get you back?"

"The sink. Through the Dragon's Sink, Reed. You've been there." Her breathing slowed, and she seemed to settle into the corner. "Once, when you were still in Starlyn's womb." She sagged, like a puppet without strings.

Ryder reached over to take her wrist, checking her pulse. She sat quietly, her black curls framing her face, making her eyes look huge.

"She's alive," he said. Some of the tension went out of him. Ryder was more worried about Eden then I would have guessed. "She's just so slow now, so different."

I couldn't worry about her now.

"Stay here and take care of her. Ryder, throw me the backpack. There are only certain places I can remember off trail. I know the trail, but I'm guessing at this point. Wait here for me." Rebellion flared up in his eyes. His jaw clenched. "Please? I don't think that she's herself.

This could be—" I'd almost said magic. "Just be careful. I don't know how she did it, but she was able to send that monster running or maybe chasing something. I don't know how she did it. But it was real, her power over that thing."

He nodded.

"Reed, it's got to be near where they took Lindy. Those men were looking for something, something they thought that the gryphon was guarding. Lindy was bait. The myths talk about gold in their nests. Gryphon's gold. It's probably all in one area. It's an animal after all."

I scrambled out of the Jeep.

"Dragon's teeth," I said, more to myself than anyone. A vision of ruined railroad trestles jutting up from the murk of tannin stained water shot into my mind and then the cypress knees that lined the river. It wasn't a sinkhole.

Could it be the river itself? We'd driven too far. It would have been quicker to access the trail from the ranch, but I didn't have time to double back. I slammed the Jeep's door closed and headed for the trailhead and the trail that ended in a ruined railroad bridge crossing the Tannin River.

Leaving Ryder with Eden, I charged ahead. It had been awhile since I'd hiked this far, but I managed pretty well under the damp overhang of tropical forest. By the time I made it to the bridge, I'd expected to see something, some evidence of Stillbee and the men working with him. There was nothing. I stood on the bank of the river. It ran its course as it always had, lapping at the black logs that jutted out of the water, up to the sky, the rotting teeth of a fallen dragon. Nothing. No hoof prints, no tracks. It wasn't possible that I'd beaten them here, was it? More likely, I was too late or completely off base on my theory.

I hadn't forgotten about the gryphon. Eden had managed to distract the creature with her fire lures, the Limits, but I had no way of knowing how long that would last or even what the creature would do when it caught up to them. It was impossible not to look up at the jungle canopy and bits of sky that peeked through, and wonder. Where was it?

The men who'd taken Lindy had crossed the river near here and left the little girl in the middle of the gryphon's glade, trying to draw the gryphon away from something, but what?

The last time I'd crossed the river I'd been on horseback, and there'd been a horse between me and whatever was under the black water. This time I was going to have to swim or find somewhere shallow enough to wade across. The official trail ended at the railroad trestle, but a game trail trickled off through the underbrush along the river bank. I followed the trail, hoping to find somewhere to cross that didn't look like a bottomless black pit.

I pushed ahead through the palmettos, looking for any sign that I wasn't too late. The jungle swallowed me as soon as I stepped off the main path.

I hadn't planned to be invisible when I heard the commotion behind me on the main trail, but I might as well have been. I went to my knees behind a thatch of grapevine trailing over a wall of palmettos.

Watching from my hiding place in the thicket, I saw that the trip had not gone easily for any of them. Ari's face was a bloody mess; his hands tied now behind his back. They'd had to run a rope around Cantara's rump and were practically dragging her down the trail. The men, three more like the others I'd seen at the barn, sweated and hauled at her to get her to move forward.

She was determined not to go anywhere these guys wanted. I almost had some sympathy for the guys trying to move her, but not Stillbee; I had no sympathy for him. His face was a stone as he watched one of his men—Holtzer, I realized—as he pushed Ari face first into the dirt. He calmly ordered another of the men to reach down to jerk him back up to his feet.

I waited, trying to get an idea of what they planned, but there wasn't much talking going on, just a lot of shoving and pulling and fists in Ari's face. Cantara's sides were filthy and bloody where the rope had sawed against her flanks.

Whatever Holtzer or Stillbee might have done to Eden looked to be the least of what they were capable of, but I was not going to let him disappear into some hole under the world, never to be heard of again.

It was easy to understand why I had beaten them to the river.

This was not going to happen, I thought, as I stepped from between the palmetto leaves, the Smith & Wesson 500 in my fisted hands. I had a magic of my own.

"Whatever you think you're going to do with Mr. Warrick and my horse, you can re-think it. I'll be taking them home now. Ari? Can you hear me?"

At the sound of my voice, the men froze in mid-movement, wary and calculating. I noticed that Holtzer glanced at Stillbee, who stood at the edge of the river.

My old friend kept his back to me and settled his hands on his hips.

"Reedy-Girl, I see that you're feeling better. I'm so glad. Reed—" He stopped when I swung the pistol his way. He sounded like he was holding a casual conversation in the library back at the ranch house.

I noticed a new lithe tension in Ari's body, a subtle tightening. Cantara's ear ticked back at the sound of my voice, and she snorted in recognition.

"Mister, I don't really have time for a conversation."

He faced me, rage in his face. "Master. You will call me master, just as you will call him master. Your mother called your father, your true father, master when he took her among those reeds along the river, against her will some say. And now here you are, beyond his reach for far too long, with that name that reminds him fondly of—"

He was describing rape. I saw Ari shift his balance to the balls of his feet.

"Reed. Perhaps, she remembered your father more fondly than any of us might have guessed."

I pulled the trigger. The boom of the fifty-caliber shot rattled the leaves on the trees next to me. A chunk of bridge pylon fell into the river.

"You will be quiet. I have little to no interest in your garbage. You gentlemen will back away from the man and that horse." I waggled the huge gun barrel at them, counting on them not knowing how many shots I did or did not have.

I nodded down at the gun. "Magic. My kind."

I thought I detected the first uncertainty in Stillbee's face, the face of the men dragging my horse, after the shot passed within inches of their leader's head. He looked at me with vicious eyes, anger coming off of him in quivering waves.

"Your ignorance is appalling. I've taught you better than that, Reedy-Girl." Falling back into his easy, casual cadence filled me with more than rage. Slipping in and out of character with such ease, I barely recognized the creature Stillbee had become.

I watched Ari lift his head. He looked at me for a brief moment, his eyes tender, before he turned toward the man at the river's edge.

"And you, Stillbee, you traitor, have no idea who this woman has become, who Luca's daughter has become here, in this flat place."

I hadn't realized until Ari said those words how much I had not wanted them to be true. I was not this Luca's daughter. My father was Jon Hunter, a librarian and a collector—not this cartoon character from an imaginary world I still didn't want to believe in, even after everything I'd seen. Eden had said it first, about daughters and sisters, and then she'd babbled about my mother and now Ari. He wasn't looking at me when he said those words: Luca's daughter, but I felt the truth of it. I knew it was true.

"Ari? I won't let them take you."

There was a crashing and smashing around us in the woods. I saw a group of Ari's men leap their horses over a fallen tree trunk to arrive in the middle of our standoff.

Ari stayed fixated on Stillbee, who followed me with unblinking bleary eyes. Holtzer and the men around him waited for a sign. I turned the gun on Cantara.

"I'll shoot this horse where she stands if you don't back away from that man."

Stillbee laughed and then glanced up.

"Not advisable, Girly. Boxcar's killer has found us."

I didn't take my eyes off of his, but I could feel the leaves overhead shifting as if with some strong breeze. Ari's men registered the presence of the gryphon. They flung themselves off their horses, went to ground.

Cantara lifted her head and whinnied. A tree branch came down on top of us, scattering the bad guys.

Ari dove for me, backing the two of us up from the thrashing of the horse and the madness of the fleeing men. His restraints dangled from one wrist as he dragged me down under the palmettos, curling around me.

"Be still."

I heard another crack of wood shattering and then the brush around us flattened out under a downdraft.

"Stay! And keep that gun of yours out of it. I mean it, Reed. You'll just make the gryphon mad if you hit him." And with that he blasted up out of the underbrush where we'd rolled, going after Stillbee, I guessed. Good enough, I thought, but I was here for my horse.

I stood up, keeping the gun by my side. I saw Cantara trembling in the middle of a huge, downed live oak branch, trapped in the fork of the tree limb with nowhere to go but into the river. I couldn't see Stillbee or Ari, and I was just able to keep from tripping over Holtzer, who was trapped under the fallen tree. He was dead. One down I thought. Dead was dead no matter which world you lived in it seemed.

A now too familiar roar made the air tremble, and then there came another howl, but this was different, higher pitched. At first, I thought that we were only dealing with Cantara's angry, jealous companion, but the roars started to come one after another, an echo and an answering echo of rage. The trees overhead were thrashing and cracking under the weight of the animal—I looked up and then saw two sets of wings crashing and flapping in the trees. Two. Broken limbs and branches rained down over me. I put my hands over my head and ran to my horse. Cantara heaved in her makeshift pen.

The branch was so huge, there was no way she was going to be able to jump it. She was trapped under the hail of falling leaves. I shoved the gun into the back of my pants and scrambled over the top of the fallen log, pulling off my backpack, my vest, hoping to wrap it around her eyes and calm her down before I tried to guide her out of the trap.

Chapter 41

Drowning

Monsters roared and tore at each other. The down drafts and pressure caused by their enormous wings set the river water churning. Water lapped at the banks of the river, splashing up over the sand. The middle of the river dipped and swirled like the inside of a blender. It felt like the night of the storm, that first night when Ari had found me on the trail, outside the boundary line of the first gryphon, Cantara's gryphon.

Two? Was this the animal that had attacked me, attacked and killed Boxcar? But where had it come from? The animals broke apart and hovered. Sunlight shown through their wings, and the thin membrane and bones beneath their feathers. The animals glared at each other: one blue eyed, the other with eyes of green glass. Colors. Always blue and green to decipher teams and sides and tribes. My face felt hot. My eyes burned.

How could Ari have not known that there were two creatures? With a scream, the gryphons slashed at each other. Their shrieking felt like a sad echo of the shrieking inside my mind. Another huge tree limb smashed into the churning water of the river.

But it wasn't just warring gryphons knocking the world out of tilt. Clouds shut the sun down, and I felt the first slash of angry rain, saw through the leafless tree branches that it was a storm filled with lightning. Thunder exploded before the burning light faded. The storm was already on top of us.

Cantara tried to wheel around in her makeshift enclosure. If I wasn't careful, I was going to wind up worse off than being tossed into the Tannin River to swim with the alligators. I threw my vest up over the horse's head and across her eyes. But she was too frantic, too panicked. I knew that the unfamiliar gryphon frightened her as much as the storm. I understood her fear. The storm brought back the suffocating memory of mud in my mouth and face as I lay drowning on solid ground.

When I thought I had her under control, another explosion of lightning destroyed a royal palm tree across the river. Thunder shook the ground. I stumbled forward, tripping over tree limbs teeter-tottering at the edge of the river, dangling in midair.

A hand on the back of my shirt pulled me back onto my feet. Ryder didn't waste time asking if I was okay. He'd grabbed the ends of the vest that still draped over Cantara's head; the sleeve hole was caught on one of her ears. I helped wrestle the flapping ends into a makeshift halter.

"I don't think I can get her over the branch. It's too big. We're stuck."

"The river?" he yelled, not taking his eyes off the panting horse. The war raged on over our heads: monsters with murder in their claws, and lightning, thunder, and slashing rain in the mix. How long could they possibly go at each other?

The idea of pushing Cantara out of the forked branch into the crazed water in front of us horrified me. Something about the water repelled me like it never had before.

Ryder had to shout to be heard above the noise, "What's happened to Mr. Warrick?"

"I don't know."

I saw Ryder hesitate and take stock of the situation. He pointed. "There."

They were across the river, near a still-smoking lightning strike.

Smoke curled up in spite of the gray blanket of rain.

I could just make out Stillbee and Ari, facing each other, breathing hard as if they'd had to run thirty miles to reach the far shore. I had not seen them cross the river. Stillbee held a short, lethal sword in one hand. He looked young and strong and powerful. He circled Ari, looking for an opening. Ari kept his hands up. I thought he might be saying something, but it was so hard to see.

One of the gryphons, the smaller one, dipped down through the trees, diving. It made me want to creep, crawl, run, or dig my way out of there. We were completely exposed. The other lifted away and circled.

In the gray sheet of rain, the railroad posts cut up out of the water, and I saw the dragon's teeth. The river became a black curving body, the rippling water became scales, and the railroad trestle's black teeth marked a gaping mouth.

Cantara's blue-eyed gryphon swiveled its head toward Ari and Stillbee as they danced around each other. Their movement had drawn its eye. In the middle of the swirling destruction all around, the two men had become a twirling epicenter in the forest. They were oblivious to the creature's attention. Its body hovered over the water, the muscles of its shoulders bunched and coiled. It raked through the canopy and settled above the entire scene by sitting on the tallest of the dragon's teeth.

We were trapped. The tree trunk blocked our way back. The green-eyed gryphon was perched near us, blocking our going forward into the water, even if I could talk myself into it. And Ari had squared off with Stillbee without weapon or defense. The gryphons turned on each other again. The sound of their bodies coming together was a wet thud. This time there was blood and screams of pain.

I turned to Ryder, yelling, "Where's Eden?"

"I couldn't do anything with her." He talked without looking away from the fighting animals. "I was afraid for you, but I couldn't make her stay at the Jeep." He stopped himself from covering his ears against the noise. "She followed me. She's right back there on the path." He turned, but the only person standing on the Refuge Trail was the last of the green-eyed invaders, who'd managed to find enough courage to come back to finish whatever he thought they'd started.

Cantara twirled around and slammed me up against one of the branches. It was like being hit with a brick in the gut. I'd be lucky if she hadn't cracked my ribs.

"Ryder! Get Eden. Eden knows how to control them." Ryder scrambled back the way he'd come.

Chapter 42

Collapse

Then the rest of the live oak came cascading down, burying us in greenery and the spice of splintered wood. Something slammed into the back of my head, and I was face down in the mud and muck. When I turned my head, I saw Cantara had gone down to her knees. She looked as stunned as I felt. I rolled to my side and shoved up against the rough bark of the trunk at my back. When she decided to try and get up, she was going to be a thousand pounds of slashing hooves and panic.

The gryphons fell on top of us like lightning from the sky. Cantara screamed in pain, and I tried to make like a beetle and burrow into the tree bark at my back. The branch next to me shifted under the weight of one of the creatures as it was driven back by the other. I scrabbled on my back towards the river. Using the foliage for as much camouflage as I could manage, I crawled far enough to feel the bank of the river fall away beneath my shoulders. The terror of the fighting gryphons a foot away overcame my fear of the black waves. I could feel it slapping at the back of my head. Water splashed over my hair. The storm was in my face and the raging blackness of water was at my back.

The unmistakable sound of another tree trunk shattering drowned out everything else. I scrambled to my knees, trying to see Cantara in the middle of the collapsing nightmare. I saw the tree branch that was keeping her trapped slide under the weight of the smaller gryphon toward the river. She surged to her feet, freeing herself. I watched her leap from the river's bank, front legs bent. It looked as if she were trying to jump the river or fly.

Cantara's gryphon, distracted by her escape, flew up and away from the smaller beast. He followed the mare. The water crashed over her from both sides. I saw her go under. He trailed her as she struggled.

The smaller gryphon re-grouped and coiled, tracking the horse's struggles. When it launched itself at the struggling horse, Cantara's mate whipped back and attacked like an avenging angel, driving the green-eyed one down into the river. Cantara's head sank beneath the waves. The bigger gryphon held the attacker under the water. He was trying to drown it. I thought I saw the horses' head snake out of the water.

Hands grabbed me by the shoulders and pulled me backward into the water. I saw gryphon's eyes, blue this time, track my movement, marble and glass, unblinking.

The water swamped me, lapping up over my head as the waves rushed passed up and over me. I struggled against the arms holding me and twisted as far as I could. It was Stillbee, holding me.

"Be still," he said, and squeezed me tight enough to choke off my air. "If you don't want to be picked clean, you will be still. You can't go back to Luca a skeleton."

He pressed me into the mud along the bank. All I could think of was what he'd done to Ari. "Ari! Where is—"

He gave me another hard squeeze.

Cantara screamed again.

"Help her. Can't you brainwash Eden into razzling or dazzling the gryphon with those lights or something?"

"Shut up, you stupid girl."

The gryphons flapped up, claw to claw, from a broken pile of trees crisscrossing the span of the river. He pushed my face against the mud and hunched over me, flattening us out. His body protected mine while I snatched at the roots that protruded from the riverbank.

Then he was gone, swept away by a river gone mad as I held on for all I was worth.

Chapter 43

Bitter Worlds

I still had mud in my hair. It was starting to harden as it dried, and it itched. We had retreated to my uncle's library. After Ari and Ryder collected me from the riverbank we'd dragged ourselves back to the Jeep, and taken the teenagers to the River House to let Eden recover. She was alive, but still completely entranced. Ari's men we sent to the bunkhouse. Holtzer's men were long gone.

After reassuring ourselves that Ryder could keep Eden safe, Ari offered to drive me home to grab a fresh batch of clothes. Riding in the passenger seat, I realized that I could not go one more minute without answers. As we parked and walked into the front door of my childhood home, I turned ruthlessly on Ari.

"When were you going to tell me? No, better question: How were you going to tell me? Oh, hey, Reed, your entire backstory is a lie, wrapped in an urban legend, blended with half-truths, which happen to be all true."

He had the good grace to look ashamed. "Haven't you asked it, the better question? How? That's the right question, How? How were we supposed to explain this to you?" He walked further inside, guiding our conversation into the library.

"Who's 'we'? How many people in this town are in on it?"

"Reed, even now it's so hard to explain," Ari said, struggling for words. "This place isn't 'in' on anything; they *are* it, all of it.

'Taintsville. It taint here, and it taint there." He gave me a half-hearted smile.

I turned to the stone fireplace and looked up at the elegant scrolling letters: words in Latin that had defined my life in ways I had not understood.

"Refugees of war from somewhere I have no names for," I said. It was hard to talk about, simply because I didn't have enough vocabulary, place names, coordinates on a map. I turned to look at Ari. "And what's the old man's story? And those men with him?"

He didn't flinch when I said it, but it was close. To his further credit, he looked me in the eye when he started speaking, "He owned a small place out on the river. He was there the day your mother and I and the others came through the Dragon's Sink."

"That name again, the 'Dragon's Sink,' but not the bridge trestle, apparently."

"No, but they serve as a kind of marker." He continued, "Mr. Stillbee was fishing for catfish when he saw a woman half-dragged, half-carried out of the jungle. And the others, wounded, beaten, bleeding, and," he said, shrugging, "he became part of the story from then on."

"Yes, and my uncle?"

"Yes, him too, your mother's brother."

I thought about the lovely carvings he'd created from the stumps and crosscuts of cypress trees, decorated with wonderful, swirling designs and letters and symbols.

"Him too," I said, half to myself.

"My mother, already pregnant, and my father . . . and I mean, Jon Hunter, did he know?" The specter of a man named Luca lurked in the darkness of every corner in every room of my home.

"Of course," Ari said, "They met at the library. Your mother would go there every Saturday to learn all she could about the place that was to be your home. Jon worked there. He loved you and your mother very much."

"A librarian?" I almost laughed. A man of letters.

"But why wouldn't someone tell me?" I tried to run my hands through my hair, hit mud. "You let me come home from war and no one tells me, didn't warn me, of the dangers in my own backyard." I let my voice trail off. "Because there was someone here who was supposed to tell me, my uncle. But he died before he could, and then Mr. S. kept me in the dark, on purpose. How did we not see this, not see him coming?"

He looked uncomfortable at that. "Because he was just a man, a man from this world who happened to be there at the right time. I've been watching over you for so long, making sure you were cared for. Stillbee never seemed anything but a devoted caretaker. He loved your mother, father, and Uncle Rulan."

"But my mother, my father . . . I was a little girl when they died in that car accident, under that blinking caution light on Highway 46."

My parents were like a faded negative to me; I'd been too young to understand what had happened to them; A hazy memory of being petted and loved and fussed over remained, and then it was Uncle Rulan and the man I still thought of as my childhood friend and being homeschooled until high school.

"Eden said that she brought that thing to remind her of home. That all she ever wanted was to go home."

"The gryphon was a complication we hadn't expected until Eden showed me what she'd done by bringing the egg with her. Eden is bewitched. Luca has her under his power now. She believes only what he tells her to believe."

"And that man, the one they called Luca? Stillbee said things to me about him."

"Not man, mage," Ari interjected as he walked forward to stand next to me at the fireplace. "A powerful dark mage now. But once we were friends, when we were children, the three of us: Ari, Luca, and Starlyn until . . . " Ari stared into the cold fireplace.

"Reed, we don't have much time. I need to speak with you, so that you'll understand, maybe, a little bit." He hesitated and then added with venom in his voice. "Luca will come for you. That he hasn't yet means he thought he could accomplish what he wanted without direct involvement. Maybe he didn't succeed today, but he won't stop. He will not stop. And Mr. Stillbee and at least two more are still out there."

"Maybe they drowned in the river."

I let the sting of a scrape on my forearm distract me. All kinds of bumps and bruises ached. I looked at Ari and asked, "Did you know there were two monsters out there?"

Chapter 44

All

"No. Another mystery. Some questions I can't even answer. Not yet," he said. The muscles in his jaw jumped. "Reed, I wanted to tell you all of it."

Bending my arm, I examined the source of the pain, thought about blowing on it. The silliness of that action had me close to giggling. It was a bad sign. Exhaustion, stress, and worry threatened to take over. I bit my lip, trying to hold on.

He didn't look like he felt much better than I did.

"Okay, Ari. But I don't even know where to start, and I want to be fair," I said. "I'm really trying, but I'm working without a net here. I don't even know where to start. I know I was repeating myself but—"

"Reed," he said, flicking my comment away with flip of his wrist. "We can discuss all the fairness and rightness of this someday, and I want to. I do. But right now, I need you to know that Luca, the man called Luca, will not be satisfied with the failure he experienced today."

"I don't understand. Stillbee talked crazy. Like this man was in his pocket talking to him. He said I was his daughter, that my mother—"

He took an enormous step toward me, tossing the kitchen towel to the ground, intense and frustrated, and I could feel the worry vibrating through his hands. Heat rushed into my cheeks, remembering the last time he'd touched me.

"You are in danger. I know him. I've known him . . ." His sentence trailed away when he saw me looking at his hand on my arm and then up to his face. I brushed my hand over his face, tracing the bruises with my fingertips. "You weren't there. After I was shot. You didn't come to the hospital. I can't believe Stillbee wanted me dead."

"Hush. Shhhh." He pulled me into his arms and held me carefully. When I flinched, he lifted my hand and kissed a scratch on the back of it. "Reed. They told me that you'd asked for me not to visit. He said that I would only upset you. I promise you that leaving will never be my first choice." He whispered into my hair, "I promise you."

He pushed me back, looked into my face.

"What, my eyes? A lot of people comment, if they notice. Holtzer noticed."

"Can you remember, exactly what he said?"

"He just called them unusual."

A frown flitted across his face. "In our world, the eyes are more than a window to the soul. They brand us, the way skin color does here in this world. The blue eyes of my people, the high sky people, and the green of Luca's people."

I tried to touch my face. He caught my hand.

"Evidence of a crime," I lamented.

"No." He shook his head. "It's proof that you are a dazzling woman born of your mother's love for you."

"Love." It was a whisper.

"I can't think about that right now. I need to hear what you have to say about this man you say is my father."

He pulled me over to the big leather couch, and without letting go of my hands he sat next to me. We sat close, thigh to thigh, hands interlaced. He stared down at our hands when he spoke in a voice that sounded strange and far away.

"We were boys when the Black Magi came and forced us into a torch unit." His voice slowed, remembering it. "They called us Ash Masters, gave us just enough magic to destroy with. Ash Masters," he grunted, "but it was just another name for butchers. They threatened our families, our villages. They gave us power when we were too young to know how completely it could control us. What Luca said about before," he choked. "We were too young. It took Luca. Would have destroyed me, except for my wife."

I must have gasped. His arms tightened around me. I felt his lips at my ear.

"Don't. Please."

We sat close, listening to each other breathe. The clock ticked, measuring our lives.

"I was hardly older than Ryder. We were children, and she saved me from horror, from ruin. I ran from the blood as soon as I could. I went home and tried to live a peaceful life next to a reed marsh, near the river with her and the girl I thought of as my little sister, your mother, Starlyn. But then he came for me." Ari paused, gathering the strength to continue. "I had gone with some others to hunt. While I was gone . . . " He stopped talking and ran his hand down my arm where the scratch still burned, drawing the pain out of my arm with his hand. I could feel some of the tension leave my shoulders and back.

He started again. "While I was gone, Luca came with the Black Mage. They found your mother and my wife by the river. Luca raped your mother."

I tried to stand up, pushing against him, but he pulled me back with his big hands. Insistent but gentle.

"They took my wife. You can't understand. She was heavy with our first child. They took her," he said, starting out strong and then hesitating. His hands on mine squeezed. My fingers ached. I don't think he noticed. "They took her and cut the baby from her body when she wouldn't tell them where I had gone. I came home and found . . . "

This time I did sit up, grabbing his arms. He sat ramrod straight next to me, staring into space.

"I had done such terrible things that I thought that perhaps," he said, breathing heavy in the quiet of the room. Dust motes drifted through still air. "That the great gods of vengeance had decreed that I deserved this. And maybe I did. But not your mother. Not the baby."

I sat up straighter, the pain in my arm forgotten. His words poured over me and into me like a thick, cumbersome cloak, too heavy but necessary against some painful chill.

I pressed my forehead against his and held his hands against my chest.

"We went to war then, Luca and I. But it was always a foregone conclusion: our defeat, the tribes who came against the Black Magi. War is air for Luca and his master—what they breathe, what they use for the bones that form a cage for their black hearts." Silence fell hard. He continued, "For me, it was revenge—pure, simple, easy. I never wanted Luca to have his child, just as he'd stolen mine from me. For your mother, she fought out of fear; it was fear that he would find out about you and come for you. When we finished, it was your mother who knew the way between the worlds. A powerful seer your mother, and a true healer. She saw you here, in this world, and not there with him. And so we followed her, what was left of the band I had dragged together after there was nowhere else to go. We came here to this world."

He reached one hand up to touch my face. "To this moment and to you." He ran his hand over my arm again. The pain in my arm was gone. All that was left was a growing, spreading warmth that moved through my skin.

"How is it that someone raised on such pain has become someone with such tenderness in his hands?"

"Reed, this can't work."

Something clenched tight in my chest.

"I held you in my arms when you were nothing but a bundle."

I felt him pulling away from me, pushing me back. He stood up in front of me, the memories still a heavy weight in the air, on his face.

"You need to understand that I am worlds older than you. I am bitter, worlds away from you, and now I've brought that nightmare into your life. But I promise I'll stand between this place and the forces of the Black Magi that have followed me here.

I closed my eyes and tried not to cry for him, his loss, and his broken world.

Chapter 45

River House

We made the trip back to the River House in silence. I drove. When we made the turn from Snow Hill onto River Front Road, Ari reached across the gulf between us and touched the back of my hand on the gearshift.

I stopped the Jeep in the middle of the road and turned to him. He pulled me into arms, and in that simple, quiet moment I felt the intensity of his emotions: grief, loss, despair. His lips moved over mine—heat and longing and the fragile tenderness of hope.

"Maybe," he said. It came out dreamy and soft.

It took me a moment to realize he was speaking.

"But, he'll be back. He'll send his army if he has to. Even though Cantara's gryphon killed the other. Drowned it in the river. For you. He'll be back for you," he whispered against my lips. "He'll take you if he can. I won't let him."

Curiosity cut through the fog. "How could either gryphon kill the other? I thought they were immortal here. Didn't you say it couldn't be killed? Didn't—"

A car horn blared behind us. A typical sound from the normal world, it jolted us both back to the immediate concerns. I settled back into the driver's side of the Jeep, checked my rearview mirror, and felt heat flush my face. Behind us, Sheriff Jackson Rogers glared at me from his truck. He must have seen us kissing. He seemed disgusted, hurt, even enraged as he swerved his cruiser around us and took off.

The sight of him there, behind us, with all that angry condemnation in his face, was too much.

Chapter 46

Shock Wave

The river house waited in the clutch of the towering live oaks that crowded its walls. We were blind for a minute when we walked from the sunlight into the gloom. Silence surrounded the house: no river sounds, no insects chirping, no animals moving. Silence. Something about the quiet sent Ari flying up the steps and through the screen door. The front door hit the wall with a crack.

Following him as fast as I could, I tripped and hit the ground. I went knee first into a puddle that soaked my pants through. Blood. There was blood on my pants. The smell of pennies coated my tongue. Jumping up, I blasted into the room. Eden. Ryder. Their names roared through my head.

"Reed Baye Hunter, don't you dare look at me like that. Don't." Sheriff Jackson Rogers stood over the unconscious bodies of Ari's sister and Ryder. My heart sank when I saw the pistol he was holding in his hand.

Ari's tension flowed off of him in waves, and then it was gone. He stood cooly surveying the scene.

"Sorry Reedy, but he promised me something I can't have here. More. He promised me more."

I barely heard him. "Jackson, you've hurt them. What is this? What are you doing?"

Ari made a move toward his sister, who looked like a princess struck down by a thousand-year sleeping spell, except for the blood on her t-shirt; she looked like a beautiful, dead princess. Ryder moaned. He was alive. At least he was alive.

Jackson swung the gun toward Ari.

I waved my hands. "Hey. Hey, more what? Tell me. Help me understand this."

Two other men, who'd been hiding in the shadows like cockroaches, stepped into the room. Their green eyes were filled with nothing. It reminded me of the way Eden's eyes had been when I'd last seen her, on the trail. Jackson frowned at them and then focused on me.

Ari ignored the man with the gun, going to his knees next to the teenagers. After that, no one moved. The air felt like frozen fog. A clock, unseen, ticked, ticked on and on and then fell silent.

"Tell me."

Ari bent over Eden, putting his hand on her head.

I slid sideways to keep Jackson from seeing too much of what was happening on the ground where Eden and Ryder lay. I tried to convince myself that I could see Eden's chest move.

My gut twisted when I turned to look at the only friend I thought I had left in the world. My high school crush. The Sheriff of 'Taintsville.

He started to fade back to see what Ari was doing. I took a step toward him and yelled, "Tell me! You aren't one of them. I know that."

He shook his head a little bit, the way a confused dog might. "But my father was. He came with your mother and Ari. Luca promised me time. He's going to give me time."

My mouth dropped open with confusion. Had everyone gone crazy? Hadn't I just made the same request? First Eden, and now my friend betraying us all. "Time? Time for what?"

"Living," he said, the way he used to when I was being slow in science class. "Time for living, Reed. My life here, my entire life, was ruined by one simple mistake. Stillbee and Luca promised me time to live a new life."

The men's eyes tracked to Jackson at the sound of their leader's miserable name. Their green eyes glowed like cat eyes.

"What makes you think he can?"

Jackson shrugged. "What do I have to lose, leaving this place?" He shrugged again. "Stillbee's coming too. He feels the same. My dream died in that car crash, and I've been doing nothing here but marking a calendar. And you," he said, studying me quietly. "Tell me you don't want to know the world of your mother. Luca'll take the horse, and you too. Might as well come willingly."

Anger boiled through me. "My mother's world? Don't talk to me about a place she had to run away from to save me. Don't."

"Then he'll *take* you, the traitor, and the mare." Jackson laughed an emotionally vacant laugh. "Gentlemen, please help Mr. Warrick up. And Eden, if she's still breathing. And Warrick, play nice. I won't miss again." He waggled the end of his gun. The sniper. I hadn't been the target on the porch of the community center at all.

The men turned to Eden, Ryder, and Ari. The house settled into silence. Ari let his hand drop from Eden's head, glancing over his shoulder at the two goons coming for him. Eden still hadn't moved. Her face glowed white; she looked carved from marble.

Enough. What had I been to him? A friend? A target? More? I stepped toward him. He didn't seem to hesitate; he aimed the gun straight at my chest and fired.

Did his hand shake just a little bit? His arm stiffen? Harder to kill someone you've known forever.

The shot went wide, skimmed past me, and blew out one of the massive walls of glass that lined the living room. A sweet, clean breeze filled the room while chunks of glass tinkled free from the frame.

The clutch in my chest loosened as I stumbled back from him. The shock sent a cold chill down my spine, and then the flush of fresh anger pushed me at him again. This was too much. In a weird kind of slow motion, I saw him raise the gun, aiming at my face. He squeezed the trigger—another miss. Maybe his hand hadn't been steady? But it felt more like something or someone else was intervening, protecting me.

At the same time, Ryder was on his feet, head down, arms spread wide as he threw himself into the goon squad.

Ari's hand came up. There was the hint of shimmering light radiating from his hand. It reminded me of the shock wave of an explosion—there but not there—a deadly power that moved unseen except for the effect it had on the environment around it. The image of the floor lamp quivered as the glimmer wave flew from Ari's palm. It hit Jackson like a crowbar. He collapsed in on himself and then flew back into the scrum of writhing men on the ground.

Ari grabbed Ryder by the shirt collar, dragging him back. He slammed his hand into the first goon's chest—light exploded. The man went out as if he'd been switched off.

I grabbed for the gun Jackson had dropped. It was so hot it burned my hand, and I had to let it fall back to the ground.

Ryder cursed, dangling from Ari's extended arm. The boy looked like a pissed off praying mantas. The other goon scurried backward like a frightened crab away from Ari's extended hand. There was panic, horror, and desperation in his face. Sure. When you could see death coming for you with an outstretched palm, there would be some worry there. One of Jackson's men flipped to his stomach and knees and came up like a sprinter, throwing himself through the blown-out window.

Ari shook Ryder like a naughty puppy, then ordered him to take care of Eden. His focus shifted to Jackson.

Silence.

The room settled into an odd, empty quiet. The air felt thick. It was like being wrapped in cotton batting, making it hard to draw a breath. Ari knelt next to Eden and Ryder.

"Jackson, please." I couldn't help myself. Surely there was still a piece of the man I knew inside him somewhere.

"What makes you think he won't destroy your mind the way he's destroyed hers?" Ari's face was stone as he pointed to Eden's limp body.

"No! Do not speak. Don't." Jackson tossed his handcuffs to Ryder. "Lock yourself to Gone Girl there." Turning his cool gaze to Ari, he continued, "Get up. Your bed buddy here can't handle many more gunshot wounds." He shoved me forward with the end of the gun. He shot me a disgusted look. "We're taking your Jeep, and you're driving."

Protest

Jackson ordered me to drive to the main gate of Gilded Oats Ranch, where I'd first gone after Lindy. He sat behind me, making sure that I wouldn't take any opportunities to derail his mission; he kept the barrel of the rifle against my neck. One of his men rode shotgun—literally.

They'd tied Ari with a twisting rope of grapevine and a garland of some sort of shredded grass that I didn't recognize. Ari looked exhausted, pale and worn.

What had they done to him?

The sight of Ari fading under the binding they'd used on him infuriated me. I had no idea how to help him. I was powerless and useless. There were too many variables, too many questions that I had no answers for. Think, Reed. Think. I had until we got to the front gate of Gilded Oats to figure something out.

I could have saved myself the trouble. The main gate of Gilded Oats Ranch was blocked shut.

They were back, the Animal Liberation Front of Restless Pimple Poppers, or whatever they called themselves. Apparently, the terror of the last attempted protest had faded with time and the short attention span of the very young, and they'd brought reinforcements. The reinforcements had brought signs: Stop the Slaughter. End the Bloody Nightmare.

I'd never been so grateful to have a picket line stopping traffic and causing pain in my backside.

"What would you like for me to do, Sheriff?" I didn't wait for an answer.

I slammed on the brakes and whipped around, pushing the rifle barrel off my neck with my forearm. Then I faced forward, putting my hands on the steering wheel. If the protesters looked at me, they'd see a girl trying to get home, normal like.

"Put that thing away unless you want that crowd of hormone-fueled do-gooders to call the real cops after they watch my head explode all over this windshield." I met Jackson's stare in the rearview mirror. "I mean it."

He lowered the rifle.

"I don't see a lot of options," I said.

In the mirror, I watched Jackson study the fanatics as they yelled and spat their outrage against exotic animal ranching. The lines of his face shifted and hardened as he mulled over his choices. He slid closer to Ari.

"You can't hurt these stupid kids. Don't even think about it," I said.

A sound like ground gravel erupted out of his throat. "Don't you tell me what I can and can't do. You know nothing about me."

"Well, it's true that what you're doing makes you a traitor and a creep, but it doesn't make you a killer. Jackson please," I said, trying to reassure myself. "You're not really a killer, are you? You're not. I won't believe it. Even after what you tried to do to Ari—"

Something like pure slime passed over his face when he smiled at my statement, and then I knew.

"You have killed." My fingers started to ache I was gripping the steering wheel so hard. "Who?"

He gave me a sick half smile.

He reached for the Jeep's door handle, the gun an extension of the hate in his face. I waited long enough for him to be half in and half out of the Jeep. He hadn't thought it through. I smashed the gas pedal to the floor. The Jeep bucked forward, spraying dirt out from the rear tires like a rooster's tail. I hit the horn.

The protesters scattered like the smart kids I knew they were. Jackson rolled out of the backseat of the Jeep, and Ari used the joke of their twisted vine restraints to choke out the man in the front seat.

The cryptic Latin motto scrawled across the front gate flew over the top of the Jeep's hood when we crashed through.

Item eighty-three on the To-Do list: Replace gate. Better hinges. Fresh paint.

The craziness of that thought almost got to me, almost made me laugh, except that the seatbelt cut into my shoulder when the Jeep shuddered forward. Going to have a massive bruise tomorrow. I hit the release on the seatbelt and had my door open before the Jeep stopped rolling.

I stumbled over the thick ridge of sand that stayed pushed up along the edge of the main road, scrambling like a crab on all fours away from the still groaning car engine. But Jackson was nowhere on the road. Ari and Jackson's goon were gone too. I spun back to the Jeep. It was empty. If only I'd seen where they'd gone, which way into the Refuge they'd run.

Girls screamed, more from excitement than from real fear.

"Call 911. Someone call for help," I ordered.

Their shouts and questions dragged at me when all I wanted was to search for the road for Ari. "Where did they go? Did anyone see where they went? Where?"

Ari's big black SUV skidded up. Ryder jumped out, a head taller than all the kids in the protest group, waded through the group yelling, "Listen to me. You've got about ten minutes to clear out of here before the authorities show up." Jackson's handcuffs dangled from one of Ryder's wrists.

I wedged my foot in the wire of the fence and climbed high enough to be above the milling group.

"He's right. Move along!" A police siren sounded from the distance. "Now! Before I press charges. And. I. Will."

"This isn't going to get us anywhere," one of the pimple poppers agreed. "We should get going while we can."

"Good plan." Ryder jerked his thumb toward the highway.

"Shut up, Ryder, we know that you work for these butchers. Don't you?" The crowd started groaning out a chant.

"One, two, three, don't shoot Bambi."

Ryder's accuser and head chanter was one of the shorter girls, whose uniform consisted of a T-shirt that read "We Are All Animals Now" and a pair of skinny jeans that threatened to cut off circulation to her more vital parts. Ryder tried staring her down, but it was the faint wail of the siren that started her feet moving.

"We won't forget this," she spat while flipping her hair back with style.

Before they'd all filed out of sight back to the main road, I was off the fence and grabbing the front of Ryder's shirt. "Which way? Did Ari go after them or with them? Did you see? Do you know where they're heading?"

Ryder put his hands over mine. He was speaking, but I couldn't hear anything he was saying. Panic buzzed through my head like a roaring fountain.

"Reed, I didn't see. I didn't. Let go. Reed, let go," he said, prying my fingers open. "Let's roll. Let's find them." His earnest calm reminded me that he was a young man surrounded by drama twenty-four seven and a good guy to have around in a panic. He held up his wrist, showed me the handcuffs. "Her wrist is so tiny. I just slid it off. She's almost not here anymore."

I nodded and took a deep breath.

"Is she still—"

He nodded quickly. "She's okay. I left her sleeping. I was afraid for you."

His words were designed to soothe, but his face told the lie of it.

"Check the glovebox in the Jeep. There might be a gun." I stared at the ground, hoping to see something in the jumble of tracks and drag marks. Dirt rolled away in mini dust clouds at my feet. Dust coated the tangle of weeds and underbrush. I glanced back at Ryder.

He pulled a Ruger target pistol out of the back of his jeans.

"A twenty-two? I hope you've got more ammo, because you're going to have to empty that gun and then toss it to make your point." He pouted.

His face flushed red as he went to search the Jeep. He shoved the body of the goon out of his way before he started to search. Finally, he yelled at me over the roof of the trapped vehicle. "Nothing."

I spun in a frustrated circle, desperate for a sign, anything that would help me know where Jackson and Ari were headed. Back to the river, surely; back to the gryphon's main territory, and here was Ryder carrying a pop gun.

We were back to the new reality and rules I didn't know, couldn't understand, and ancient history written with magic. I shivered in the growing heat.

Ryder joined me at the first curve in the trail, the pistol held out in front of him.

"I can't take you out there with only that thing." I pointed at his pistol, pulling him along back to the gate. "Give it to me. We need more firepower. Go and stop the cops from coming to the front gate. The last thing we need is the police finding a body in the front seat of my Jeep under a crashed gate. Can you do that?"

The sirens stopped, somewhere on the long access road to the highway. It was hard to imagine what craziness that group of do-gooders might be telling the police.

"Ryder, maybe those nuts are buying us some time. Help me get this gate off the back of the Jeep. I'll figure out what to do with our guest. We've got to go back to the house for weapons. We need weapons."

He helped me wrestle the gate off the Jeep's bumper, and after he stuffed the gun into the back of his jeans, I froze. "Ryder? Why are you really here?"

He did not meet my eyes when he said, "Eden. It was Eden. She didn't, need me, anymore, and I thought you could use my—" He stopped talking and clamped his jaw shut. "Eden is dead," he finally said.

"I'm sorry." It was a stupid, pointless thing to say; even I knew that.

Chapter 48

Teen

The house was still and musty; I hadn't done much housekeeping lately, that was for sure. It felt like coming home from an extended trip to a place where no one lived. Standing in the entryway, I found the empty silence depressing. A bang from the kitchen started my heart thumping in reaction, and I felt the rush of adrenalin set me on edge.

I had to make a decision. Should I take the time to go up to my room and get my service revolver? Another bang. I reached for one of my uncle's walking sticks from the stand next to the door. I'd take my chances; a little hand-to-hand was starting to sound appealing right about now.

Stillbee was sitting at my kitchen table, drinking a glass of milk. I wasn't expecting that. I busted out laughing, but even I could tell it wasn't a happy sound. He looked younger, less wrinkled, bright eyed, and alert.

"I thought you'd be lurking out in the woods with some mythical traveling cloak or spell or an amusing assortment of crystals or what nots provided by mythical men from beyond the pale. "

"Now, why would I do that, Reedy-Girl? I've never found 'what nots' to be all that effective." He swallowed a huge gulp of milk and then took another Oreo from the bag in front of him. He contemplated the cookie in his hand. "These are quite tasty. I might miss these."

I was in no mood for a heart to heart with this man.

"What do you want? I can't believe you're sitting here while a corrupt sheriff is out doing your dirty work, or is it Luca's dirty work?"

He held the cookie up. Dust motes danced through the musty air. An array of my uncle's handguns rested on the table next to the bag of cookies.

"Ah, Jackson. Such an interesting addition to Luca's plan. Your mother, however—" he began.

My blood turned to cement when he mentioned a woman I barely remembered. How dare he talk about her? He must have seen me stiffen with outrage. He set the glass of milk in front of him and held up the cookie in his hand. With the tip of his finger, he drew curious shapes on the table top. Something about them felt familiar.

"I don't want to hear anything you have to say on the subject of my family." I gripped the cane tighter. "I've heard quite enough lies out of you for one lifetime."

His eyes followed the movement.

"That's just it. This life is so short. There magic rules." He set the cookie next to the glass, uneaten. "Come with me, meet your real father. What adventures we'll have. They need warriors like you and wiry old guys like me."

He picked the cookie up again. "Do you think I'll miss Oreos and roads and technology? At first, it was all about bringing you back, when I first started being taught by Luca from beyond. When he showed me how Ari and your mother had deceived him and stolen you away. That sweet little thing all pregnant and dirty in the mud by the river. I wanted to help her, protect her then. How was I supposed to know how treacherous she really was?"

Enough. I spit as sharply into his hateful face as I could.

"Really, Girl?" Suppressing his rage, he calmly wiped his face and continued, "Your father and uncle were nice enough, but they really never let me in on the real gifts your mother shared. The raw power that was there. Such potential. Luca showed me, and then I knew that being the kindly, babysitting caretaker might pay off in the end. All while your uncle read his life away. It's really too bad what happened to him while you slept."

There it was. Truth. Stillbee was more than crazy. He was a killer.

"Do you really think it will end with you getting your fondest wish, whatever that may be? What makes you think you're going to leave here and that will be the end of it?"

He contemplated that stupid cookie as if it was going to talk to him, and then slid a look at me.

"When you were born and I held you for the first time, I knew you were something special. It wasn't long after that when the dreams began, when I started to hear a voice, his voice. Back from where you're from, life had become a world reduced to ashes and the bitter taste of fear because of these people, these rebels. You can teach them what it is to be safe, to trust the great magi. You can tell them that the threat is over."

I took a step toward him. "Did it ever occur to you that you might be a big part of that threat? These people are a threat to no one. They're planning a Harvest Festival and parade, you fool."

He smiled a crooked, wry smile. "Tell me, will Cantara's offspring lead the way followed by its father?"

I brought the cane up, but I was slow and tired. He was on his feet tearing it out of my hands before I could bring it down on his smug head. He smashed it down on the kitchen table. The cane had never been a great idea. He grabbed my wrist.

"And if Prince Luca wants this world too, then I'll help him get it. He may want this world that Ari discovered. He'll take it just the way that Ari took you."

I jerked against his grip on my wrist. He slapped me across the face.

"This world, where impossible love is possible. That ridiculous Holtzer tried to lure out the gryphon to find its gold for me, back when my aspirations were so narrow minded and small. But when I knew that the mare and the gryphon had mated, I knew I could have the ultimate treasure, the true gold of the gryphon's nest. To own a hippogriff, I'll be safe forever. Even Luca will give me the respect and power I deserve."

There was madness in his gaze, a weird jumpy light.

"Ari will stop you. They all will." A vision of the holiday committee popped in my head. I hoped they could stop him.

The quiet of the house settled around us.

"They can try." He smiled again.

"And I'll stop you."

He slapped me harder. I put my head down and slammed my head into his gut.

With a grunt, he shoved me into the kitchen wall. A picture of a butterfly sitting on a daisy smashed to the ground behind my back. My chest collapsed as the wind rushed out. He peeled me off the wall and pushed me away from his side, never letting go of my arm. When he yanked me to him, he came close to dislocating my shoulder.

"Come now! I'll show you what it is to be the master of winged death. Luca has taught me so much."

I snorted before I could stop myself, licking blood from my lower lip. What a pompous prick. If only I'd seen the monster under the façade.

He snapped at me, "How do you think Eden came to be able to control the gryphon? With her vapid looks? Luca taught me, and then I entranced her. Don't question me again."

It didn't seem like the time to point out that all I'd done was make a rude noise, no questions asked. My shoulder throbbed, providing all I needed in the way of a reminder. Suddenly, he let go of me, reaching for one of the guns on the table in front of him.

"So much for other worldly magic."

"Again, you're not listening. There's all kinds of magic, Reedy-Girl." He held the gun comfortably.

The banging on the front door echoed through the house, made me jump.

I waited for his direction.

"Go. Find out."

I knew it couldn't be Ari; he wouldn't knock. And I doubted it was Jackson.

Stillbee followed me through the hallway. There was a wiggle of denim and patterns in the side windows of the front door. They were back. What was Ryder thinking? The protesters were knocking on my front door.

I threw the door open. Stillbee drifted back out of sight, pressing against the foyer wall, gun raised and pointed. The noise outside the door—their stomping and chanting—made me worry that they'd spook the man with the gun. Stillbee made no noise, but I felt him there as surely as I felt the sweat drying on my neck.

There were about a dozen of them now. If Ryder was there, I couldn't see him. They started their chant up again.

"Hey there!" I shouted. I had to. Finding my house had given them a fresh rush of courage, and it sounded like a pep rally on my front porch for a losing football team—complete with a couple of true believers trying to keep the others going. I tried again. "Hey!" Nothing. They continued to wail.

In a sudden lull, Stillbee's muttering registered. He didn't sound supportive of my visitor's animal rights concerns. He shoved me aside and pushed through the door to stand on the front porch.

"Shut up, right now! You're on private property, and you're trespassing."

Stillbee kept the gun out of sight, hidden behind him. The kids fell back before his angry, crabby presence. "You heard Miss Hunter, the owner and proprietor of Gilded Oats Ranch." He did nothing to demand their attention except stand there, and it worked—something about his unblinking hostility, his expectation of total obedience.

Here was an idiot playing at becoming a tyrant, thirsty to command, control, and force obedience.

My stomach sank at his public hostility. The way he said my name in front of a bunch of dopey teenagers, but their passion and earnestness made his betrayal seem all the more real to me.

"You should leave . . . now," he continued, never once raising his voice.

"We aren't going until we know the animals here are protected from your murdering hunters," said a girl I didn't know. I recognized Lindy's sisters, standing behind the ringleader. They looked embarrassed to find themselves on my front porch. The leader was one of the more flamboyant kids in the group: hair cut so close to her head I could see scalp, earrings lining the curve of her earlobes, a face full of stubborn jaw clenching and grimaces.

"Who are you? Where's the boy at the gate?" I piped up. Where was Ryder?

"Enola. Like the plane that carried the atom bomb, Enola Gay."

I shook my head.

"Like the bomb plane. And we're bringing our explosion of truth."

I watched Stillbee's gaze swing toward the brave, stupid girl. His eyes settled on her, eyes unblinking and cold, like icy, frozen marbles. Madness. There was madness in his face. I tried to step between them, but he shouldered me out of the way.

"Shut up." Disdain dripped off the words as he spoke.

The girl sucked in her next breath but then drew courage from some deep well. "No, I won't."

He shifted to the balls of his feet, his hands twitching. I started to reach for him. I hardly knew what I was going to do. Drag him back into the house? Punch him in the mouth? Ask him, "Pretty please. Don't crush the little pests?"

I had no idea what he was capable of, not actually, what twisted power he possessed, but then she said the very thing that assured her little band of protesters some actual, honest to God leverage:

"We have the horse, the one from the flyer, and we want the reward." Stillbee's body stiffened with shock.

Enola looked more confident and belligerent when she saw the way her announcement surprised the big man in front of her.

I put my hand up to stop her from saying anything else. I pointed at a boil of dust coming up the road, anything to distract the group.

Someone jogged toward the house, kicking up a dust trail as he ran. It was Ryder. His face was flushed, and sweat darkened his hair.

Out of breath, he gasped, "Sorry, Miss . . . Reed . . . I tried to stop . . . them, but they doubled back, and I got," he bent at the waist and sucked in a big gulp of air, "stuck talking to the cops about the mob. These kids got by me."

I waved him off. "I want my horse back," I said to the girl.

She narrowed her eyes at my request and said, "That's what we were counting on."

A boy behind her, with a fairly moth-eaten Mohawk, shoved another copy of the "Have you seen this horse flyer?" at me. I reached out and snatched it away from him, trying not to let the armed, angry man next to me see the way my hands shook.

"Listen, I don't have fifty-thousand dollars for a reward." I peeled up the corner of the sticker. "Look! It's a sticker, a joke. I haven't got a clue who would do . . ."

Ryder made like he had something to say. I waved him off.

The girl's lip pooched out like a toddler's, and it made me remember the way Lindy's face turned into a thundercloud when she was crossed.

"I just don't have that kind of money."

"I do." Stillbee's face transformed. His smile dripped warmth and invitation, and almost reached his eyes. "If recompense is what you require . . ."

"Re . . . com . . . what? If that means money, I'm there." She crossed her arms over her chest and let another pout finish her thought.

The old man next to me stuck the gun in the back of his pants, grabbed the girl by the arm, and dragged her down the front steps. The others stepped back like happy puppies waiting for a bone as the two of them walked into the yard.

Chapter 49

Attack

Neither one of them looked back at me, but I wasn't going to let this happen: her going off with him, alone. No way.

"Stop!" I was halfway down the steps before I saw it. When the bird-shaped shadow collapsed and then flared out again as the gryphon flapped its wings, I screamed to the group, "Inside, now! I mean it. Hurry!" There was bloody panic in my voice. "Mr. S.! Let her go. Ryder, get them inside. Please! I mean it. We can't be dragging off the protesters. Let her go."

But he didn't, he walked her farther out into the yard straight toward the gate. A couple of the kids caught my panic and rushed inside the front door of the house. I heard it bang against the hallway wall. Still, too many of them were busy shielding their eyes against the glare of the sun, wandering farther out into the yard, more curious than scared. I heard the girl yelp once or twice at being manhandled by Stillbee. He backhanded her when they reached the front gate. Her protests stopped short. The girl's protestor friends had quickly forgotten about her, or didn't really care.

The shadow grew bigger, swelled, pulsed as it flew closer. Finally, the girl must have seen a clear enough view of what was coming for her. She screamed in horror and collapsed. Still, he didn't let her go. She dangled from his hand as he dragged her across the road, her legs leaving ruts.

"What the fu . . ." One of the taller boys pointed and gestured for the others to come out and get a good look. Curiosity overcame fear.

"Ryder, I need you! Help me."

I raced out to the idiots staring helplessly and started shoving. "Ryder! Help me get them inside."

"Wow. That's some big bird. Hey, that's not a bird."

They pushed around me.

"What is that?" a round-faced girl asked. "What?"

Stillbee grunted with effort when he lifted the girl up and flung her in the middle of the road. The shadow morphed into the shape of a dart and dove at the girl, Enola, named for a bomb.

Stunned, she lay still. All the onlookers froze just as instantly. It was on her before she could make a sound. The gryphon's talons caught her mid-chest. She screamed again, but this time it was a high-pitched, thin sound that made me think of the goats when they were hurt. The girl's body flopped; she was gone, unconscious or dead. Screams erupted around me. I slammed through the squeaky front gate, barreling toward Stillbee.

"Stop it. Stop it from taking her." I grabbed for his arm. "What are you doing? You can't let this happen."

He didn't look at me when he stiff-armed me to the ground. "Can't? It's done." The gryphon lifted off with the body, flew a hundred feet away, and landed. Horrified, I was sure it was going to rip the girl to pieces. Instead, it tipped its head side-to-side, looking at the girl, smelling her. There was blood on her shirt, her skin like wax.

Her hand flopped and then clenched—not dead. Tripping over the ruts in the sand, I ran at the monster.

I heard my name, kid's yelling, a weird chirping sound coming from the gryphon. What had Ari said? That he'd never seen anyone run straight at a full-grown bull gryphon.

The gryphon swung its glassy eyes toward me. For a measured minute, I faltered. Then Enola groaned—alive, absolutely alive. I had to get her back before she disappeared into some bone pile.

The gryphon roared a warning: mine, all mine, you can't have her; but it made no move to come toward me. It sniffed and snorted and picked at Enola's clothes. The girl opened her eyes and froze; it was the shock that only true terror could bring. The sharp bite of ammonia hit me. She'd wet herself. The big animal lifted its head, shook its beak side-to-side, and then snorted. It hopped backward.

If only I'd had some kind of plan. I started to wave my arms; it was the best I could come up with. I'd been waving my arms in front of rampaging wildlife since I was little, but this . . .

Just as I opened my mouth to yell, someone slammed into my back, driving me headlong into the dirt. I tasted sand; my teeth crunched down on grit. Spitting and cursing, I bucked against the arms holding me.

"Stop, you ass. Stop." Stillbee's voice hammered against my ear and echoed. The air around us turned yellow, then red, and then white. Sounds stopped: the gryphon's snorting, it's warning chirps, wind teasing through the tall grass, Enola's raspy breathing—all gone. We were in a glowing cave of silence. I twisted my head out of the sand and gasped at the twisting swirls of light that surrounded us—like a bubble. It was like being inside of a bubble. Exactly.

Stillbee chuckled. "See the tricks I've learned, and it's just the beginning."

That made me angry. I bucked up against his weight on my back. "Stop! Now. He's looking for the mare, smelling for her on the girl. He'll find the horse like a hunting dog, backtracking, trailing her."

Jumping to his feet, he dragged me to mine. I heard Ryder holler, but it was muted and hollow and far away.

"They're inside," Ryder yelled. "They're all inside. Reed?"

The gryphon hopped once in the direction of Ryder's voice, flaring its wings wide.

"Help the girl, Ryder, don't leave them alone. Please. Keep them here. Call for help!"

The gryphon lost interest with the girl on the ground. I could hear her softly weeping.

Stillbee yanked at my arm, demanding my attention. "The horse. He has her scent. We are going."

The gryphon lifted easily into the air with a hard push of its wings and a whir of feathers.

The bubble was back: thicker, heavier, enclosing us. It lifted slightly so that our feet, my feet, hovered above the ground. Stillbee grabbed me by the shoulder and pinched, but the sight of the ground rushing under my feet focused all my attention. His hand on me was more annoying than painful.

He glanced over at me, smirked, and said, "This? This is nothing. To fly! Don't you want to know what else is possible, my child?"

The wonder of it dazzled me; I'd seen the electric fire of Ari's magic, the balls of fire and light that flew through the swamp and fog. I hadn't understood, still didn't, but this was . . . breathtaking. When the bubble slowed, he reached out and touched its side, sending it away from the force of his hand. I'd heard what he said: the invitation in it, the threat.

I couldn't speak. We had followed the gryphon's shadow, literally a bubble on the breeze. It occurred to me that a bubble might be as stable as the man I was with.

When the bubble collapsed, it spilled me onto the ground. I went face-first into the dirt—again. Stillbee stepped out of the popped bubble like a cowboy getting off his horse: smooth, easy, and practiced.

"Thanks for the heads up." I pushed up to my hands and knees. "So, where are we? Where's the monster?"

He ignored me and started marching off in the direction of the Tannin River Bridge trailhead. We were back in the parking lot. The bridge arched over the black water; I was back where I'd started. He never looked at me, knowing that I would follow, knowing that I wouldn't let him go after Cantara without me.

I scrambled to my feet and trotted after him into the gloom of the trail. I wanted to ask questions, but I realized that's what he was hoping for, counting on curiosity to drag me into his invitation. The only question I wanted answered was where Ari might be.

Sweat stung my eyes, burning. Oak tree roots crisscrossed and humped up across the trail. I tripped my way after Stillbee, his stumpy strides eating up the distance. We were headed toward the gryphon's stash of bodies and bones. The air hung thick with humidity. Oppressive, it was all so oppressive, and the farther we went, the harder it got to keep the sweat out of my eyes.

Somewhere, across the river, I heard a horse whinny—Cantara.

"Those kids didn't have her out here. They would never have kept her out here. They might have had their hands on her for a bit." I faded toward the sound of Cantara's voice, stopping to stand on the bank of the river. The murky water trickled past. Overhead the sky turned dark with storm clouds, like that other time, at the beginning of this mess. My heart started to speed up. Stillbee kept walking.

At the curve in the trail, he stopped, just before he lost sight of me.

Across the river a bright, bobbing globe of light drifted up from the ground—the 'Taintsville lights, Eden's limits, an urban myth made real. The power that kept the gryphon contained, or that was the theory. Cantara squealed, whether in pain or fear, I couldn't tell. Stillbee looked at me, then at the ball of light drifting through the underbrush.

He shoved me into the black water and then splashed in after me. My heart thundered; the water was a shock and a relief. There were monsters of a different kind in the water: gators, snakes, hidden deadfalls full of spiked limbs, tangles, and traps.

I sputtered out, "If you were planning to drown me, you'd better hurry." I struck out for the far side of the river.

I headed for the light.

On the opposite bank, I pulled at my soaked clothes; they clung, strangling me. I pulled off my oxford shirt, wearing only a sports bra and sweat pants I tied the shirt around my waist and kept moving. The ball of light hovered as if it waited and watched, waiting to lead us into the woods, watching to see if we followed. As soon as my shirt was tied, it moved off. I didn't look to see if Stillbee was following.

Farther than the bone pit, past Lindy's clearing, the light drifted and bounced farther and deeper into the darkest, heaviest part of the Refuge. It stayed ahead, just far enough to keep us hustling. My bare arms started to burn from the thorns and brambles.

Before I saw it, I heard it. It was the strange, tinkling sound of ground water dripping down into the open mouth of a massive sinkhole. The woods opened up here into a vine-tangled, tropical fairyland. Air plants hung in the arching green branches like spidery jewels. Ferns covered the ground, rimming the open hole in the ground. Fifty feet across, it was a limestone conduit. The light that had drawn me here hovered directly over it in the air. I suspected that this place had another name, The Dragon's Sink.

On the far side of the sinkhole, Ari held Cantara. A scrawny boy with dreadlocks shivered next to him; the kid looked about fifteen. Had Ari found the horse and the kid together? Had to be.

A rustling in the woods from behind startled me. Stillbee stopped, stared, and smiled when he saw Ari across the way.

"Why did you bring her?" Ari's voice was raw.

Cantara lifted her head and snorted. I saw the way Ari's hand tightened on the horse's halter, the way he glanced up at the sky, the way his face filled with dread when he saw me.

"Good work finding the mare. Luca will be pleased, perhaps merciful," Stillbee said.

"I'll come with you." Ari turned his eyes away from me, concentrating on the old man. "I will even bring this animal and what she carries, but you will send Reed back, with this boy, now. Nothing happens until she is gone from this place."

I stepped forward, horrified by the demand and tinged with defeat. "Ari, stop—" I began. "Where are your men?"

"Not coming. Are they Stillbee?"

"I think they might be busy trying to figure out what to do with another hole cut in the fence. Wild animals running free, getting hit by cars on the freeway. Time to call the lawyer." He giggled.

Without looking at me, he reached over and shoved me into the leaf mold and mud of the jungle. I hit a twisted root. It hurt bad enough to drag my attention away from the standoff in front of me. Wincing, I staggered up to my feet. Ari answered Stillbee's abuse by pushing the kid in front of him.

He ordered the boy, "Walk!" The kid acted groggy.

"She is not a part of this."

"This girl has something of a stubborn streak. She insisted on coming."

Stillbee cocked his head at Ari and looked at me with the creepy sheen of speculation in his eyes. "You love her. You truly love your enemy's daughter. The way he loved her mother."

Ari straightened. "Luca? He doesn't love. The Black Mage broke the love out of him. Love is impossible for him now."

Stillbee started to laugh. "Ahhhh, impossible love. How perfect is that? And my master senses that even more than the impossible has happened. Between the two of you. Does Reed know that she's carrying your child?"

Ari's eyes widened. My mouth went dry. What was this monster saying?

Suddenly, the air took on an aspect of weight and drag; it was more than humidity. It felt like a smothering blanket. Stillbee started to mutter and growl. The boy tripped and stumbled toward our side of the sinkhole. He had the look of a hunted rabbit in his eyes: frozen, blank, just this side of senseless.

I doubted he was even aware of where he was. Cantara lifted her head and snorted.

She knew what was coming: the gryphon. He would hunt her through time and mystery.

"Reed, listen to me. I need you to go from this place," Ari said.

Forgotten, the ball of light that had led us to this place began to quiver. The light trembled over the center of the hole in the ground. The air around it thickened. It was like breathing fog. I reached out to the boy, who'd stopped to watch the growing glow of light. My skin crawled when I heard the muffled sound of the gryphon's shrieking battle cry. He would find us. He would take back what was his.

It got hard to see across the opening of the sinkhole. "Ari?" I screamed. "I can't leave you. Please. Let him go. Let Cantara go too. It won't matter."

Stillbee looked at me, speculation in his eyes, then reached over and grabbed the stunned boy who stumbled near. The word bait came to my mind. He was going to use the kid somehow—as a distraction, as bait, as a lure.

No way that was going to happen. I grabbed the kid's other arm. Everything around us dimmed, shrank, and folded into the sight of my hand on the teenager's skinny arm.

"Reed! Go! You'll be dragged in—" The sound of Ari's voice seemed so far away.

I shook my head and yanked. Stillbee hadn't expected it. He stumbled off balance.

"Stillbee! I'll let the mare go." Ari held the lead rope over his head with both hands. "You'll have nothing."

Nothing! What did that mean? Wouldn't he have Ari as his prisoner? Everything, Stillbee would have everything I cared about.

The light grew and began to pulse. A sound like a short in a light switch crackled in the middle of the ball of light. The ball formed a dome over the clearing. Ari dropped his hold on Cantara's halter. She started to dance in fear. Ari raised his hand to the ball of light, spread his fingers and pushed the air in front of him. I yanked harder on the kid with one hand and shoved at Stillbee with the other.

The light bulged, contracted, and then blew apart. The air cleared for a second, and then the sky overhead exploded rain. The world turned into a gray flood of water.

"Reed, go, now!" I didn't think Ari was worried about my getting wet. Overhead the gryphon appeared in a downpour of feathers and screams. He swayed toward the man standing next to Cantara. Ari lifted his hands. I saw electricity leap from his palms.

The kid woke up. His eyes about popped out of his head, and his hands covered his ears. He pulled himself free of Stillbee and me both, then headed for the tree line. Smart boy. I turned to the old man, thinking what? That I'd be able to shove him over the rim of the sinkhole and out of our lives forever?

Stillbee's face shone through the downpour and the wet and the raging storm. He brought his hand up, like before, like when he'd commanded the magic of the bubble that had brought us here. Not this time. Not against those I loved.

Cantara stamped and snorted but didn't bolt. Ari stood still, concentrating on the sky and the gryphon. I saw it all, like an accident victim watching the car flipping its way toward me. Putting my head down, I rammed Stillbee in the middle before he could whip up anything else to throw into the mix.

He hadn't seen it coming, or didn't believe I was all that big a threat. He fell back without even trying to stop himself. My momentum took me with him. We fell straight back into the Dragon's Sink. There was the impression of slashing rain, and then swirling light, and then something caught at the shirt I'd tied around my waist. I dangled. Ari?

Screaming. Someone was screaming. Stillbee fell away from me as I was lifted up and away from him, but not by Ari and his magic. The gryphon had come to find its mate.

Cantara whinnied and nickered. The air flashed with sparks and jolts of electricity. My name rang out across the open pit.

"Reed, be still. Be still. Don't fight. Play dead."

I heard him in a haze. Adrenaline was making me jittery; every cell of my body screamed at me to fight, to run, to live.

I heard him again. "Reed, my love, please, stay—" The rest was lost in the swirl of sound and rain and light.

Forcing myself to go limp in the gryphon's talons, I watched the world go by in a rush of gray rain. Cantara whinnied and the gryphon hesitated, hovering, probably looking for her. I whistled to her. She answered. The gryphon swept toward the sound of her in the murk. The ground seemed so far away, I couldn't judge the distance.

"Ari?"

"Here. I'm here."

He sounded close. I wanted to believe it was close enough, and that I wasn't still over the Dragon's Sink. I untied the shirt and fell to the earth, remembering the last glimpse of Stillbee's face as he fell toward another world, the world of my mother's birth.

He'd been smiling.

Chapter 50

Leaving

The gryphon cooed softly to Cantara as she stepped into the underbrush. He settled into the curve of a massive oak limb, watching as we backed away from the Dragon's Sink: content and happy as long as we didn't move toward his love. He'd placed himself between Cantara and us.

"He'll protect her," Ari said. "We'll get her back, but not now. Let's go. Come now, we are going, Reed."

I had a vague sense of his hands on me, as he ran them up and down my arms, my legs, checking for broken bones, wounds, convincing himself that I was still in one piece. I couldn't take my eyes off of the gryphon, feeling its blazing eyes tracking our every move.

Distracted, a little dizzy, I reassured him, "I'm okay. We're okay." I grabbed his hand and brought it up to my lips. "I'm okay. We're okay." There were questions in his face. I know I had my own questions for him. What had he been thinking, making a deal for my freedom, for my safety?

Nodding, I gave him a smile. He nodded back and turned to the kid who'd found himself in a mess and way over his head. His dark eyes were still glassy with horror.

"Bryce," Ari said, his voice calm and firm. "His name is Bryce. Come. Come now."

Trusting me to follow, Ari led Bryce, dreadlocks and all, by the hand toward the relative safety of the trailhead parking lot. The whole way Ari murmured something low in the boy's ear, not words, exactly, more like humming or singing. Something about it was so familiar. I let the sound wash over me. By the time we hit the first twist in the trail next to the river, I knew when I'd heard it before.

Ari was singing away the boy's memories of the gryphon's presence, the shock of seeing men fall into oblivion— all the magic and the supernatural among the ferns along the dark river's trail.

I'd heard it before. He'd sung away my pain, fear, and remembering. It felt like so long ago.

I stepped carefully into Ari's footsteps and listened to his magical song. It was another kind of magician's spell that he was still here with me and that Stillbee had not gotten what he wanted. We were together, and something about that felt too easy. At the river, Ari glanced back; it was the first time he'd hesitated or checked on me. He kept a firm hand on the boy, who looked as if all he needed was a big nap.

"I'm okay. And you're still here." My voice broke on the last word, embarrassing me. Without letting go of Bryce, he stepped back to me, put his finger under my chin and forced me to look at him.

"I'm here, and I'm not going anywhere."

I dropped my face to hide the quick sting of tears. "He smiled at me when he fell. Stillbee. He smiled. And I know what that means. He'll be back. I know it. He was smiling." I shivered.

"Shhhhh, later, we'll talk later about what's to be done. Stay close. Let's go home."

At the word home, I felt something break loose in my chest and spread outward beyond even the tips of my fingers. Home. With me. He was still here, and he was staying.

"But . . ." I wanted, no, needed to tell him about the old man's face, the spy, his smiling, vicious, smugness as he slipped away from me. "Jackson and . . . Eden? What was Stillbee talking about? Me and you and . . ."

"The babbling of a madman. Shhhh. Not now. Home, come on," he repeated, more firmly this time. I nodded and stepped carefully in the outline of his footsteps as he led me out of the forest, the rain continuing to fall in a lacy mist.

But it wasn't going to be smooth going, and we both knew it, as far as I could tell. The house was going to be full of frightened, traumatized teenagers who'd seen something that had no explanation in reality— this reality—our reality.

But they were gone. The ranch house was empty. No Ryder. No Eden. No Jackson. No one. Somehow that was more frightening than finding the National Enquirer on my doorstep.

The boy, Bryce, insisted on walking on to the highway when we made the turn to the ranch road, explaining that his car was parked there. He needed to get some homework done. He seemed a bit put out with his friends, who'd promised a study session to catch up on Spanish. He walked away mumbling. We went home.

"It's not settled. Those men . . . they're still out there. Holtzer's dead but there were others. How are we going to settle this? We can't exactly call the cops." I snapped the blinds shut in the front parlor. Ari took my hand and led me to the kitchen.

"What if they find Cantara?"

"Then I wish them luck with her. The gryphon has imprinted completely. He'll kill anyone or anything that he thinks is a threat, and my men will be patrolling the trail from now until we know they're gone or dead."

"But you said—"

"Reed, I know this overwhelming. It will get easier. I promise. The one gryphon I knew of, of course, but the other . . . and that it was able to be killed . . . I . . . no, we have to think about what this could mean. Impossible things made possible."

He pushed a glass of ice water into my hands. I held my breath, willing my hands to stop shaking. He put his hands on mine as I held the glass. We stood that way for a long, slow minute; my hands on the cold, slick glass, his warm hands covering mine. Eventually, I set the glass down and reached up to trace my finger down the scar on his neck. "How did you get this? Just start there."

He took a deep breath. "I've only known one other person who tried running at a full-grown bull gryphon." His lips curved up. "And it did not end well. I'll tell you the whole story someday, if you're a good girl and drink more water." He picked the glass up again.

I found it easy to empty the glass: thirst, exhaustion, shock. "But what about—"

"Reed, just breathe." He took the empty glass from me and pulled me gently into his arms. I felt the sigh seep out of him and into me. Magic? It was getting easier and easier to believe. I felt his joy, just in being there with me, flow into my body. He lowered his lips to mine. The kiss spoke for him as a soft yellow glow enveloped us. I felt dipped in liquid gold.

An embarrassed cough broke our kiss, and I had an unreasonable moment of genuine annoyance.

Ari tightened his arms around me when I would have yanked away. Ryder shuffled his feet like an unhappy twelve-year-old. It was my turn to sigh. Time to sort through the disaster and do some damage control. I hesitantly sat down at the kitchen table and braced myself for the inevitable bad news.

Ryder, relieved when Ari pulled away from me, pulled out a kitchen chair and filled us in on the whereabouts of the gaggle of protesters and the injured girl. He'd taken her to the fire station, but by the time he'd gotten her there she was sitting up and complaining about the tears in her vintage t-shirt. The firemen had checked her out but found only superficial wounds. As for the rest, they'd scattered and were probably spreading new and exciting versions of the 'Taintsville lights myth.

Most had raced inside when the gryphon had arrived and would only have hearsay accounts. I wondered if Ari knew a handy crowd amnesia spell. He didn't seem overly worried about what they might be reporting to their friends or parents or cable news. I tried to take my cues from him, to trust that he'd let me know when blinding panic might be an appropriate response.

But the whereabouts of Eden and Jackson were my biggest worry. I sat next to Ryder.

"Ari, about your sister," Ryder said, his voice fading out. "She's gone."

I reached for his hand.

Ryder saw my look. "No. Not that. Not dead. I mean not around."

"What? But you said that she was dead, Ryder. Dead is dead," I said, and then realized that statement might not be as correct as it once was.

He shuffled his feet under the table. "And that's what I thought she was, but maybe not. You know? Come on. Things aren't exactly following the rulebook lately. I went back to see, but she was gone. And I think the sheriff took her, but I don't know where. He passed me in his truck when I went to the River House, moving fast."

"A binding spell." Ari stood, bracing himself on the kitchen table and then dropping his head. "And I didn't see. I should have seen. This world makes me slow at times. I'm sorry I wasn't there to help you with her."

Ryder gave him an embarrassed shrug.

Ari's face looked drawn. Shadows loomed under his eyes. I realized how tired he must be, another reminder at how close I'd come to losing him. I filled the glass with water and handed it to him. "Drink. It will get better."

Better

And it did. Get better.

Mr. Synder, my lawyer, made the painful trip out to my house with the happy news that he'd found some money after all, an account that he hadn't been aware of left to me by my Uncle Rulan. It turned out to be a fairly substantial sum tucked away in a retirement fund in an obscure Credit Union, The Green Swamp Credit Union of Yeehaw Junction. The paperwork had been misfiled. He assured me that he'd given his secretary a stern reprimand over the incident.

He showed up on a day when I'd had to drag myself out of bed—again. Mornings had become a test of real will power lately. I chalked it up to bad dreams and worry.

"I understand your Mr. Stillbee has taken a long and overdue vacation?" His raised eyebrows and the curious tilt of his head told me he wouldn't object to finding out more about Mr. Stillbee's "vacation" plans. "So, you're here by yourself." It wasn't a question.

"No, I have help from . . . friends, and now I'll be able to pay help, which is wonderful. Thank you so much for coming out to tell me in person. I'll get a phone. Top of the list." I stood up and swept my hand in the direction of the front door.

He sighed and resigned himself to no juicy updates.

On the way to the door, Mr. Synder and I agreed that the title dispute with my neighbor, one Ari Ben Warrick, was a concern for another day, seeing that I'd now have enough capital to keep Golden Oats on its feet for, at least, the rest of the year.

"You could still marry him and combine the properties. That's one way to think about it," he said, mopping his face with one of my paper towels. I laughed politely and tucked him back into his Cadillac.

It was that same day that Cantara showed up at my front gate, fat, sassy, and needing a good brushing. My first reaction was to check the sky, but if she was back on her own, then . . . My second reaction was to call our vet, Dr. Dunn, out to give her a good examination. After all I had money in pocket to pay my vet bill and Ari's assurances that the men of River House were keeping the gryphon safely contained in a pleasant enough glade in the depths of the endless Tannin River Forest.

Dr. Dunn clucked and checked and pronounced Cantara fit, healthy, sound, and pregnant.

"I wasn't aware you'd planned to breed your mare," he said, patting her belly. "She's not as young as I'd like, but she should be fine. When did you have her bred?"

I opened my mouth but nothing came out. It had been months, but I could still see moonlight washing the gryphon's glade with crystalline light.

"Don't you remember? You really should keep track, Reed. It's the best way to judge their delivery date. Horses go for a year. I shouldn't have to tell you that." He listened to her lungs, while I tried to pull myself together.

"So I hoped you picked a stallion worthy of her. She's a beauty."

I nodded and handed him a check for the money I owed him.

He jumped in his truck to print out my receipt and then handed me a container of fiber.

"Hey, thanks, but regularity is not really my problem."

"No," he said, tapping at his computer. "Not for you. For Cantara, who knows what she was eating out in that jungle of yours. Make sure you sprinkle it on her feed. It'll keep her from getting sand colic. It's apple flavored. Smell it. She'll love it."

I dutifully unscrewed the lid and took a big whiff . . . and promptly gagged and vomited in the dirt next to his truck.

Wiping my mouth with the back of my hand, I gulped again. He tipped his head and gave me a searching look.

"And how about you? How are you feeling?"

I stuttered, "I'm perfect. Absolutely tip and top. Got some good news today. Nothing exciting going on. Hooray."

Cantara pawed the ground, restless to be put back in her stall. I walked back to her and pulled her lead rope free, balling it up in my hand. "Should probably put her up."

"Sure," he called back to me. "And you should probably check with your doctor about your sudden adverse reaction to smells." He waved my receipt at me before handing it to me and winked. Winked.

I felt faint as I watched the cloud of dust his truck kicked up as he drove away.

Chapter 52

Voices

In the dream I was back in the desert watching the lead Humvee in the convoy dissolving into the fire of a roadside IED. I'd jumped from my truck to run to the hopeless pile of rubble ahead of me only to feel the whoosh of the RPG that destroyed the vehicle behind me, the truck I'd been riding in.

Facedown in the dirt, fire licking at my back, I'd heard my name and a woman's voice telling me to crawl and keep crawling, away from the death, the fire. And I had. Her voice had been as tender, as patient, as gentle, as any child's mother . . .

Except it was a dream of a memory, and I had forgotten the voice—my mother's voice.

The medics had found me under a pistachio tree, fifty feet from the wreckage with a burn shaped like a tongue of flame up my back. For two weeks, the medical staff said that I'd raved about a woman who'd spoken to me, a woman with bright, blue eyes.

Coming awake from the dream with a gasp, I realized I hadn't told anyone about hearing my mother's voice under a pistachio tree in the sand. I'm not sure I'd even remembered until now, and my mother's name scratched into the face of my true enemy as a warning? Had there been other moments when she'd reached out to me, looked over me? Another kind of ghost light from beyond the here and now.

At the fireplace Ari stood looking at me over his shoulder. "Hi."

330 · LINDA L. ZERN

"Where've you been?" I asked, but I already knew and told myself I understood.

He'd been swamped with tamping down rumors, innuendos, and out-and-out lies, patrolling the endless miles of impenetrable jungle. Tomorrow. I sank back into the couch in the library; we'd talk about the proper construction and manipulation of urban legends tomorrow.

"Out. But I'm here now. A nap?"

He pulled a footstool next to the couch.

"It's early afternoon. I've never known you to be the napping kind, except when we first met that is." He took my hand and smiled. "Are you feeling alright?"

I thought about it a minute. "Yeah, I really am." I squeezed his hand. "And I think . . . I hope you'll think so too after I tell you . . . something important." He leaned close and pressed me back into the leather with a kiss.

Against my lips, he whispered, "I'm here, Reed, and I'll love whatever you have to tell me." He sat up straight. "Besides, the Harvest Festival committee is still waiting for your answer on being the grand Marshall of the parade."

"Right. Absolutely. Can't wait to meet with them, with all of them." I started to laugh, took a deep breath, and told him that the birth of Cantara's hippogriff, a creature born of myth and moonlight, would not be the only miracle born at Gilded Oats in the coming year.

ABOUT THE AUTHOR

Author Linda L. Zern lives, works, and dreams in Central Florida.

Writing her way through the genre list, the author began with a children's chapter book, *"The Pocket Fairies of Middleburg,* followed by an illustrated inspirational book, *The Long-Promised Song,* and continuing with a children's middle grade historical fiction, *Mooncalf.*

Also included in the list of her works is a collection of short blog posts and essays titled, *ZippityZern's: A Collage* and *ZippityZern's: Fifty More.* Her humor blog essays@ www.zippityzerns.blogspot.com are a fan favorite and Humor Press national award winner.

Ms. Zern's latest novel is a young adult, realistic, dystopian action/adventure set in Central Florida called *Following the Strandline*, a sequel to *Beyond the Strandline*. Inspired by the classic *Alas Babylon* by Pat Frank, the author revisits the apocalyptic collapse of the power grid and the destruction of society in this romance "prepper" thriller series.

Ms. Zern has had experience publishing with a small press, the self-published platform, and Indie publishing through Create Space. A complete bibliography of her work can be found at <www.zippityzerns.com>

CONTACT INFO: zippityzern@comcast.net